FOX & RABBIT

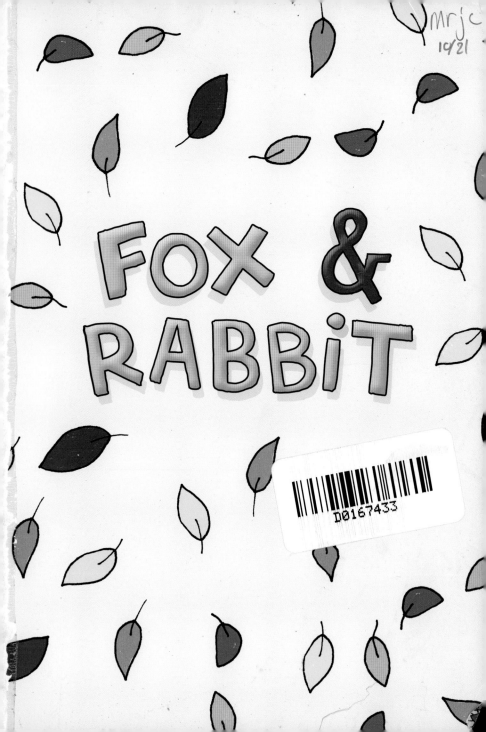

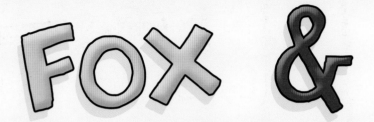

FOX & MAKE BELIEVE

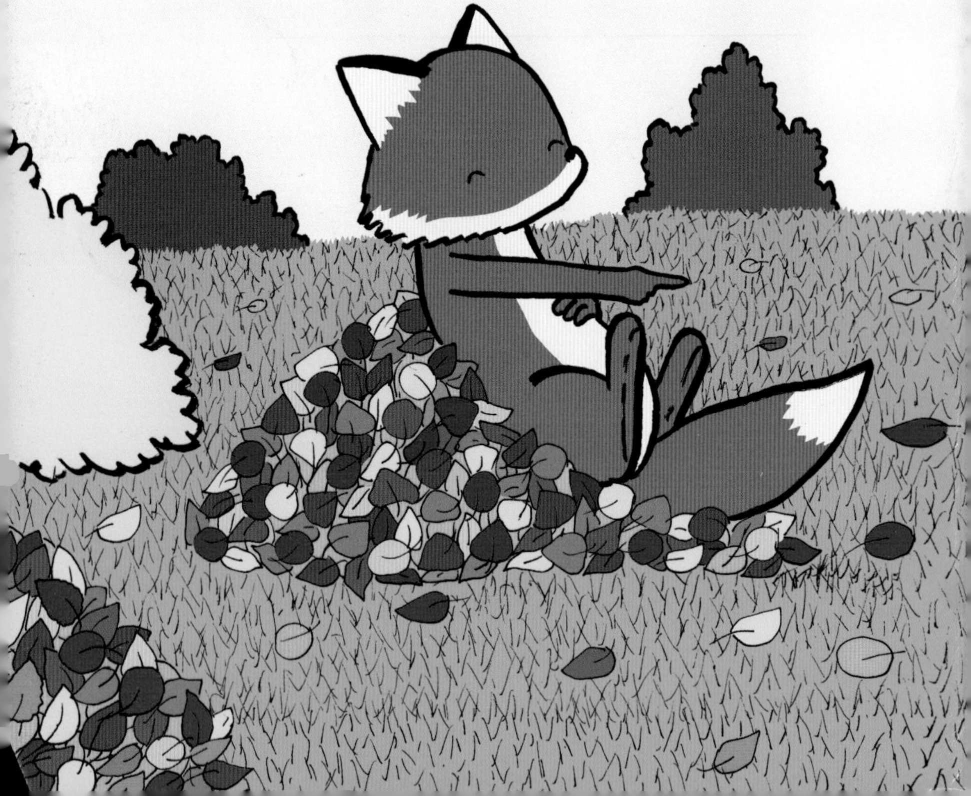

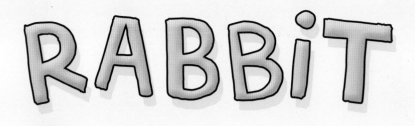

RABBIT

by Beth Ferry

illustrated by Gergely Dudás

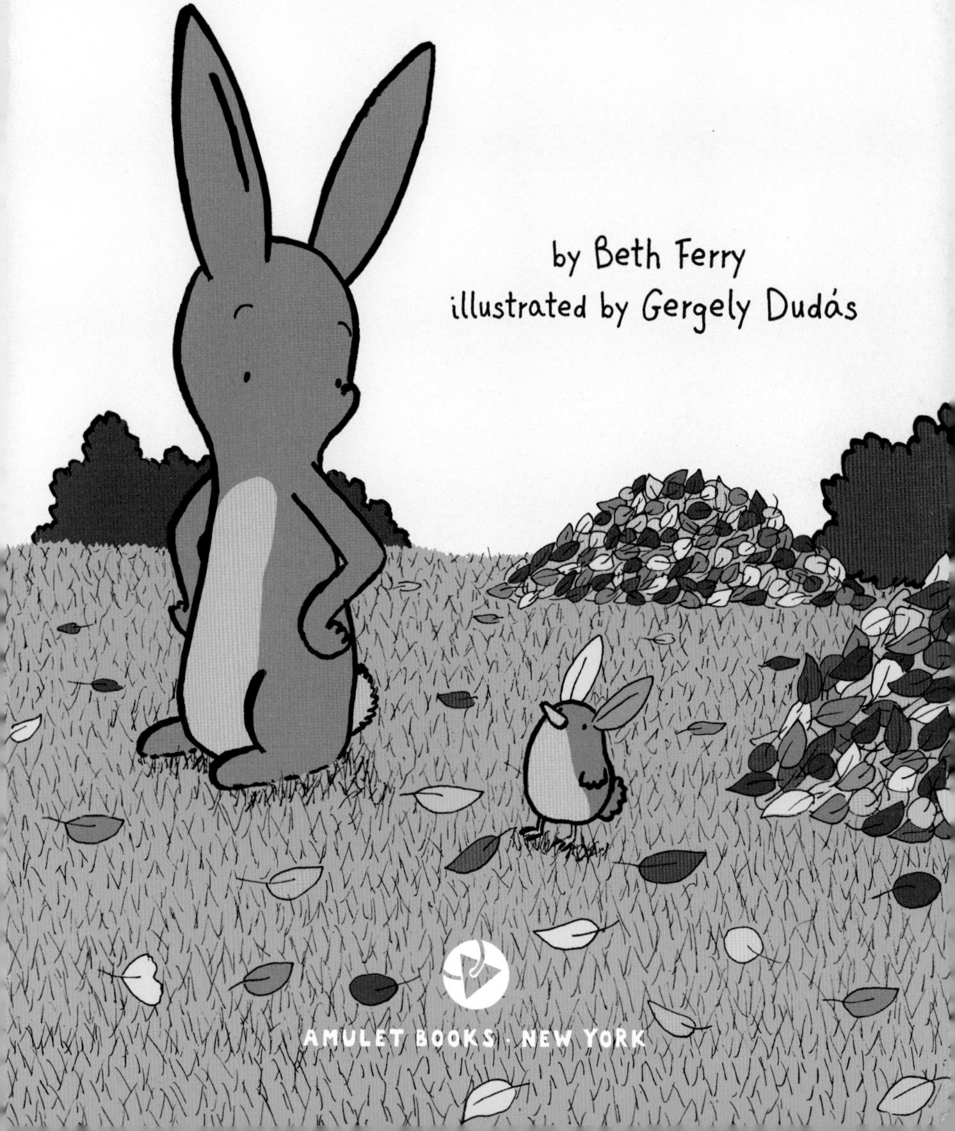

AMULET BOOKS · NEW YORK

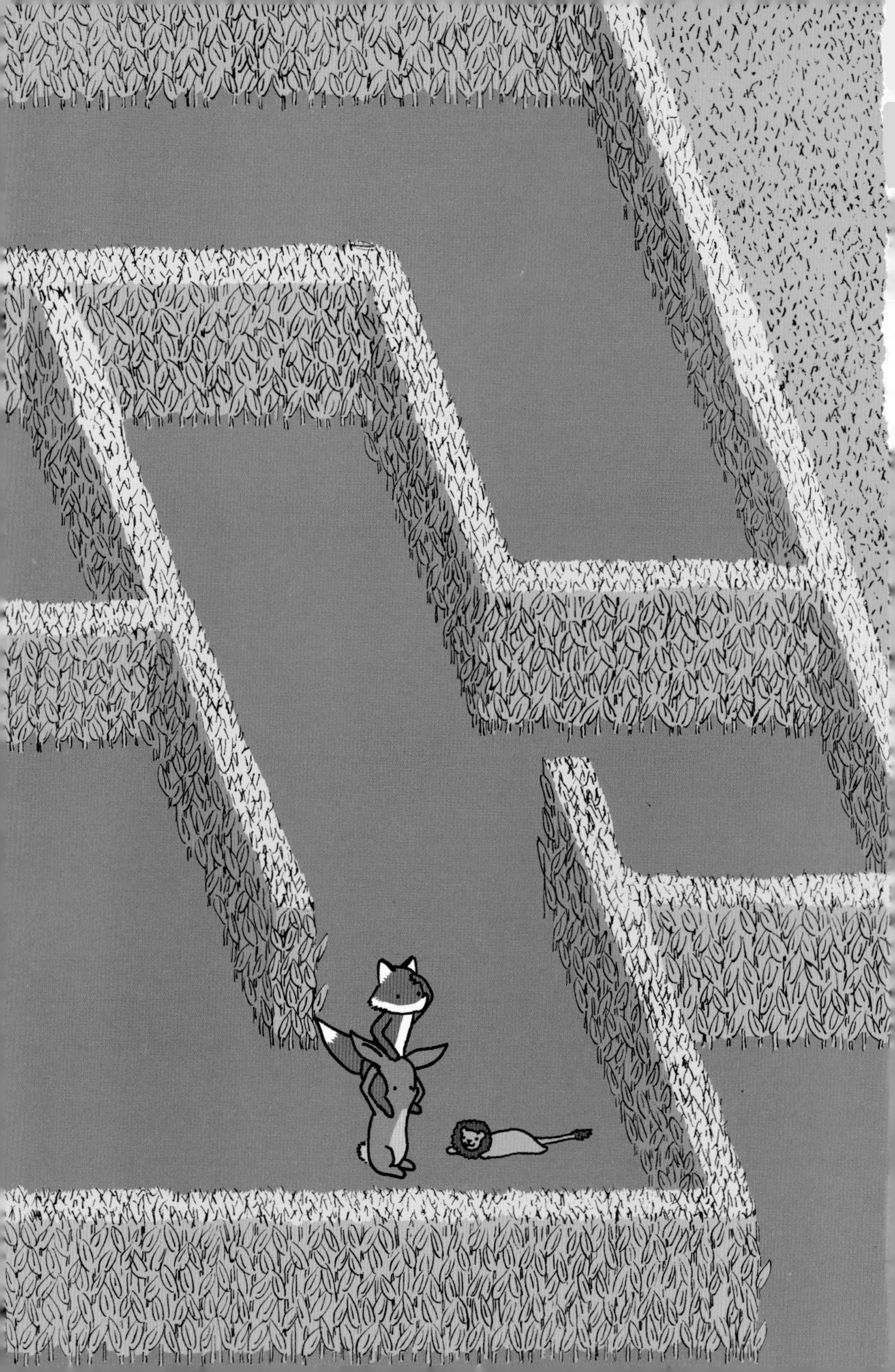

CONTENTS

STORY ONE

MONEY,
MARSHMALLOWS
& MMMMMM

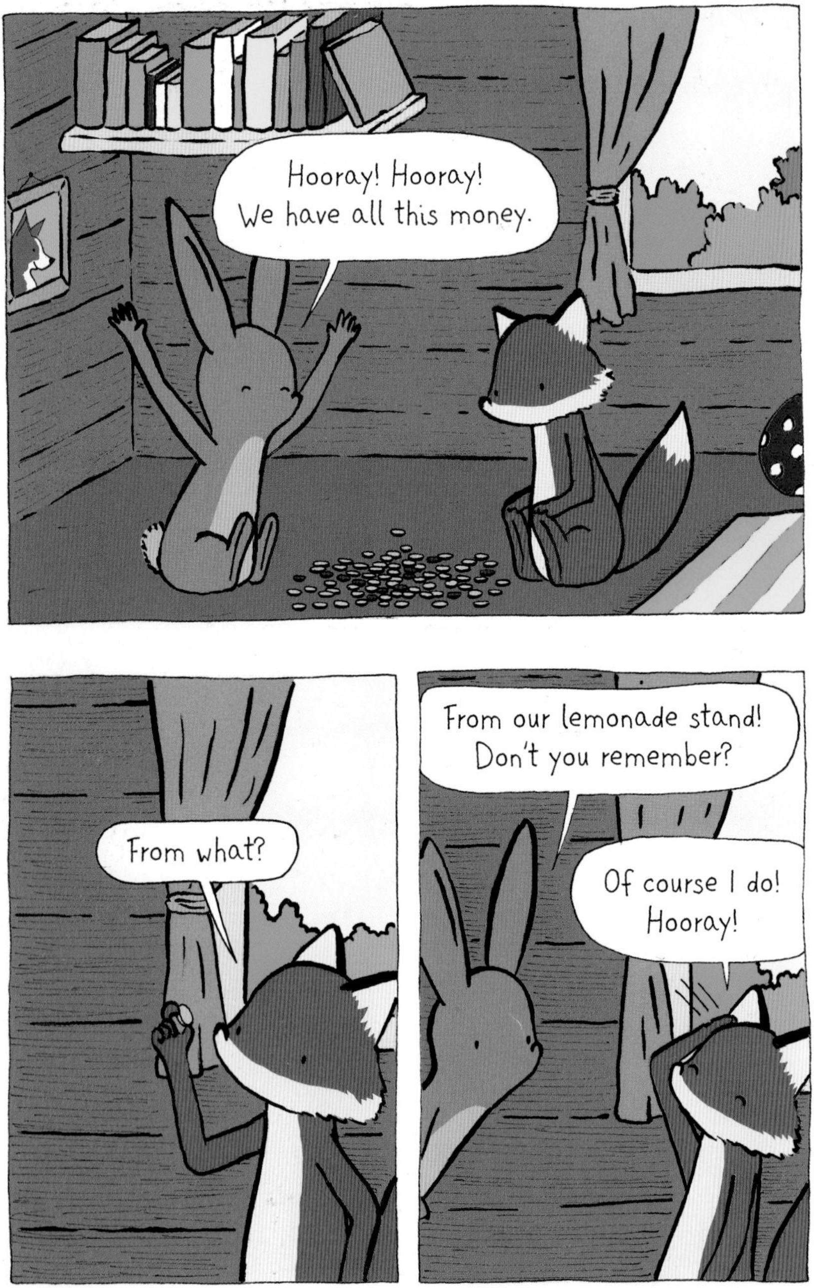
Hooray! Hooray!
We have all this money.
From what?
From our lemonade stand!
Don't you remember?
Of course I do!
Hooray!

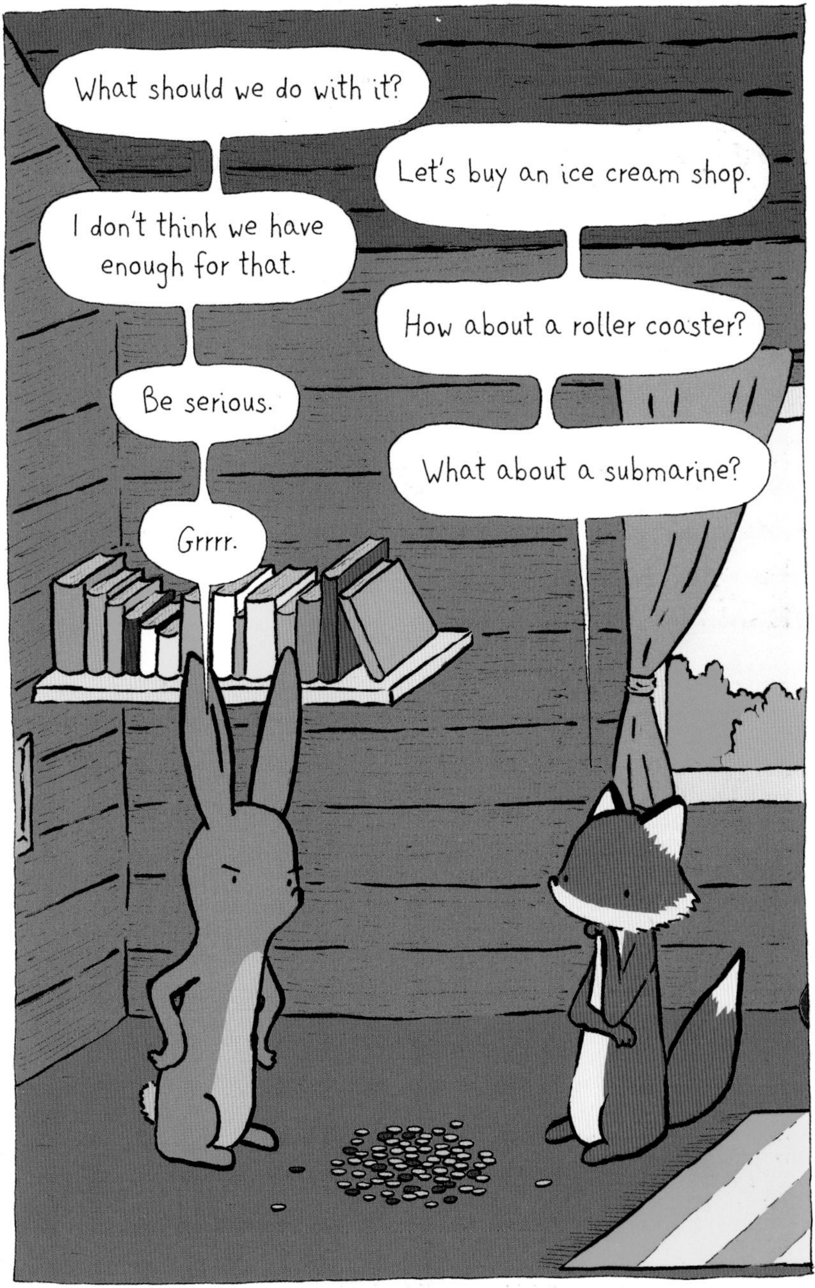
What should we do with it?
Let's buy an ice cream shop.
I don't think we have enough for that.
How about a roller coaster?
Be serious.
What about a submarine?
Grrrr.

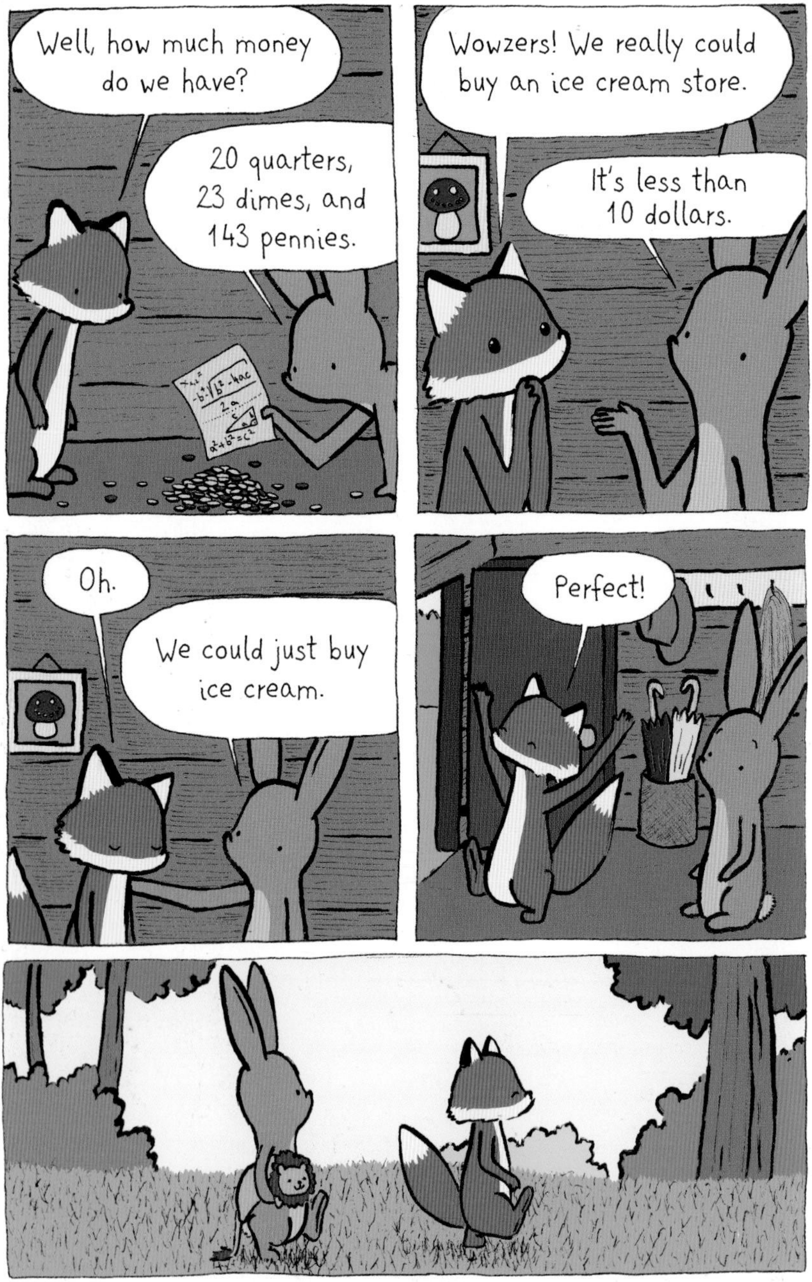
Well, how much money do we have?
20 quarters, 23 dimes, and 143 pennies.
Wowzers! We really could buy an ice cream store.
It's less than 10 dollars.
Oh.
We could just buy ice cream.
Perfect!

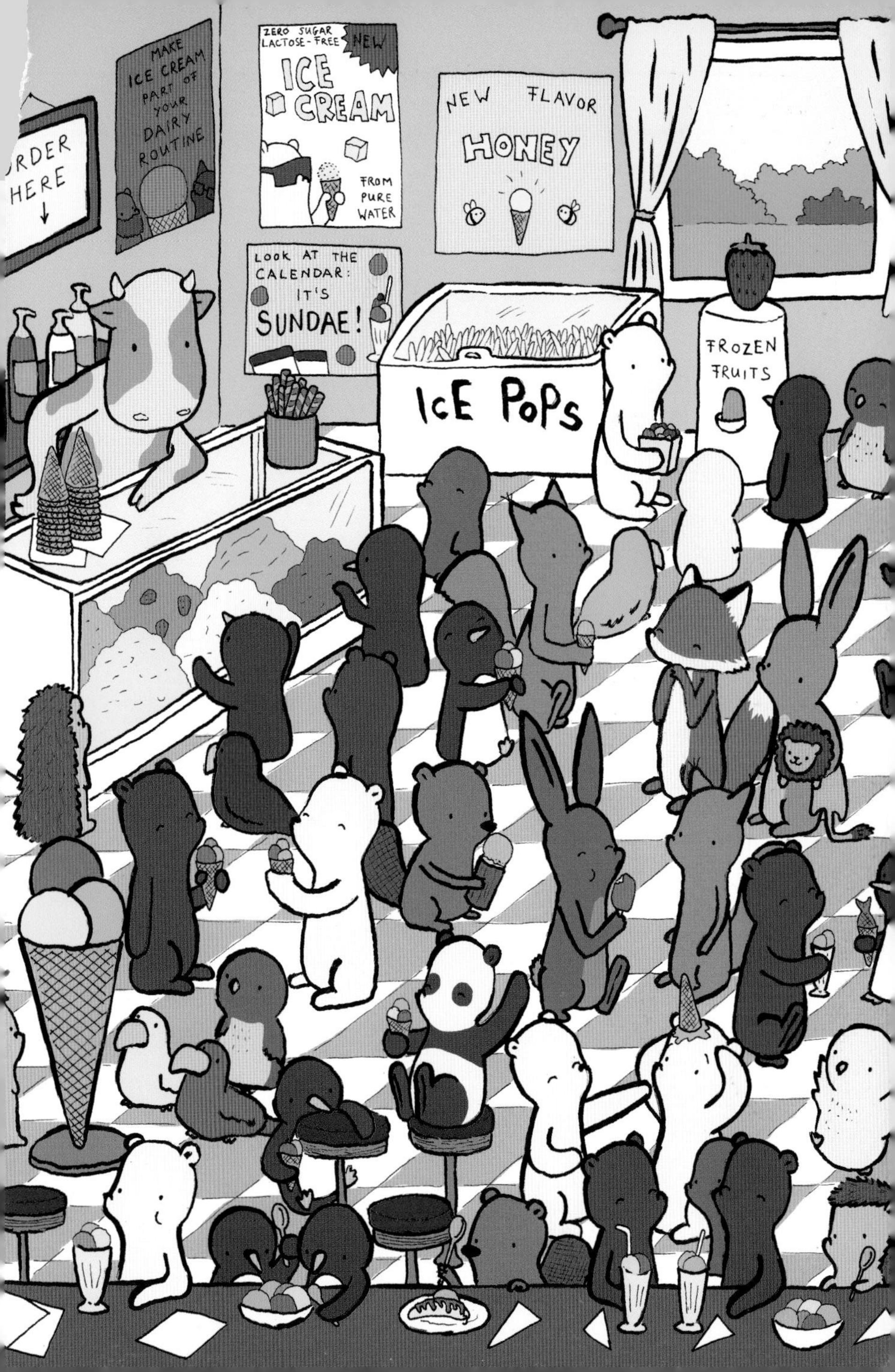
ORDER HERE
MAKE ICE CREAM PART OF YOUR DAIRY ROUTINE
ZERO SUGAR LACTOSE-FREE
NEW
ICE CREAM
FROM PURE WATER
NEW FLAVOR
HONEY
LOOK AT THE CALENDAR: IT'S SUNDAE!
ICE POPS
FROZEN FRUITS

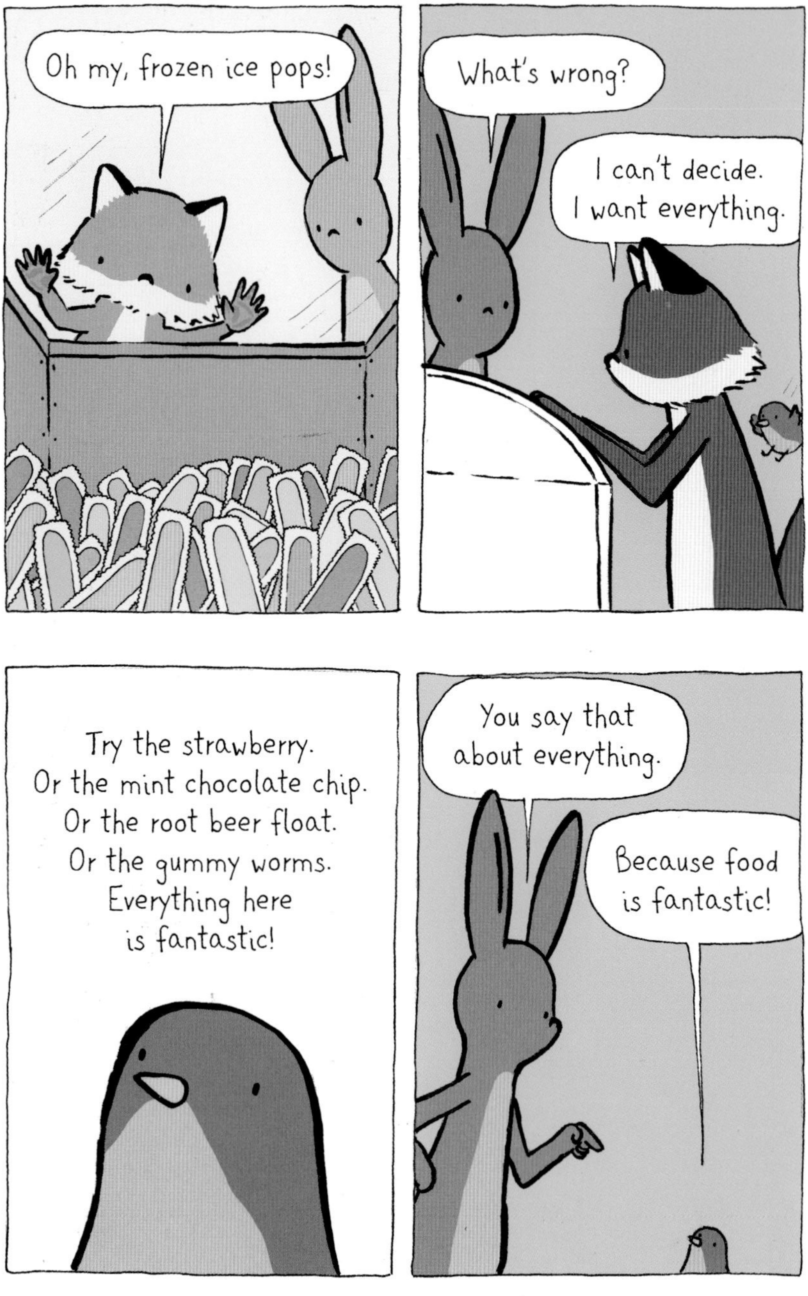
Oh my, frozen ice pops!
What's wrong?
I can't decide. I want everything.
Try the strawberry. Or the mint chocolate chip. Or the root beer float. Or the gummy worms. Everything here is fantastic!
You say that about everything.
Because food is fantastic!

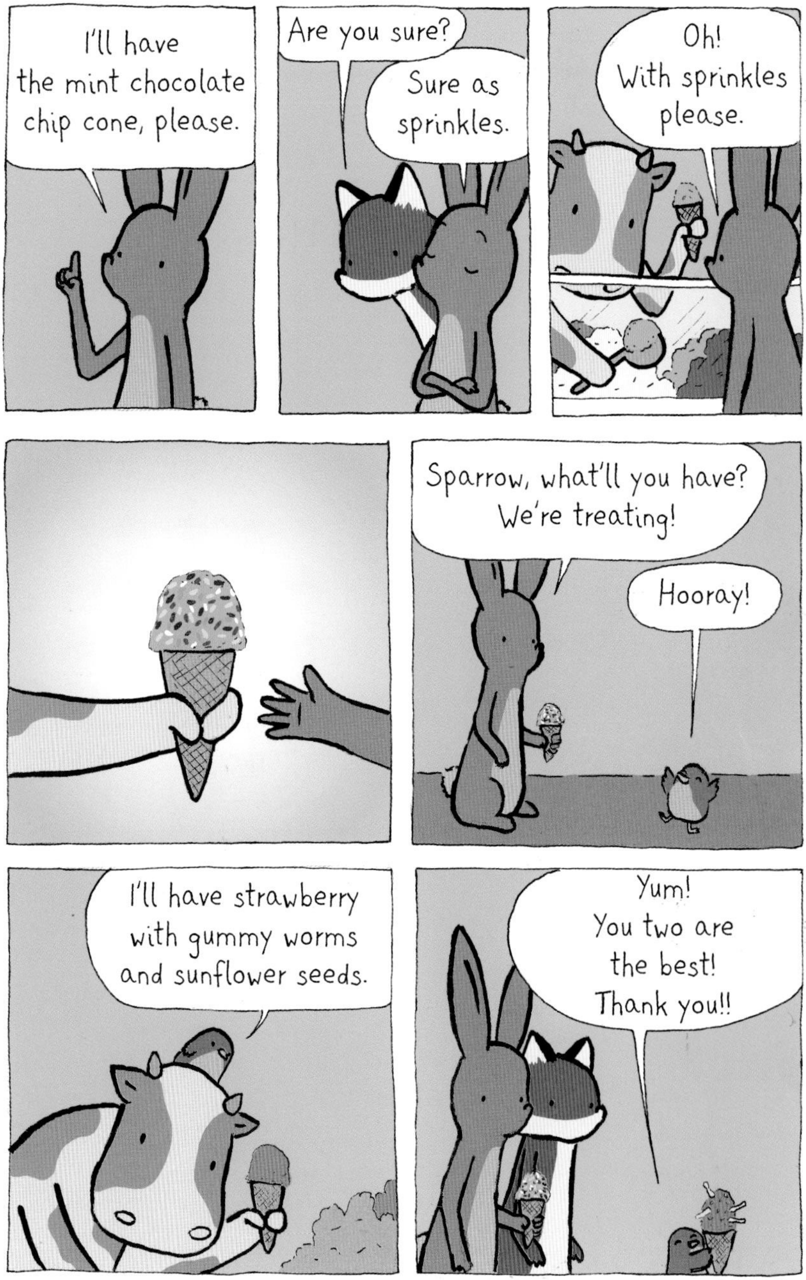
I'll have the mint chocolate chip cone, please.
Are you sure?
Sure as sprinkles.
Oh! With sprinkles please.
Sparrow, what'll you have? We're treating!
Hooray!
I'll have strawberry with gummy worms and sunflower seeds.
Yum! You two are the best! Thank you!!

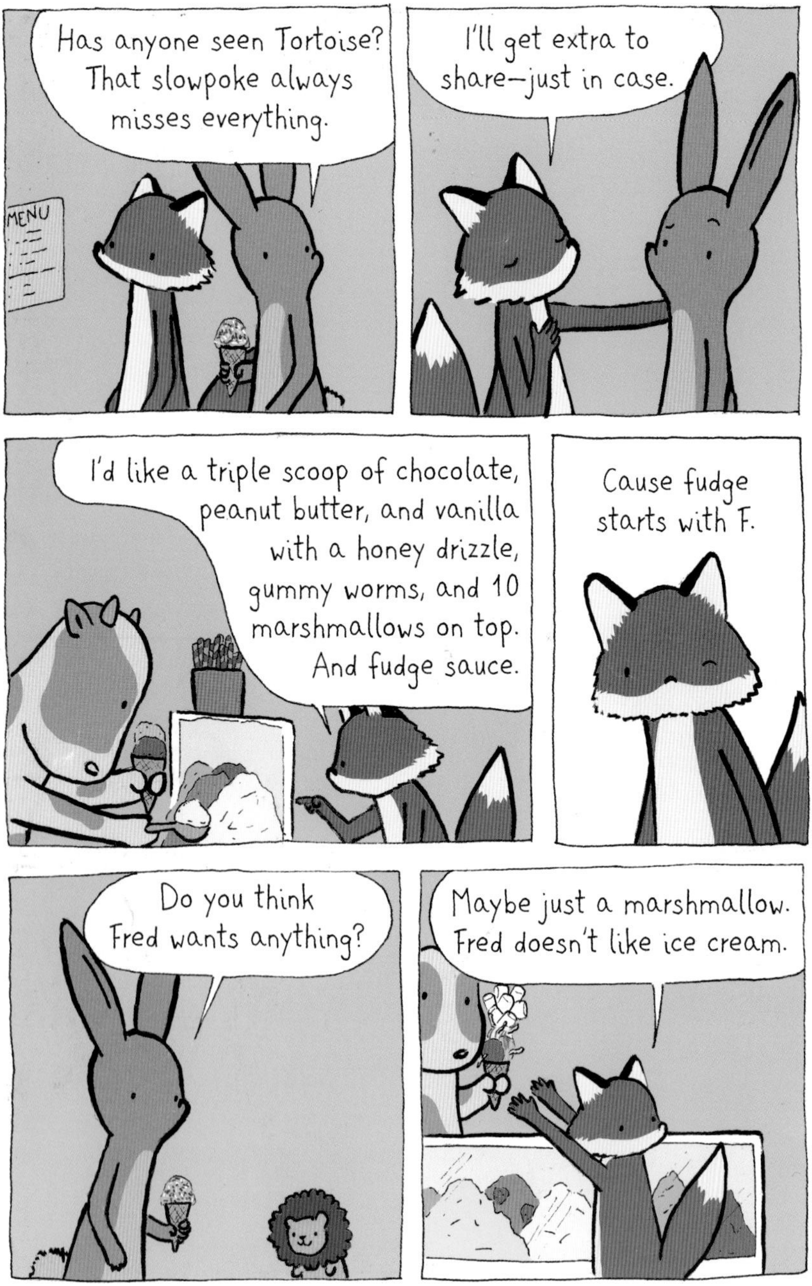
Has anyone seen Tortoise? That slowpoke always misses everything.
MENU
I'll get extra to share—just in case.
I'd like a triple scoop of chocolate, peanut butter, and vanilla with a honey drizzle, gummy worms, and 10 marshmallows on top. And fudge sauce.
Cause fudge starts with F.
Do you think Fred wants anything?
Maybe just a marshmallow. Fred doesn't like ice cream.

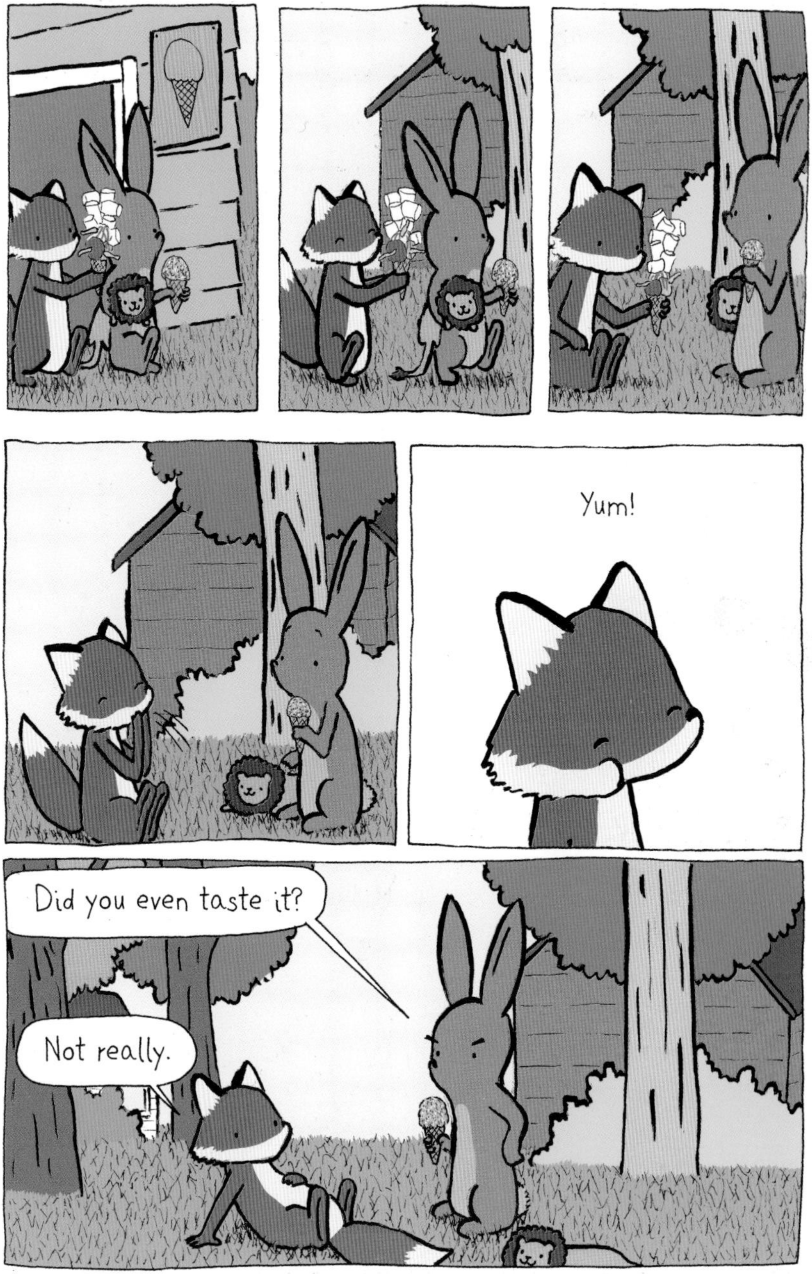
Yum!
Did you even taste it?
Not really.

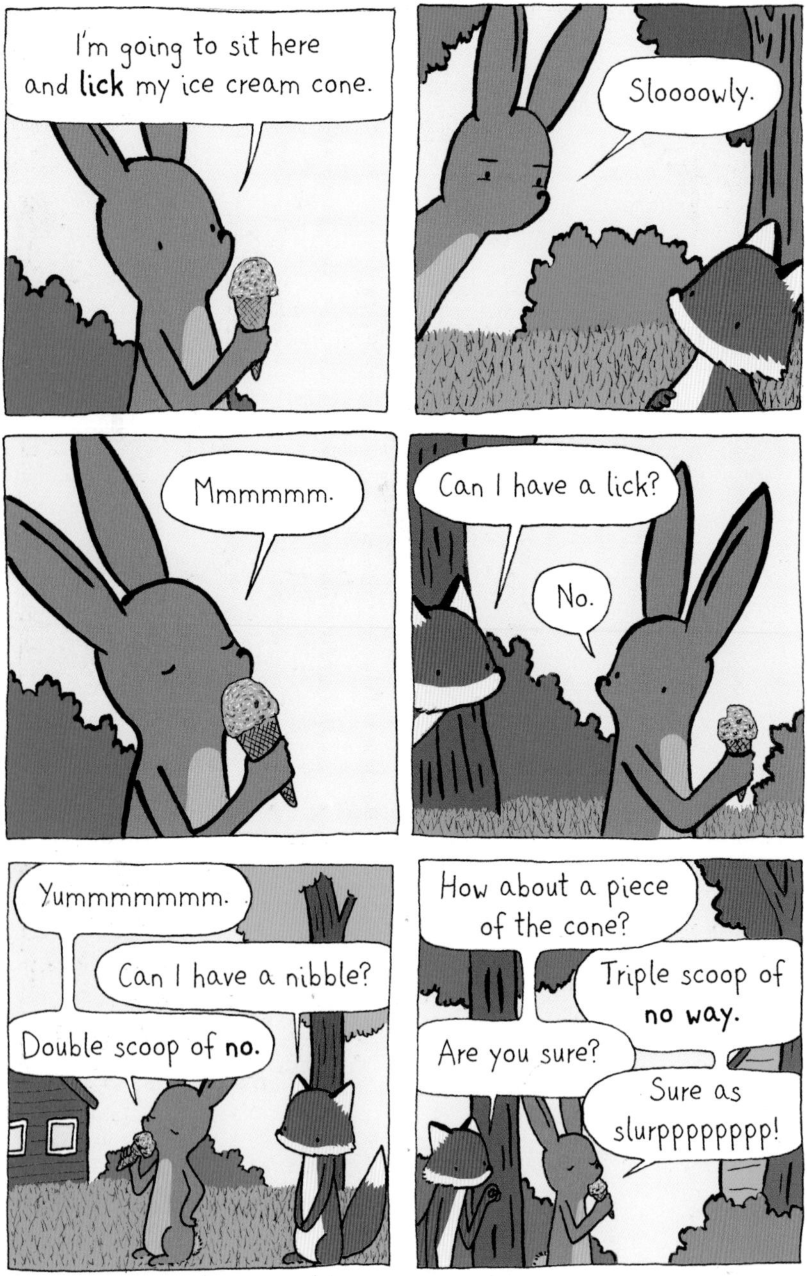
I'm going to sit here and **lick** my ice cream cone.
Slooowly.
Mmmmmm.
Can I have a lick?
No.
Yummmmmmm.
Can I have a nibble?
Double scoop of **no.**
How about a piece of the cone?
Triple scoop of **no way.**
Are you sure?
Sure as slurppppppppp!

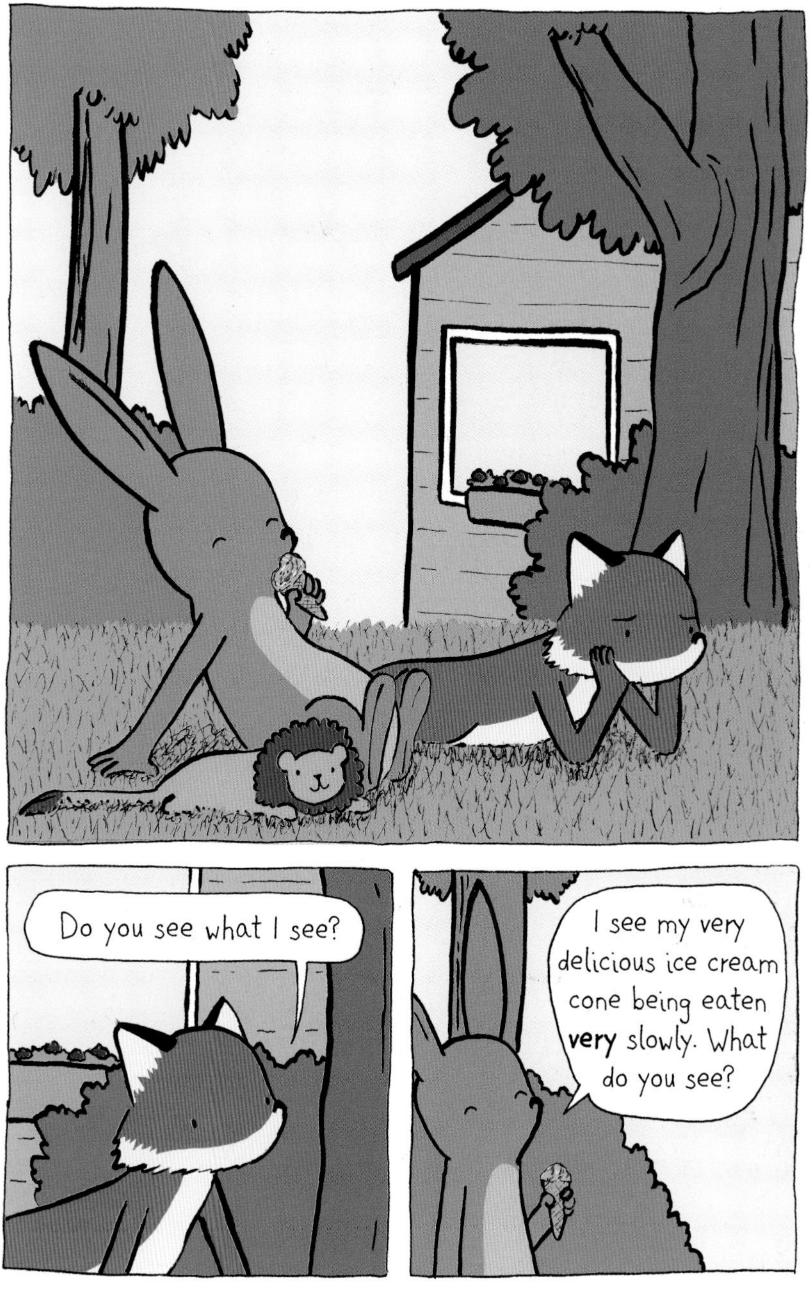
Do you see what I see?
I see my very delicious ice cream cone being eaten **very** slowly. What do you see?

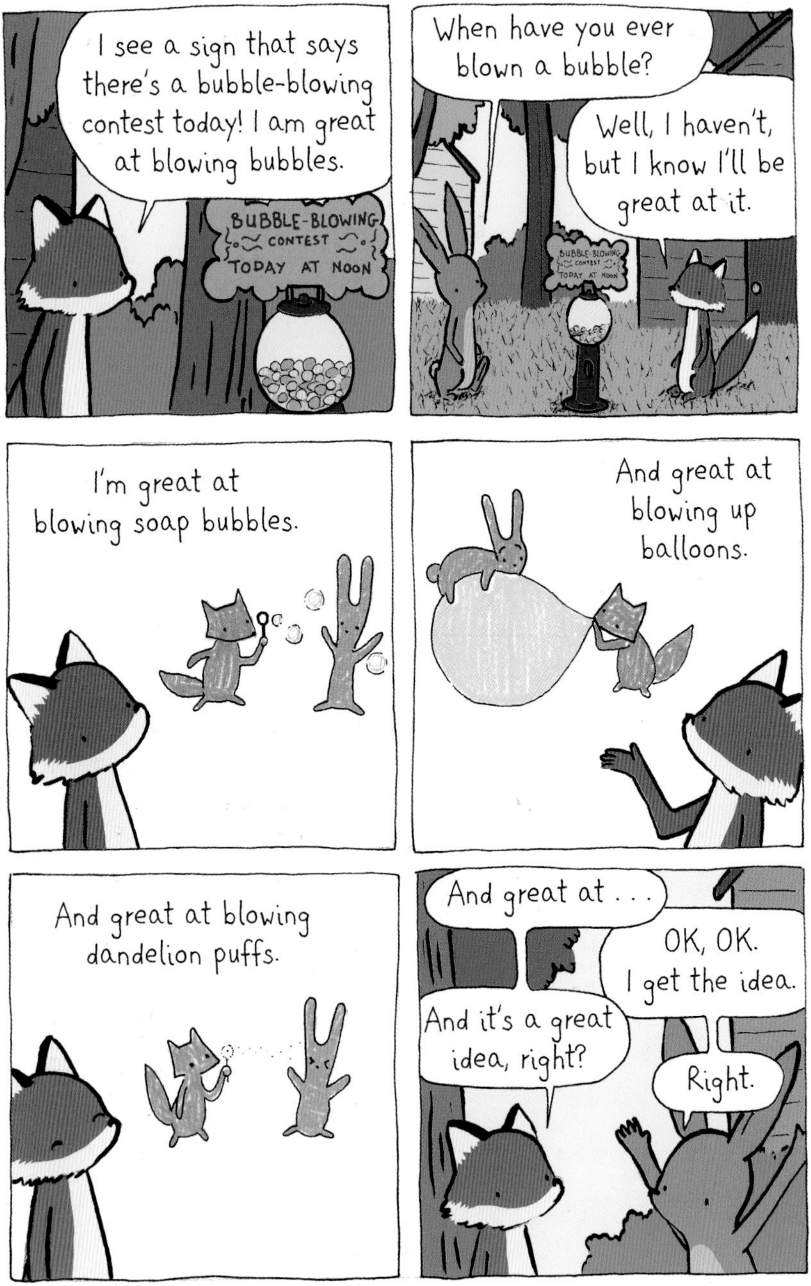

I see a sign that says there's a bubble-blowing contest today! I am great at blowing bubbles.
BUBBLE-BLOWING CONTEST TODAY AT NOON
When have you ever blown a bubble?
Well, I haven't, but I know I'll be great at it.
BUBBLE-BLOWING CONTEST TODAY AT NOON
I'm great at blowing soap bubbles.
And great at blowing up balloons.
And great at blowing dandelion puffs.
And great at . . .
OK, OK. I get the idea.
And it's a great idea, right?
Right.

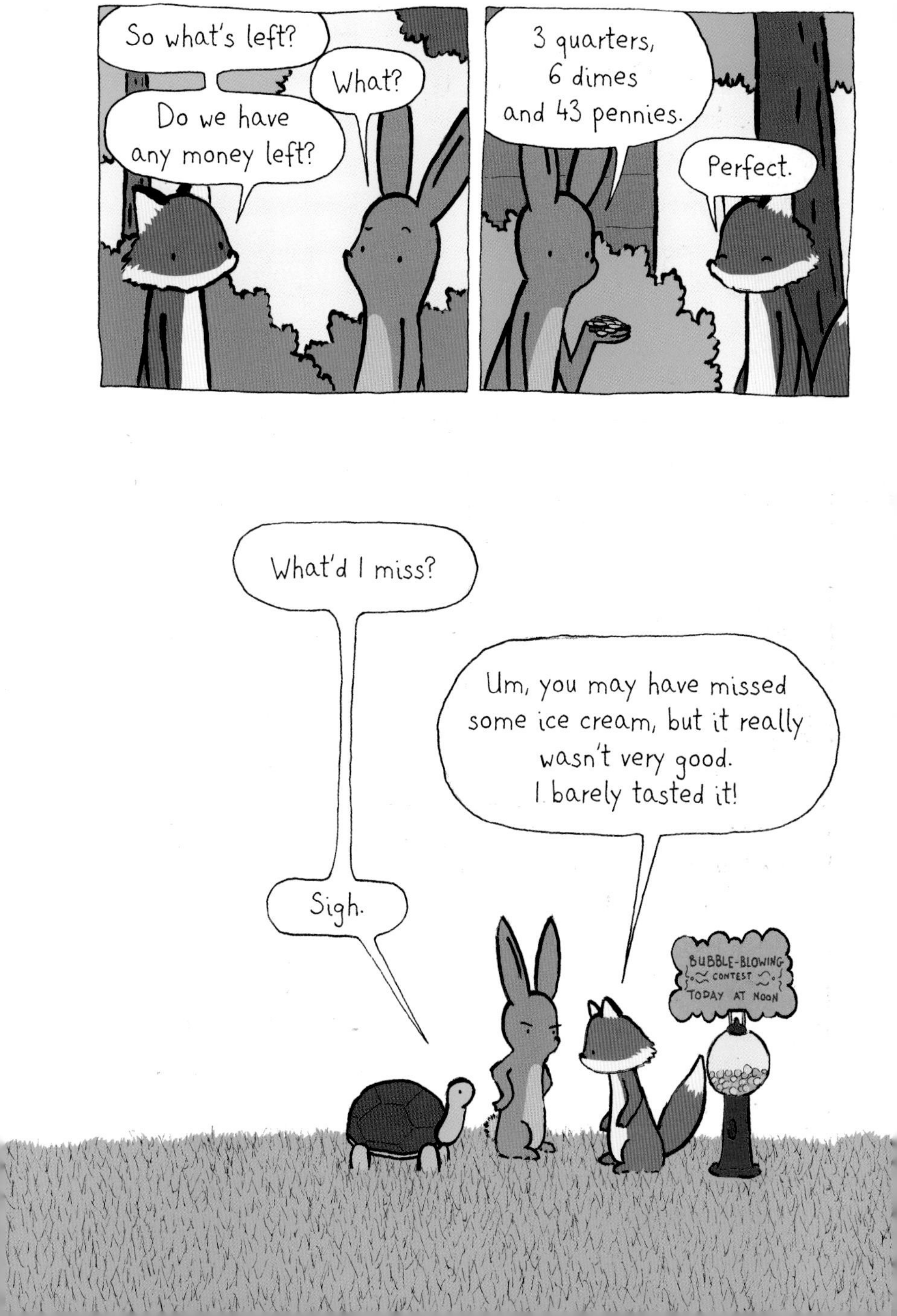

So what's left?
Do we have any money left?
What?
3 quarters, 6 dimes and 43 pennies.
Perfect.
What'd I miss?
Sigh.
Um, you may have missed some ice cream, but it really wasn't very good. I barely tasted it!
BUBBLE-BLOWING CONTEST TODAY AT NOON

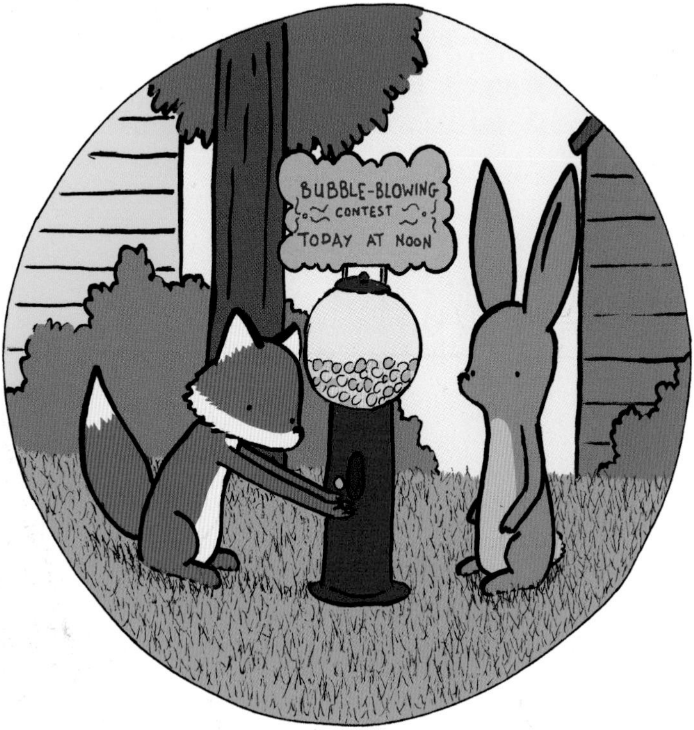
BUBBLE-BLOWING
CONTEST
TODAY AT NOON

STORY TWO

GUM, YUM & CHUM

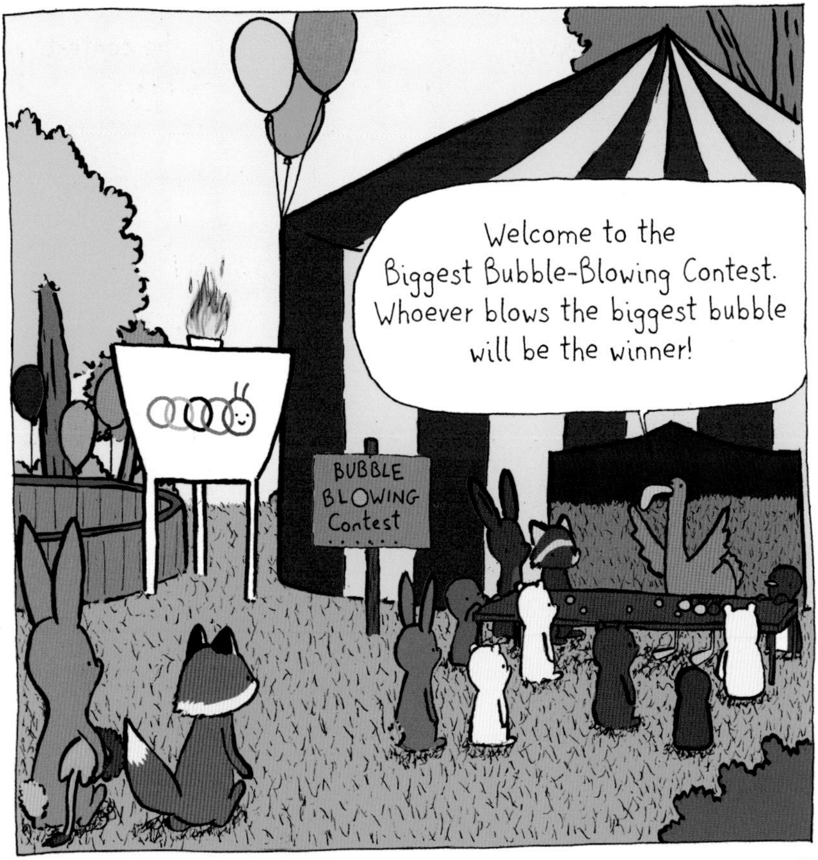
Welcome to the Biggest Bubble-Blowing Contest. Whoever blows the biggest bubble will be the winner!
BUBBLE BLOWING Contest

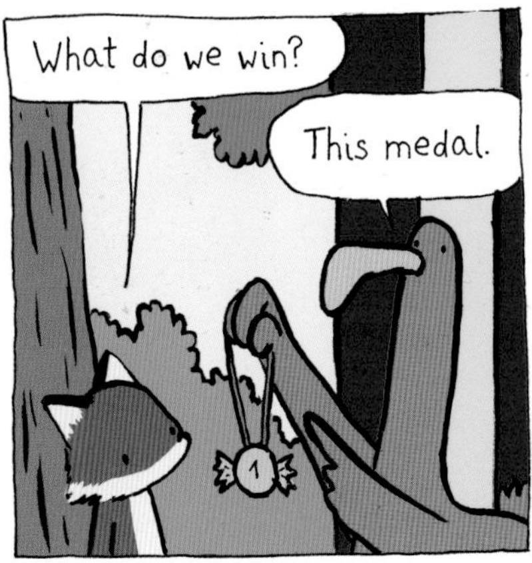
What do we win?
This medal.

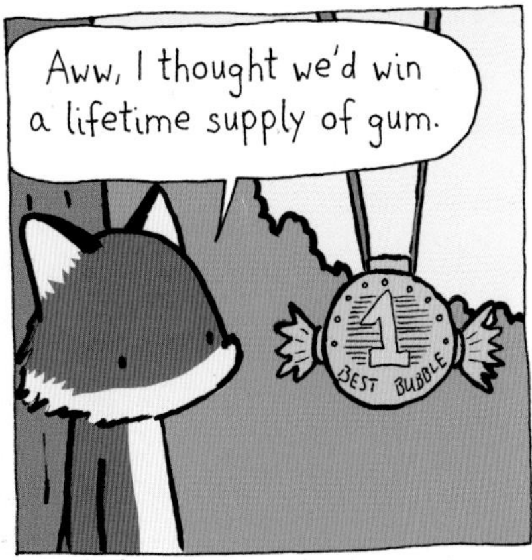
Aww, I thought we'd win a lifetime supply of gum.
1
BEST BUBBLE

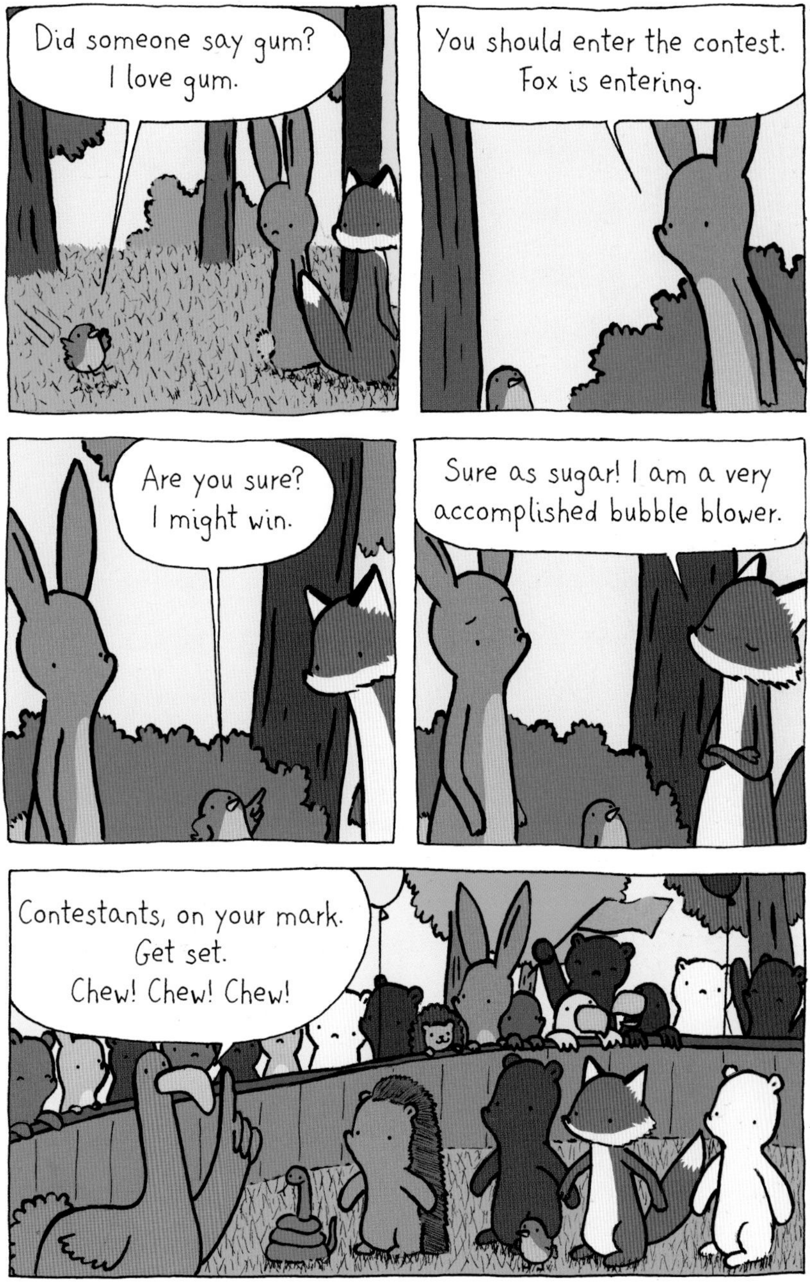
Did someone say gum? I love gum.
You should enter the contest. Fox is entering.
Are you sure? I might win.
Sure as sugar! I am a very accomplished bubble blower.
Contestants, on your mark. Get set. Chew! Chew! Chew!

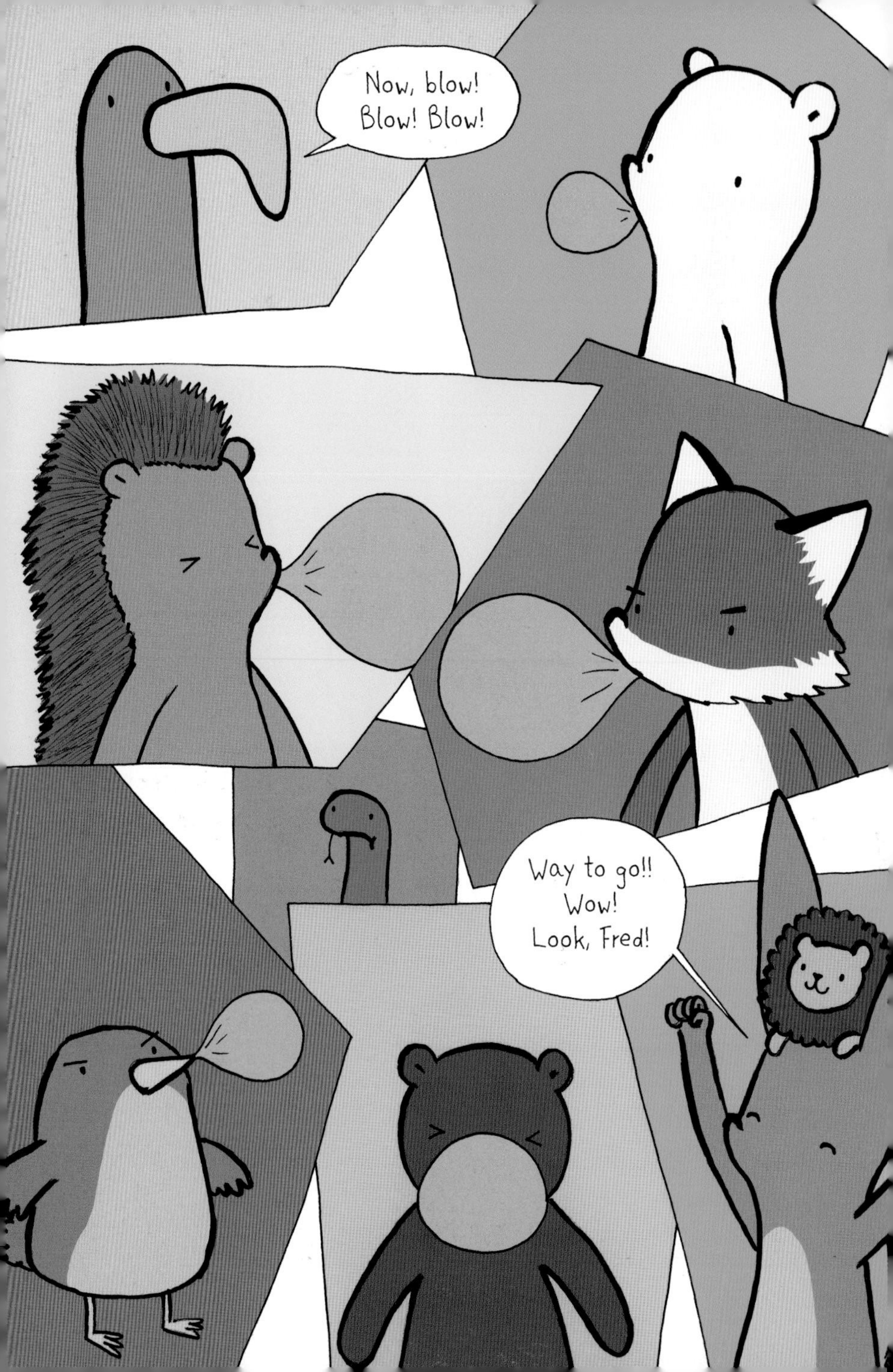
Now, blow! Blow! Blow!
Way to go!! Wow! Look, Fred!

Oh no!

HELP!

Bubble gum emergency. Help!

This is no time to think about eating, Sparrow. I am covered in sticky pink gum.

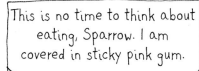

I know just the thing. Peanut butter!

No! Peanut butter will get the gum out.

I read it in my *Food That Fixes Things* magazine.

Are you sure?

Porcupine is the winner!!

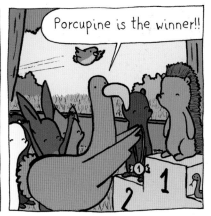

Sure as super creamy peanut butter! I'll be back in a jiff!

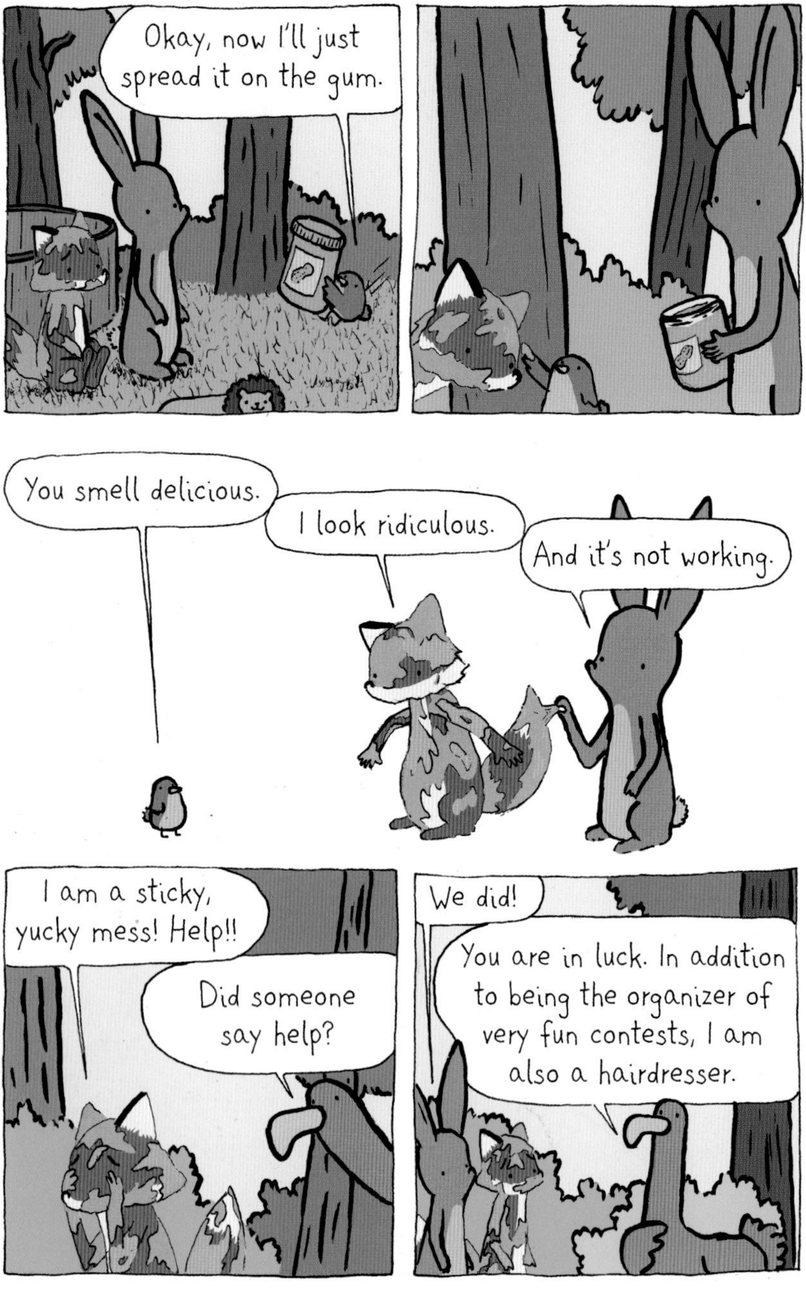
Okay, now I'll just spread it on the gum.
You smell delicious.
I look ridiculous.
And it's not working.
I am a sticky, yucky mess! Help!!
Did someone say help?
We did!
You are in luck. In addition to being the organizer of very fun contests, I am also a hairdresser.

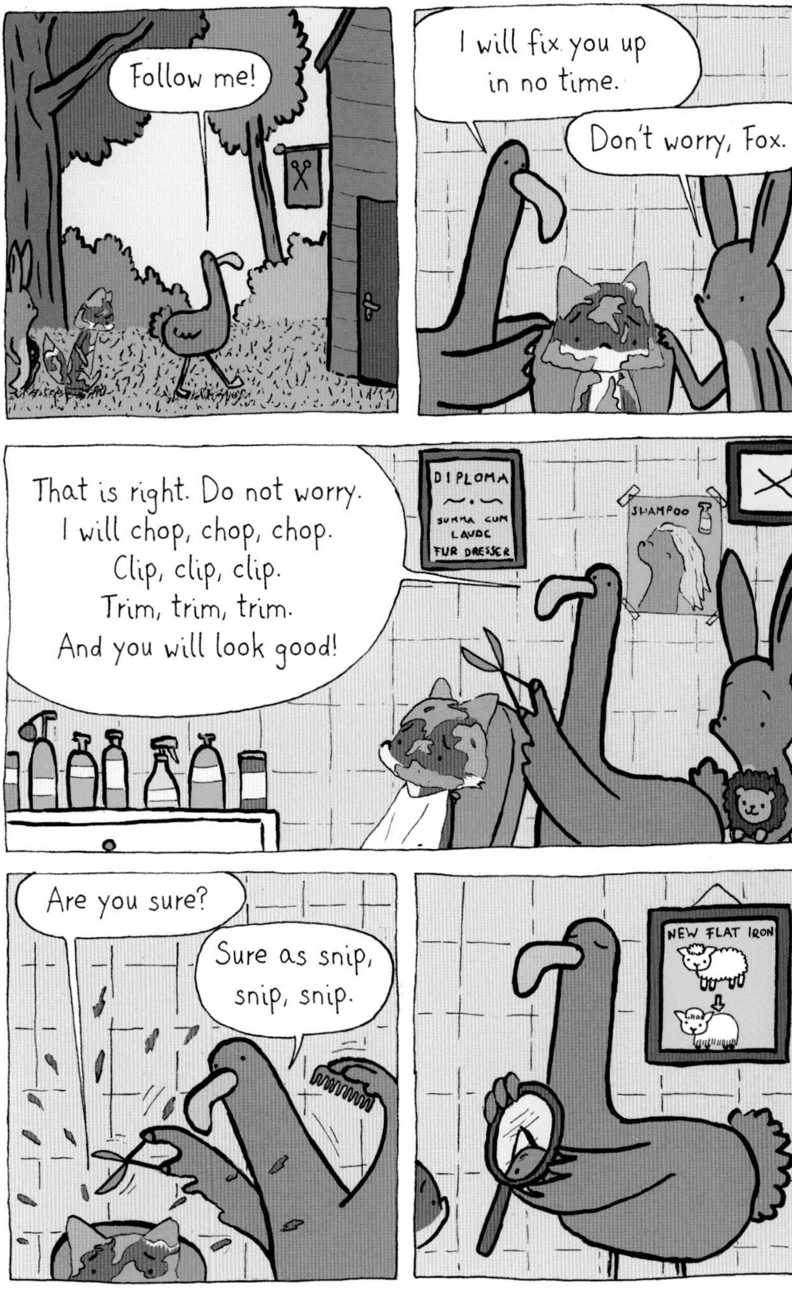
Follow me!
I will fix you up in no time.
Don't worry, Fox.
That is right. Do not worry. I will chop, chop, chop. Clip, clip, clip. Trim, trim, trim. And you will look good!
DIPLOMA
SUMMA CUM LAUDE
FUR DRESSER
SHAMPOO
Are you sure?
Sure as snip, snip, snip.
NEW FLAT IRON

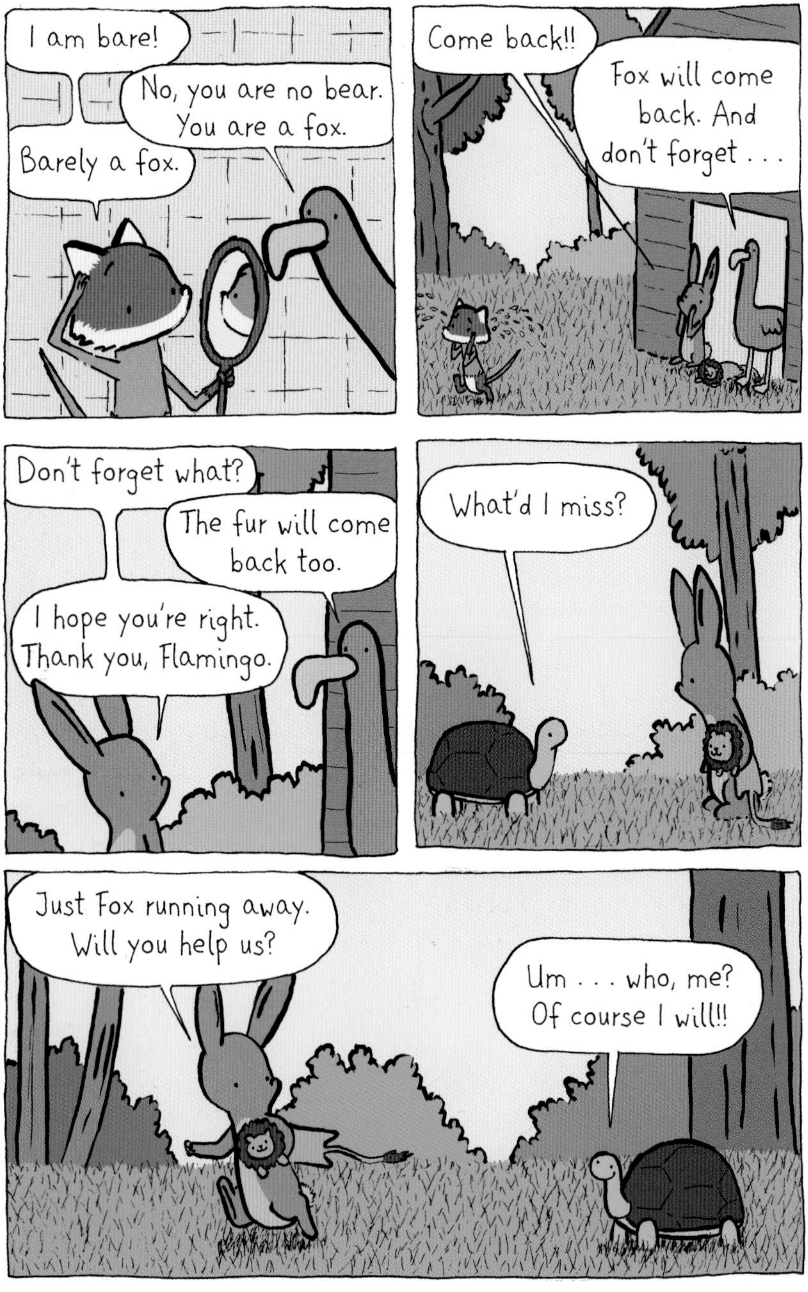
I am bare!
No, you are no bear. You are a fox.
Barely a fox.
Come back!!
Fox will come back. And don't forget . . .
Don't forget what?
The fur will come back too.
I hope you're right. Thank you, Flamingo.
What'd I miss?
Just Fox running away. Will you help us?
Um . . . who, me? Of course I will!!

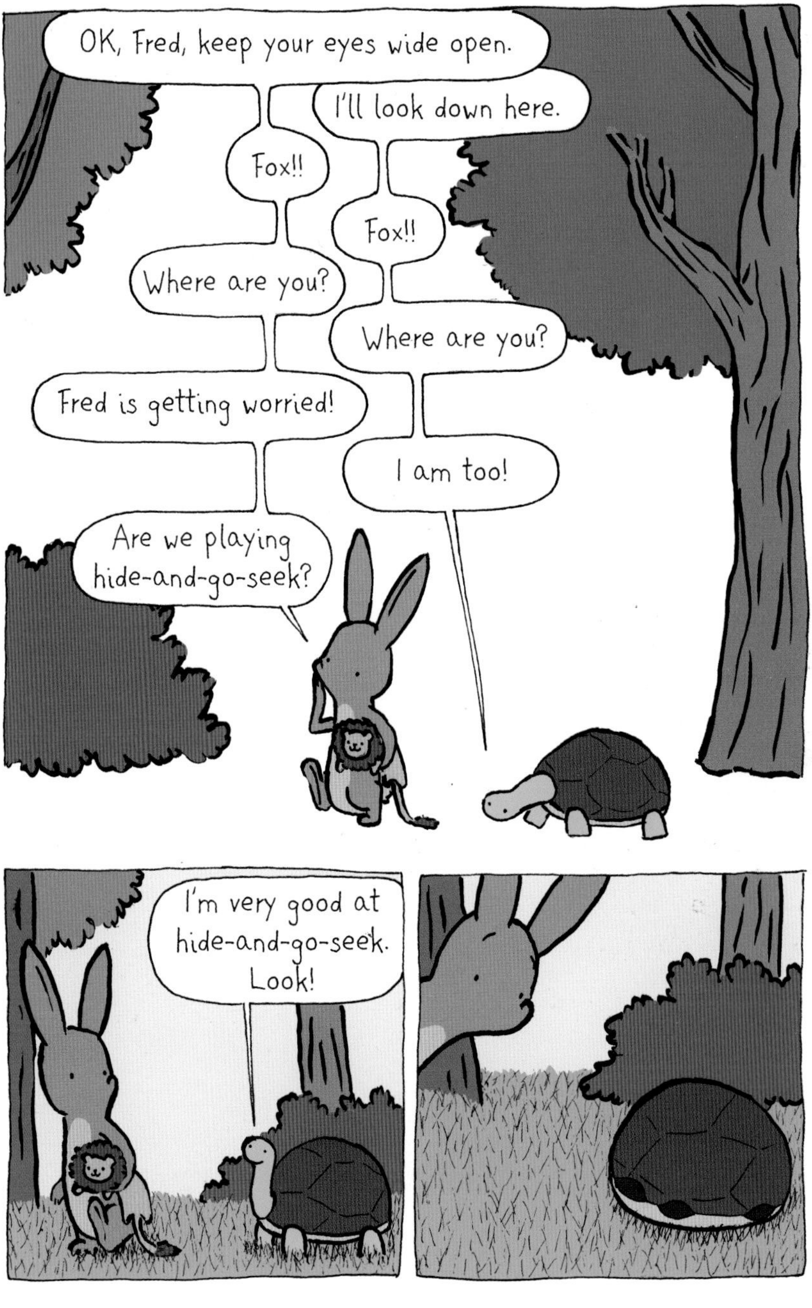
OK, Fred, keep your eyes wide open.
I'll look down here.
Fox!!
Fox!!
Where are you?
Where are you?
Fred is getting worried!
I am too!
Are we playing hide-and-go-seek?
I'm very good at hide-and-go-seek. Look!

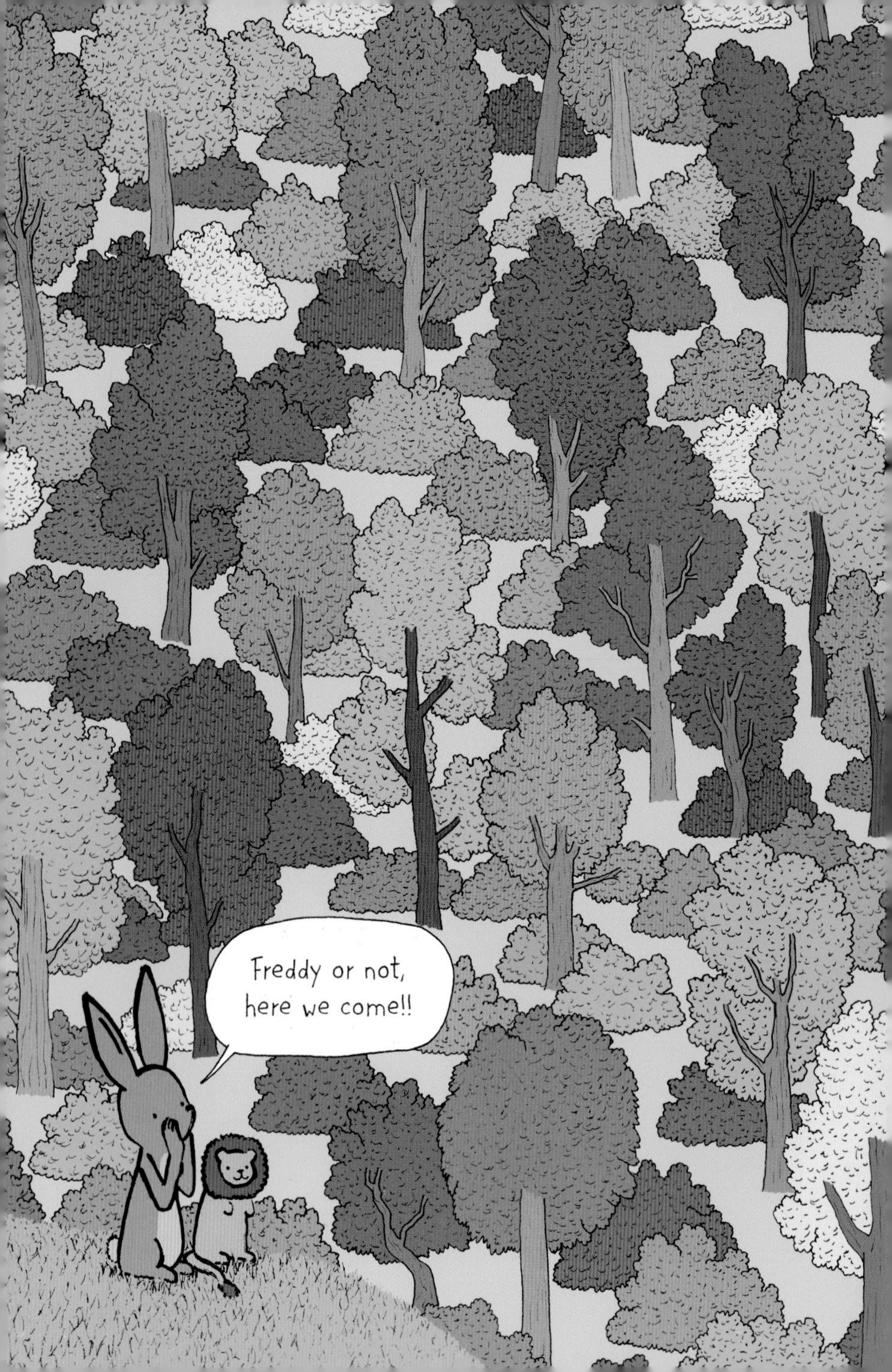
Freddy or not,
here we come!!

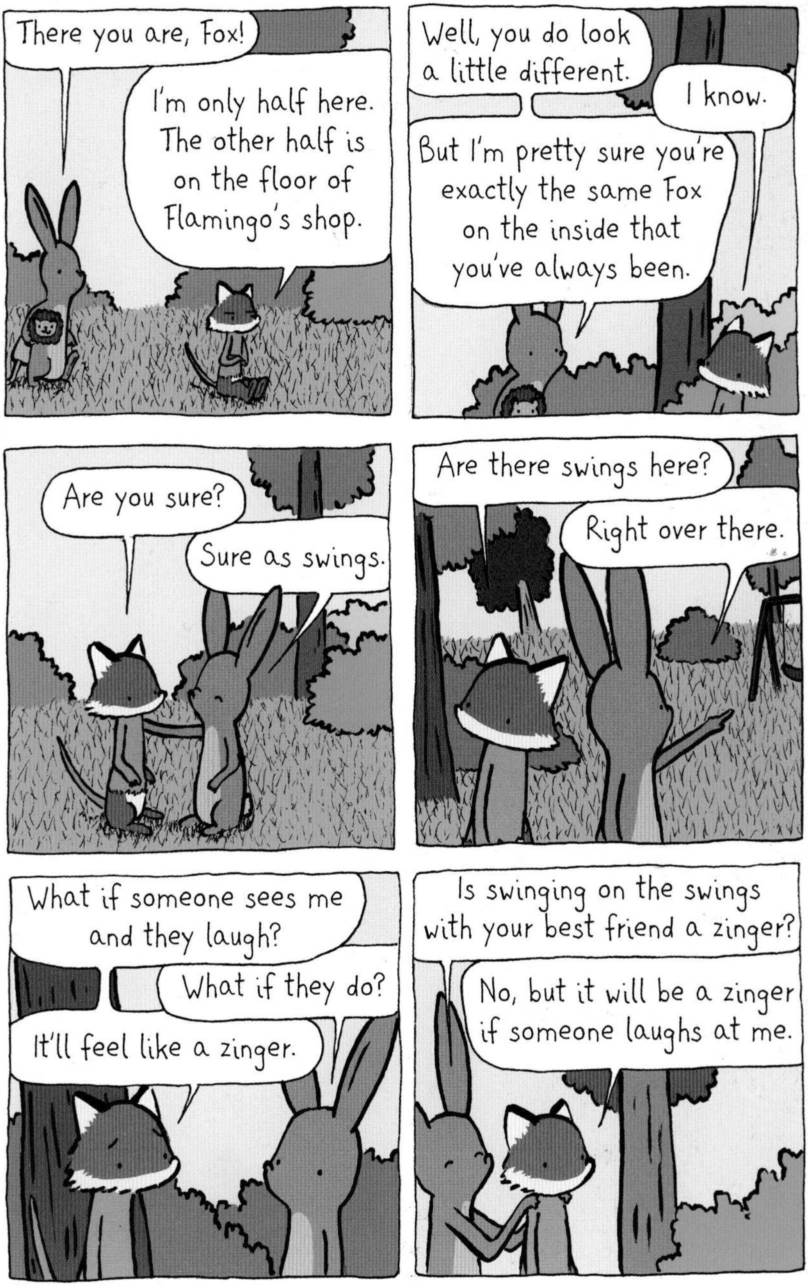
There you are, Fox!
I'm only half here. The other half is on the floor of Flamingo's shop.
Well, you do look a little different.
But I'm pretty sure you're exactly the same Fox on the inside that you've always been.
I know.
Are you sure?
Sure as swings.
Are there swings here?
Right over there.
What if someone sees me and they laugh?
What if they do?
It'll feel like a zinger.
Is swinging on the swings with your best friend a zinger?
No, but it will be a zinger if someone laughs at me.

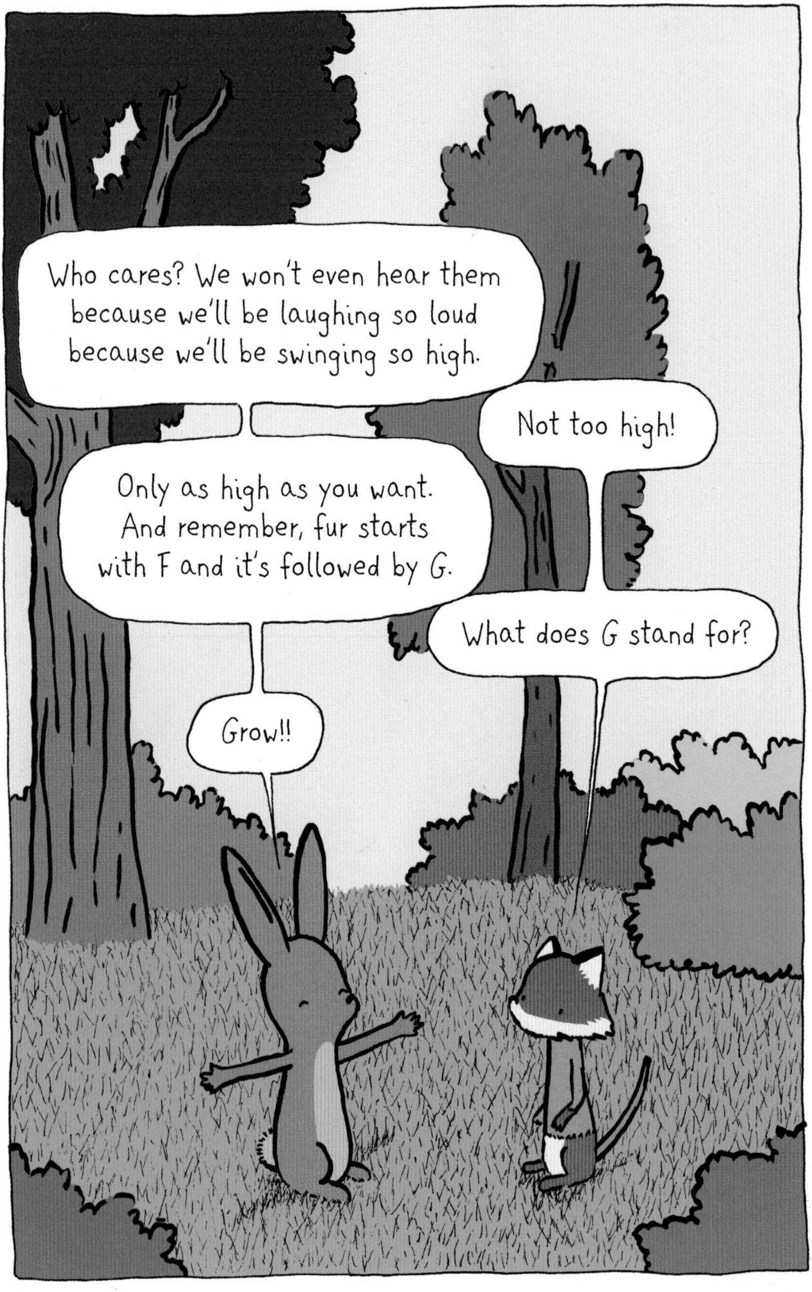
Who cares? We won't even hear them because we'll be laughing so loud because we'll be swinging so high.
Not too high!
Only as high as you want. And remember, fur starts with F and it's followed by G.
What does G stand for?
Grow!!

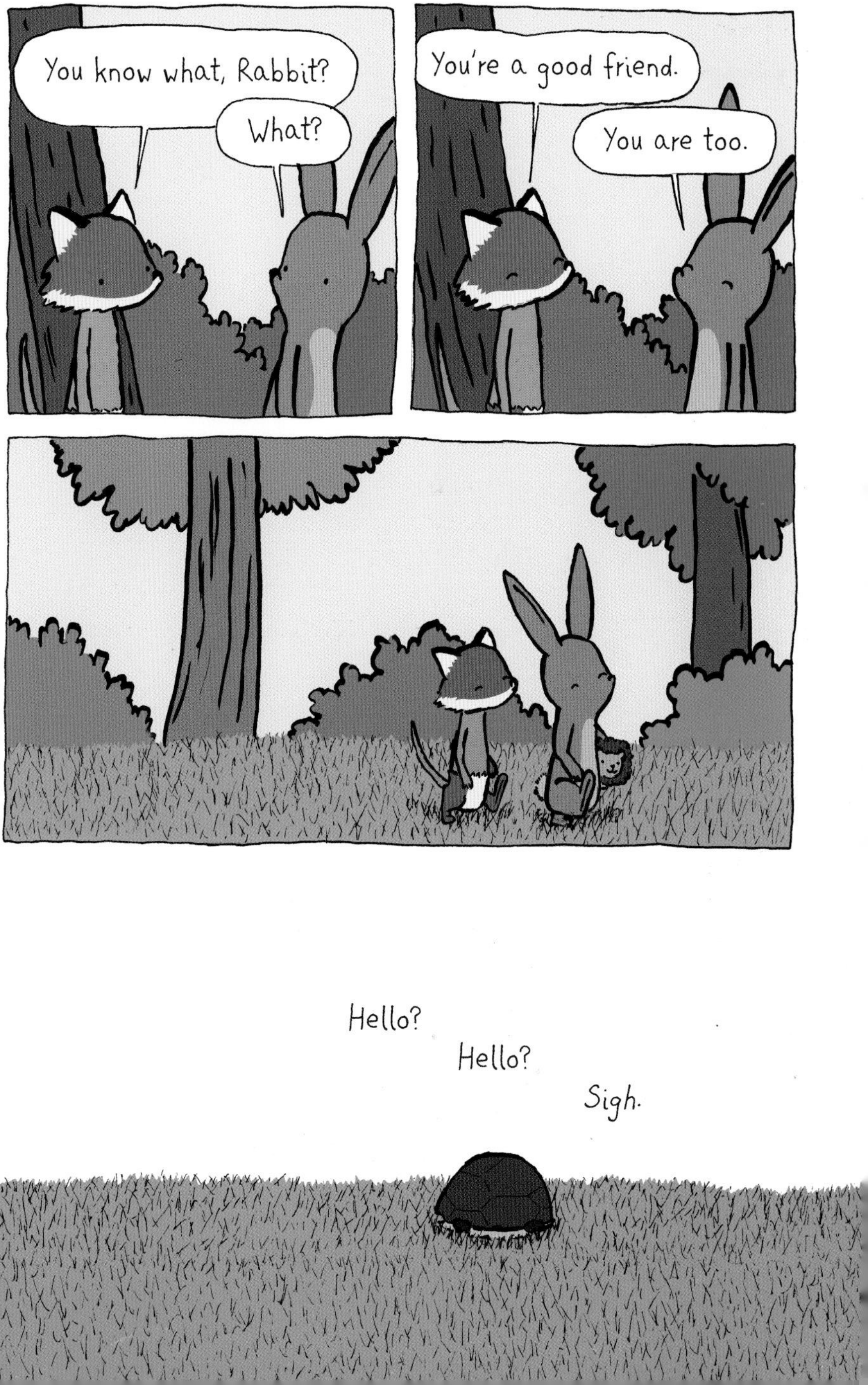
You know what, Rabbit?
What?
You're a good friend.
You are too.
Hello?
Hello?
Sigh.

SWINGS, WINGS & SCARY THINGS

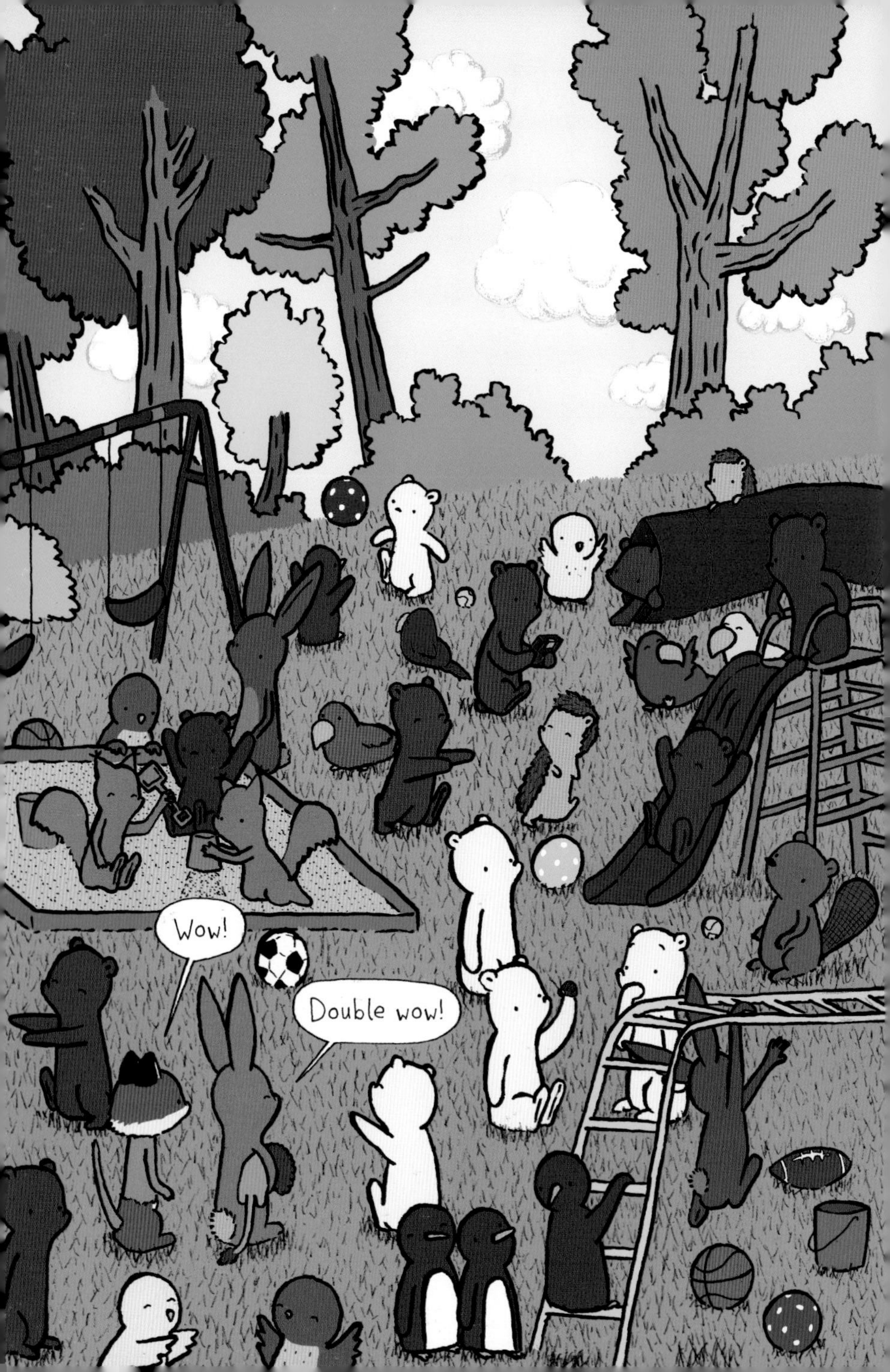
Wow!
Double wow!

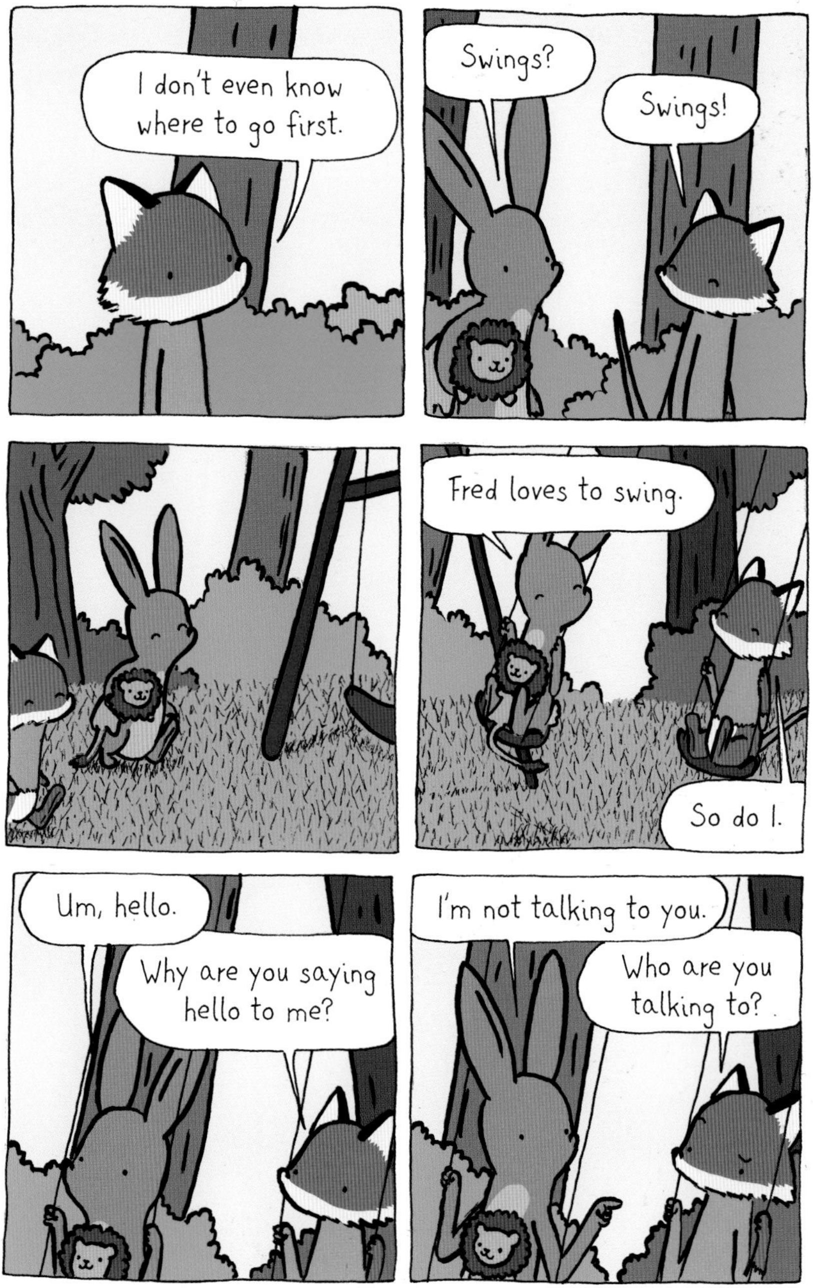
I don't even know where to go first.
Swings?
Swings!
Fred loves to swing.
So do I.
Um, hello.
Why are you saying hello to me?
I'm not talking to you.
Who are you talking to?

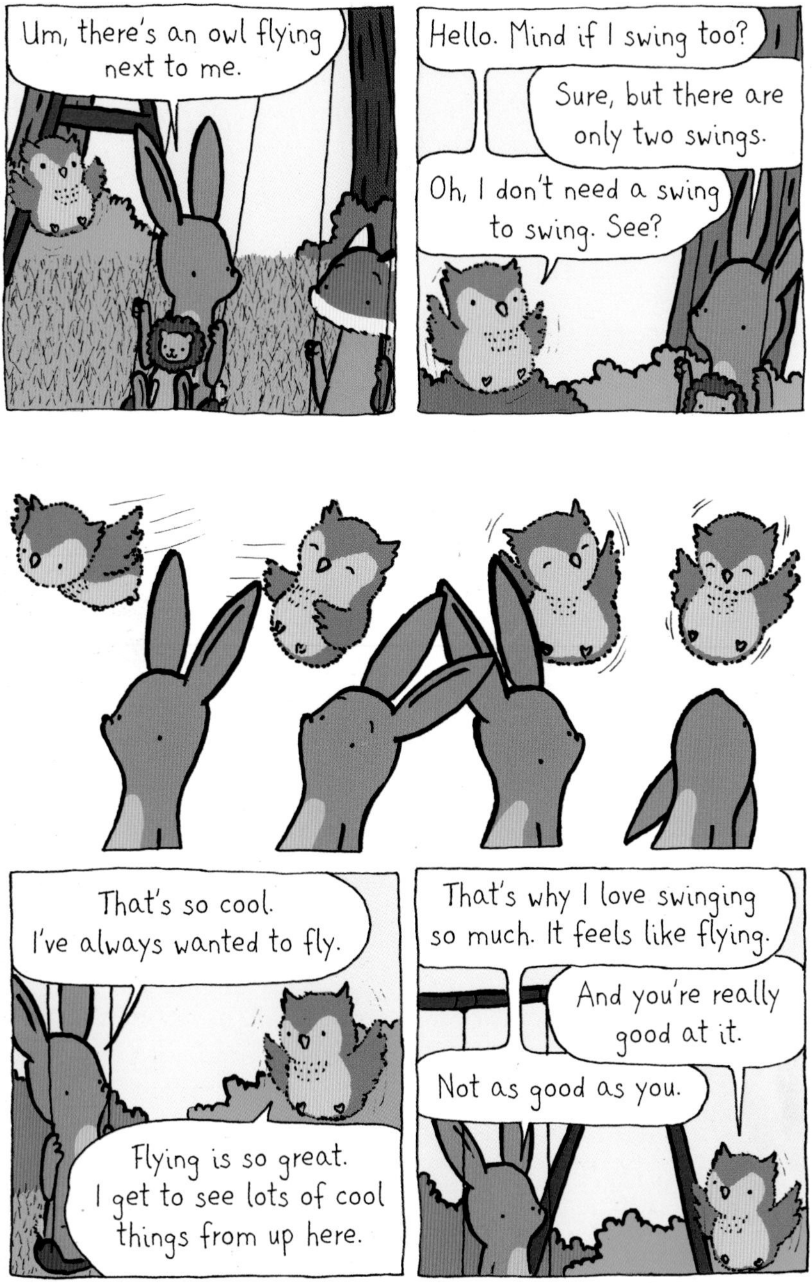
Um, there's an owl flying next to me.
Hello. Mind if I swing too?
Sure, but there are only two swings.
Oh, I don't need a swing to swing. See?
That's so cool. I've always wanted to fly.
Flying is so great. I get to see lots of cool things from up here.
That's why I love swinging so much. It feels like flying.
And you're really good at it.
Not as good as you.

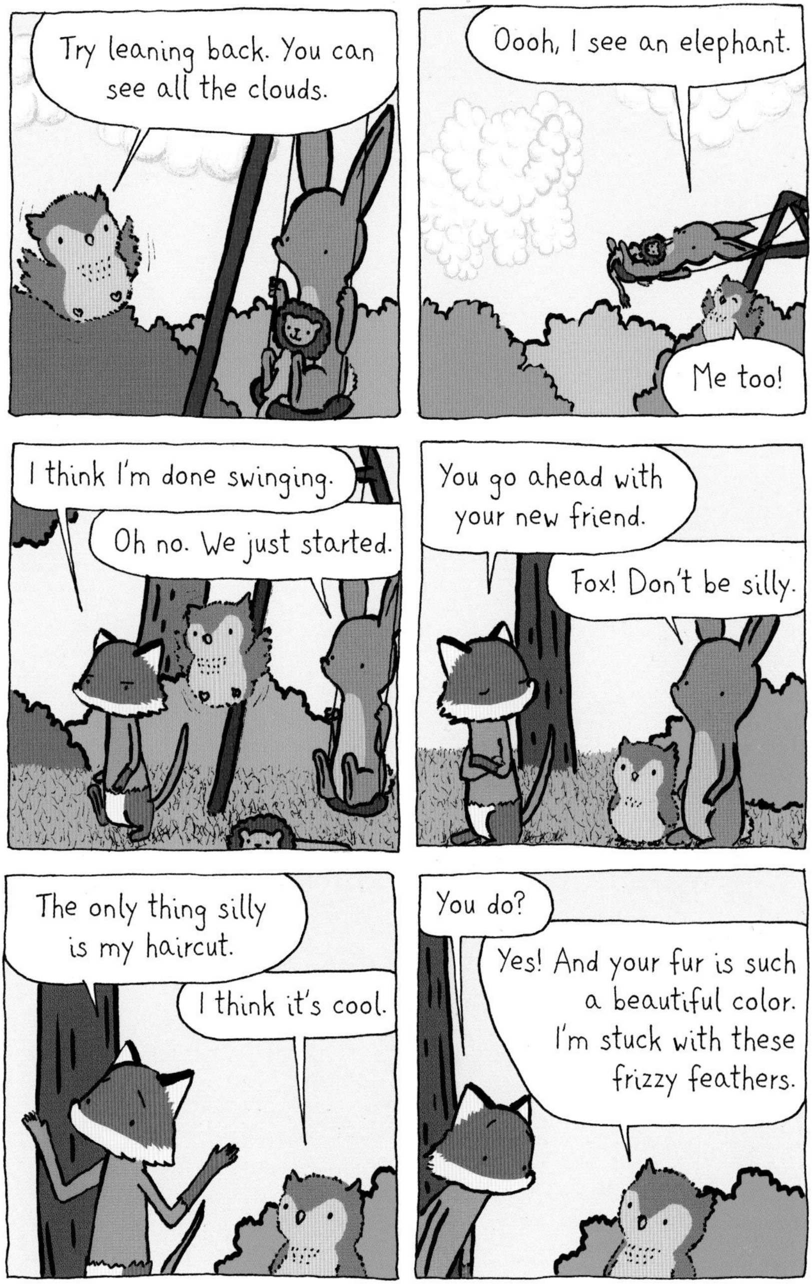
Try leaning back. You can see all the clouds.
Oooh, I see an elephant.
Me too!
I think I'm done swinging.
Oh no. We just started.
You go ahead with your new friend.
Fox! Don't be silly.
The only thing silly is my haircut.
I think it's cool.
You do?
Yes! And your fur is such a beautiful color. I'm stuck with these frizzy feathers.

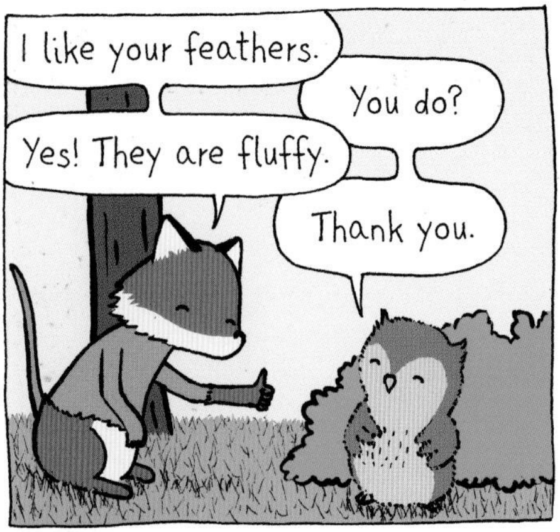
I like your feathers.
You do?
Yes! They are fluffy.
Thank you.

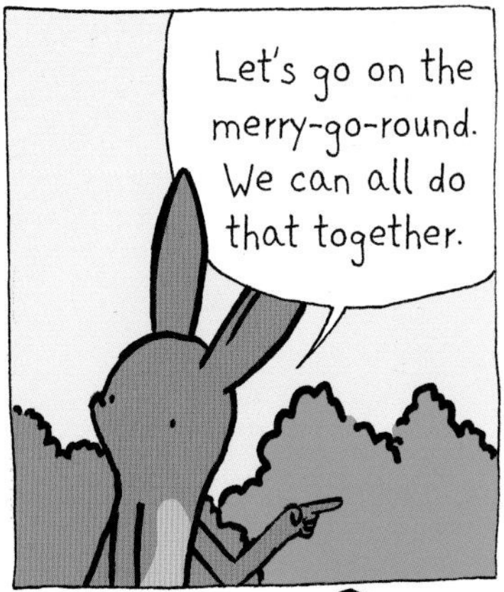
Let's go on the merry-go-round. We can all do that together.

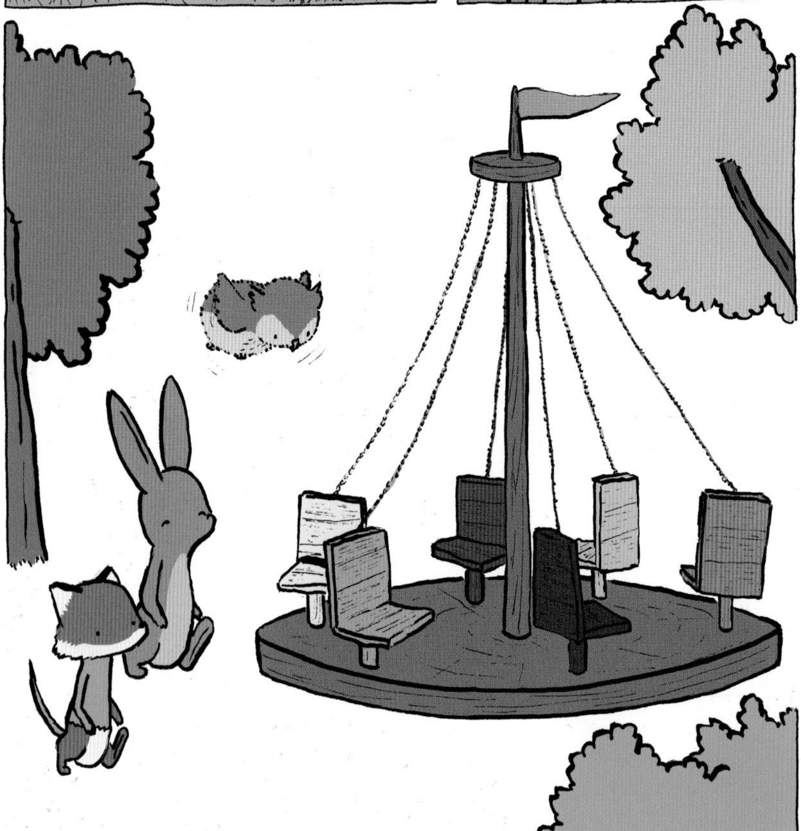

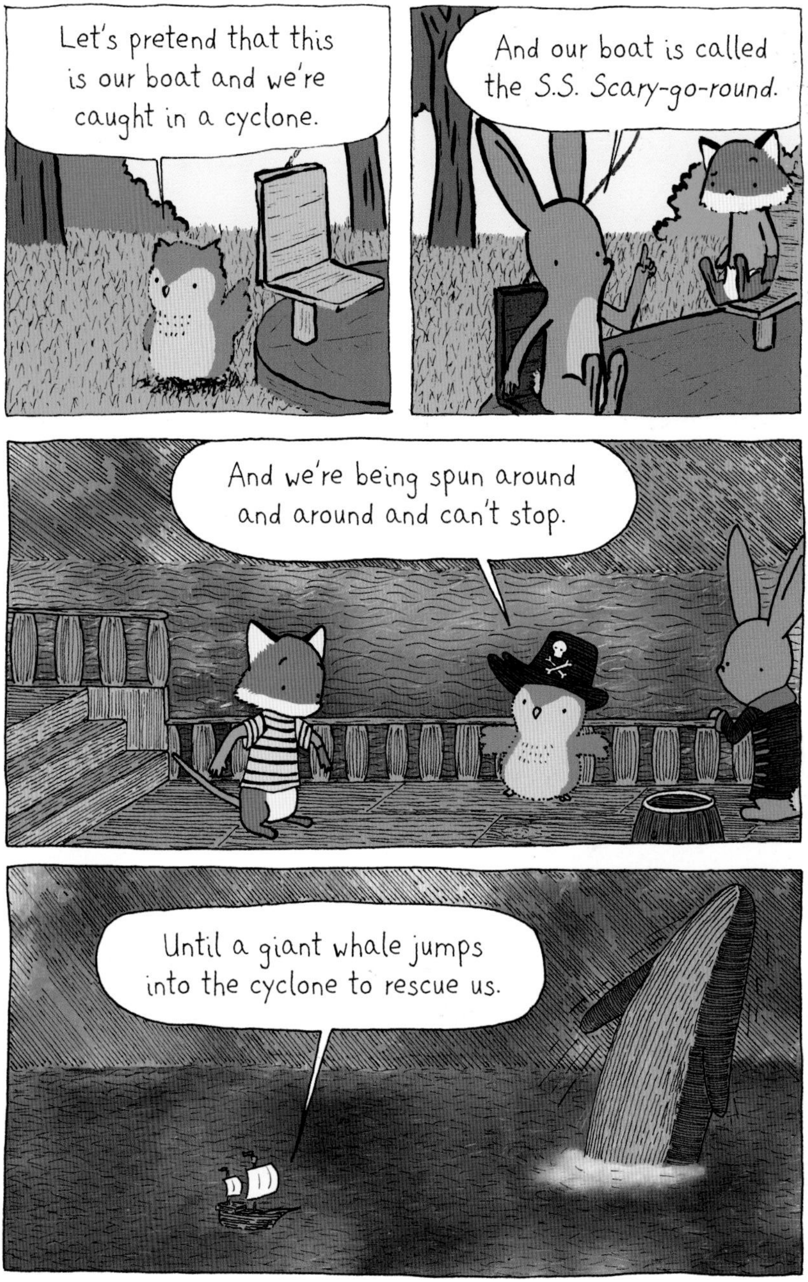
Let's pretend that this is our boat and we're caught in a cyclone.
And our boat is called the S.S. Scary-go-round.
And we're being spun around and around and can't stop.
Until a giant whale jumps into the cyclone to rescue us.

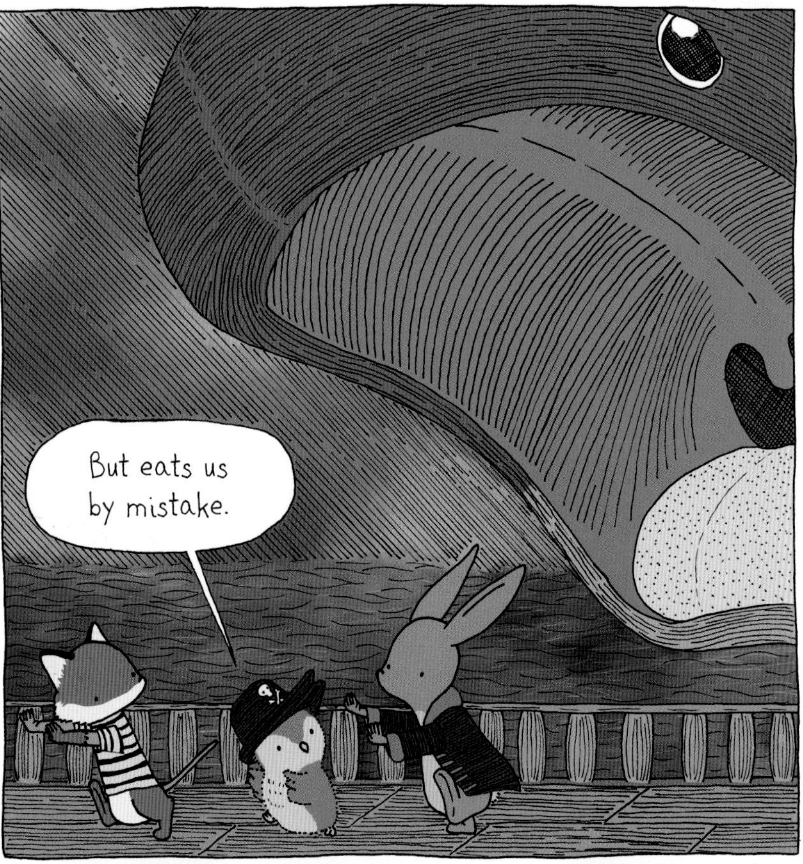
But eats us by mistake.

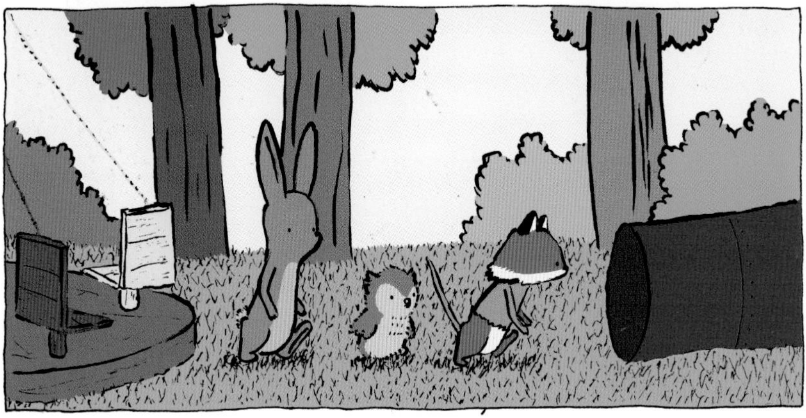

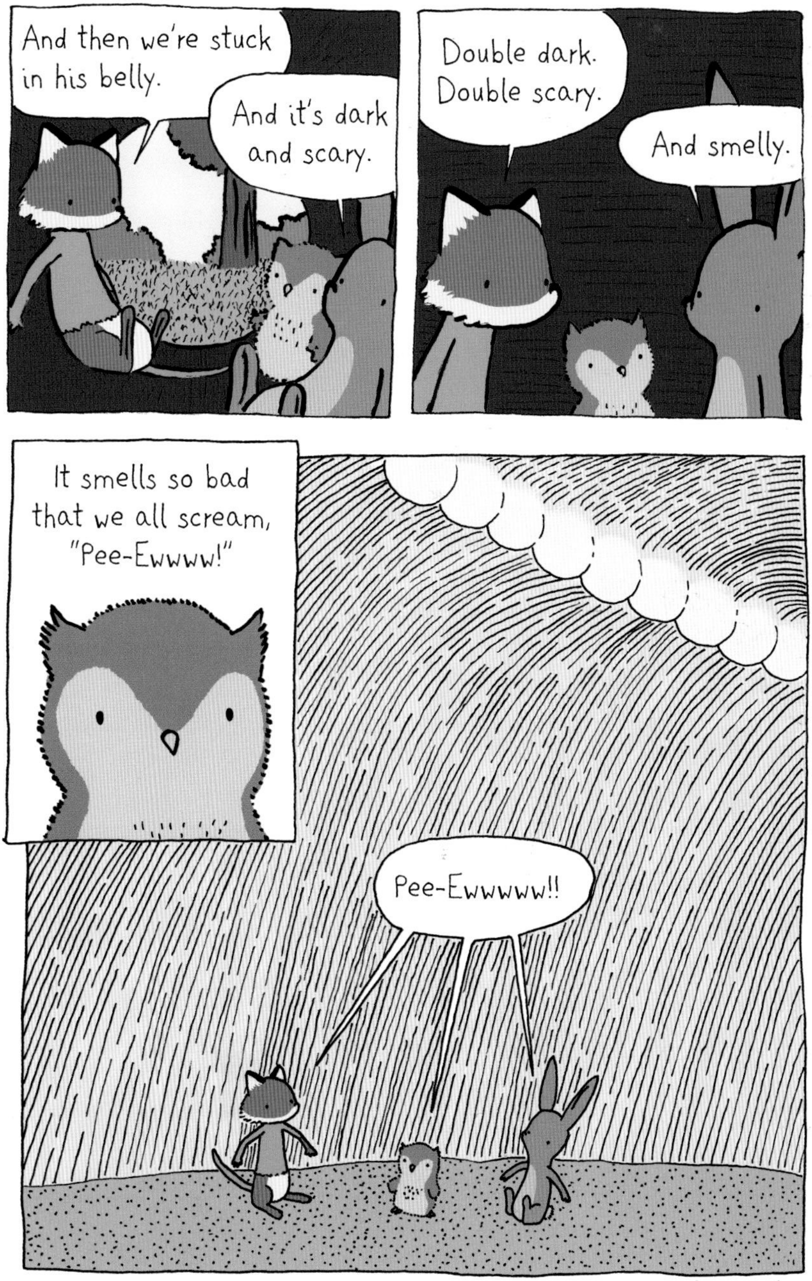
And then we're stuck in his belly.
And it's dark and scary.
Double dark. Double scary.
And smelly.
It smells so bad that we all scream, "Pee-Ewwww!"
Pee-Ewwwww!!

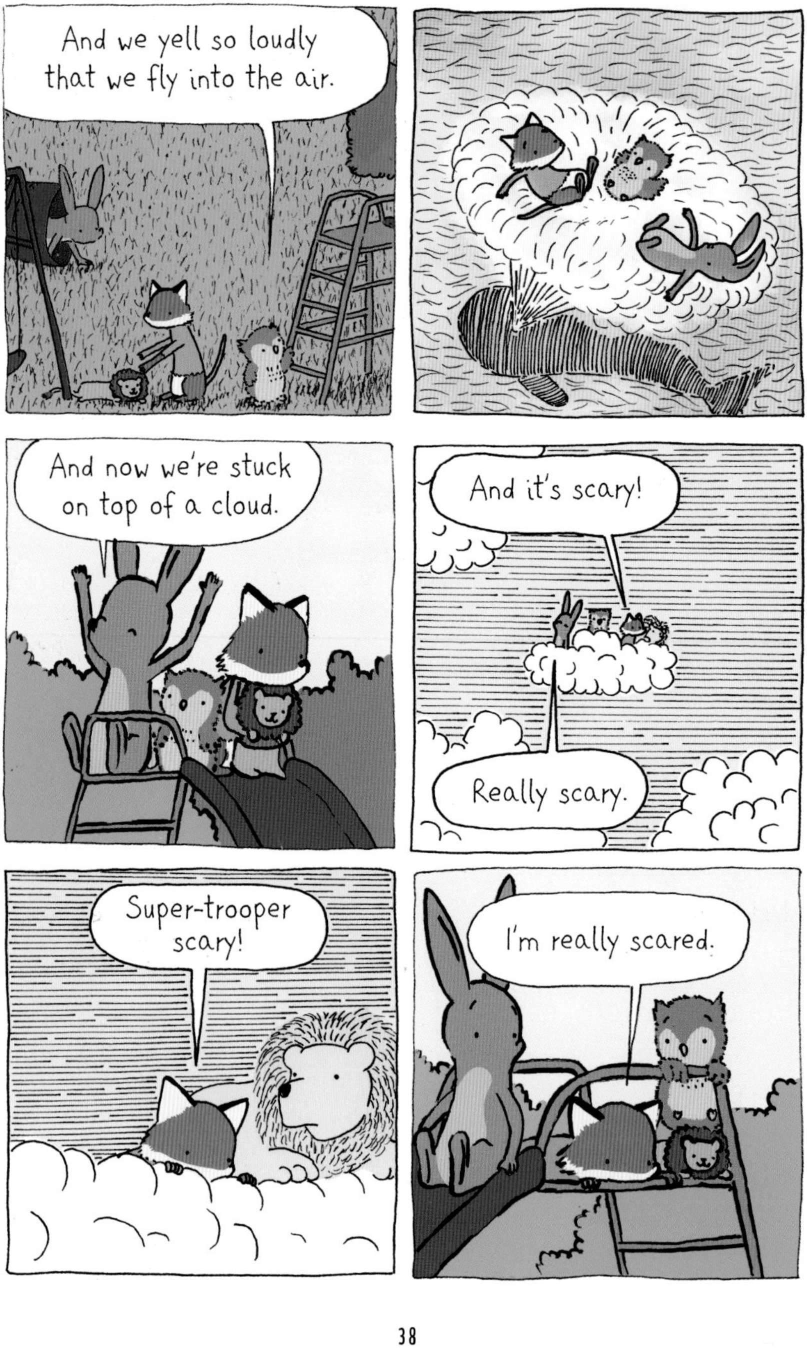
And we yell so loudly that we fly into the air.
And now we're stuck on top of a cloud.
And it's scary!
Really scary.
Super-trooper scary!
I'm really scared.

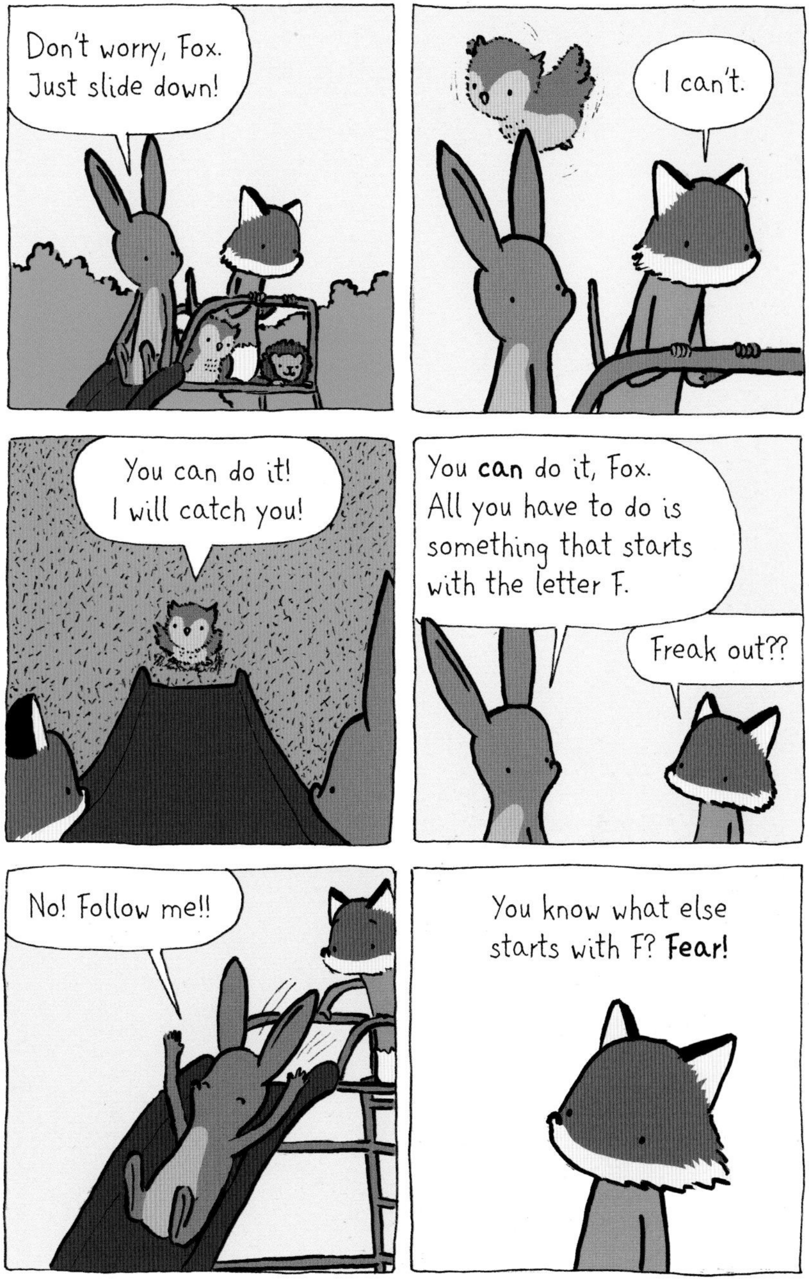
Don't worry, Fox. Just slide down!
I can't.
You can do it! I will catch you!
You **can** do it, Fox. All you have to do is something that starts with the letter F.
Freak out??
No! Follow me!!
You know what else starts with F? **Fear!**

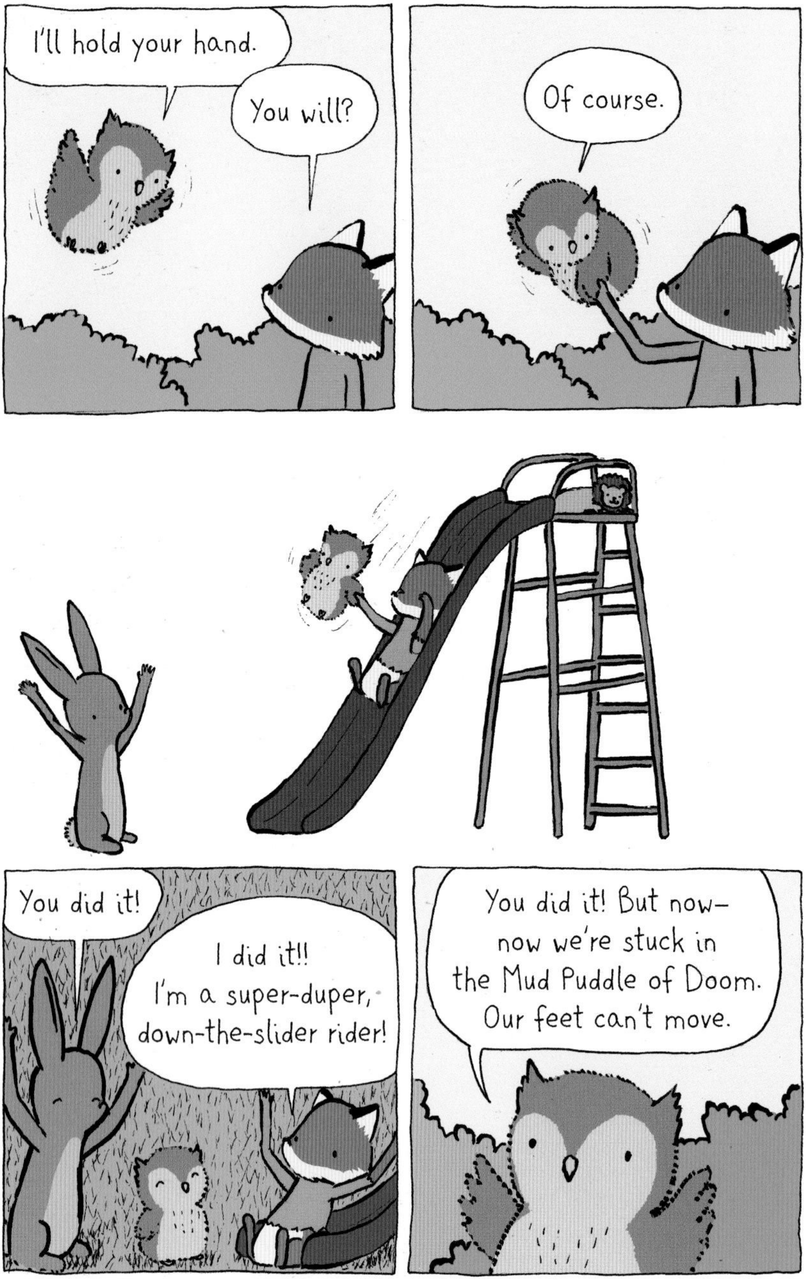
I'll hold your hand.
You will?
Of course.
You did it!
I did it!! I'm a super-duper, down-the-slider rider!
You did it! But now—now we're stuck in the Mud Puddle of Doom. Our feet can't move.

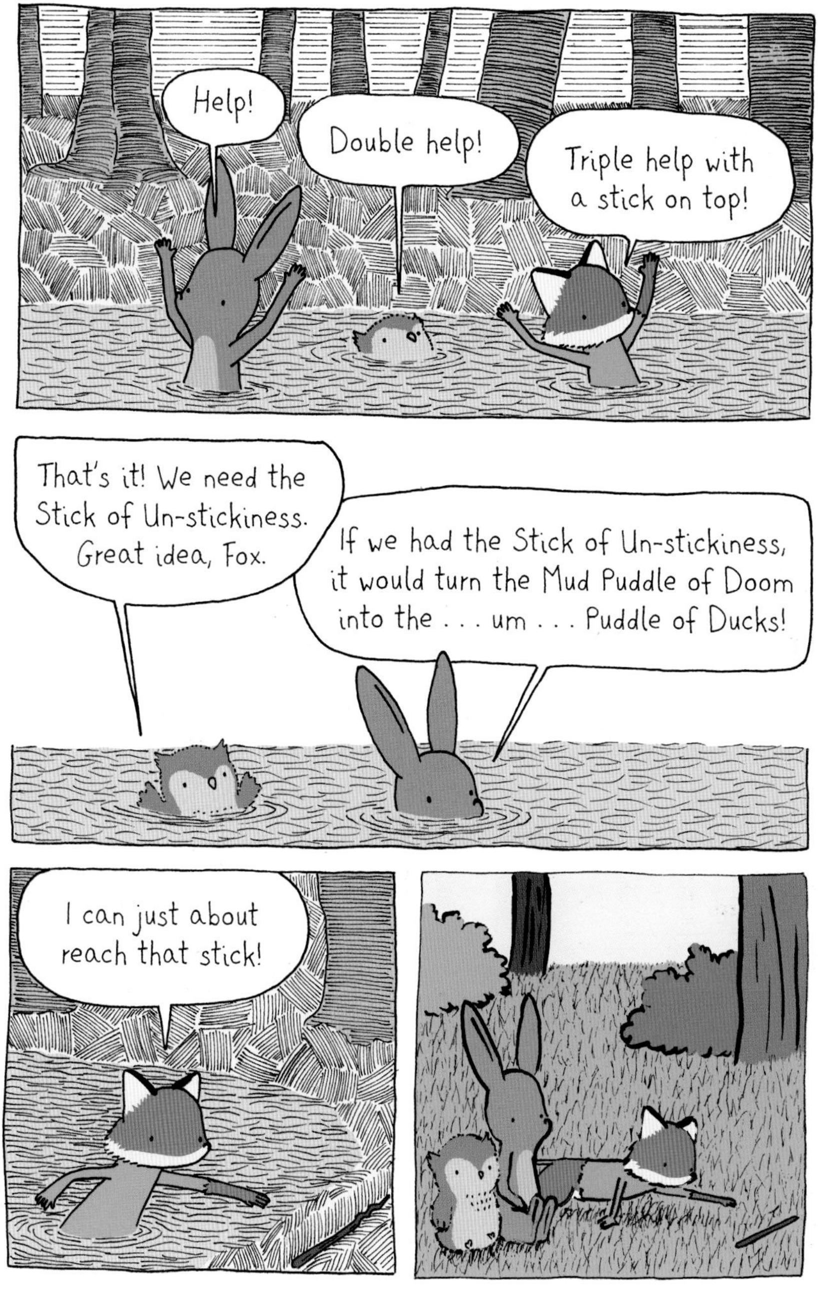
Help!
Double help!
Triple help with a stick on top!
That's it! We need the Stick of Un-stickiness. Great idea, Fox.
If we had the Stick of Un-stickiness, it would turn the Mud Puddle of Doom into the . . . um . . . Puddle of Ducks!
I can just about reach that stick!

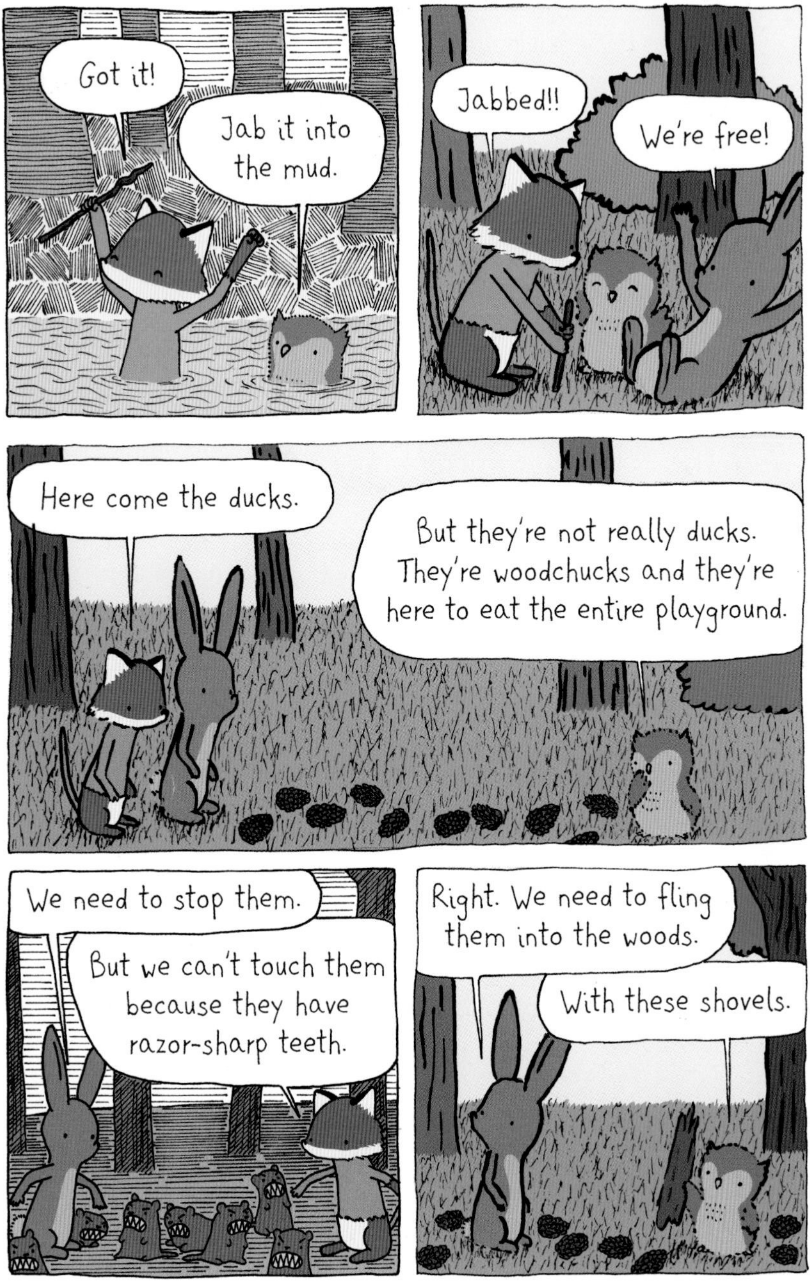
Got it!
Jab it into the mud.
Jabbed!!
We're free!
Here come the ducks.
But they're not really ducks. They're woodchucks and they're here to eat the entire playground.
We need to stop them.
But we can't touch them because they have razor-sharp teeth.
Right. We need to fling them into the woods.
With these shovels.

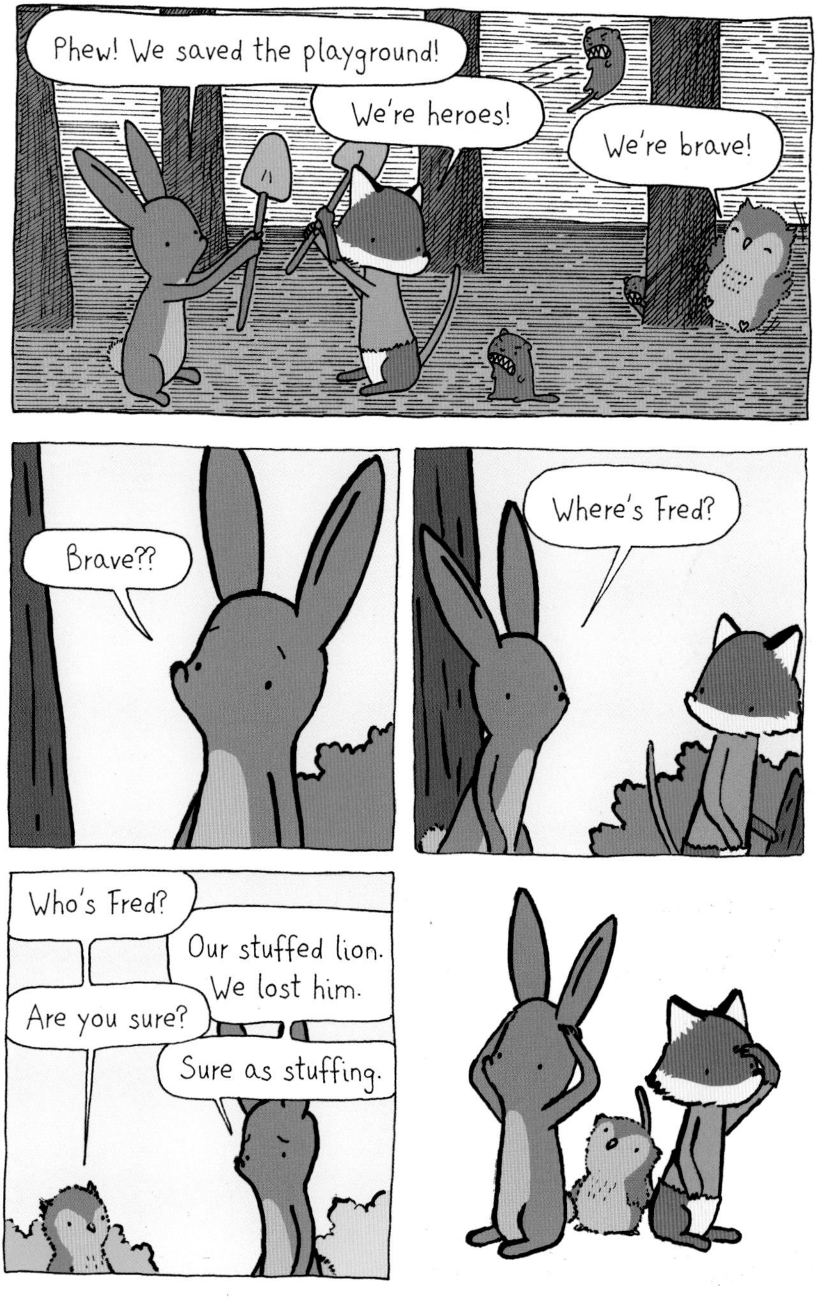
Phew! We saved the playground!
We're heroes!
We're brave!
Brave??
Where's Fred?
Who's Fred?
Our stuffed lion. We lost him.
Are you sure?
Sure as stuffing.

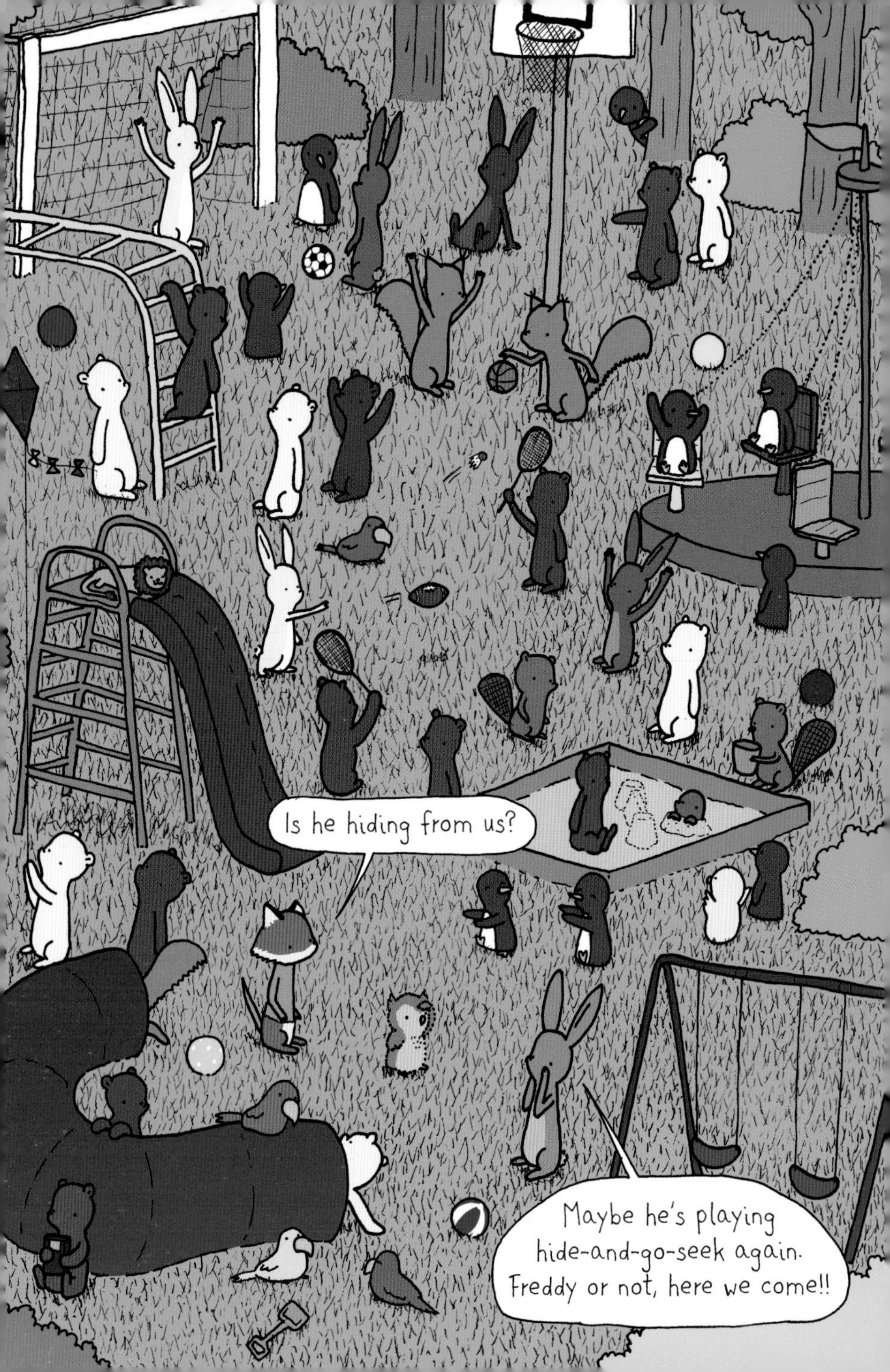
Is he hiding from us?
Maybe he's playing hide-and-go-seek again. Freddy or not, here we come!!

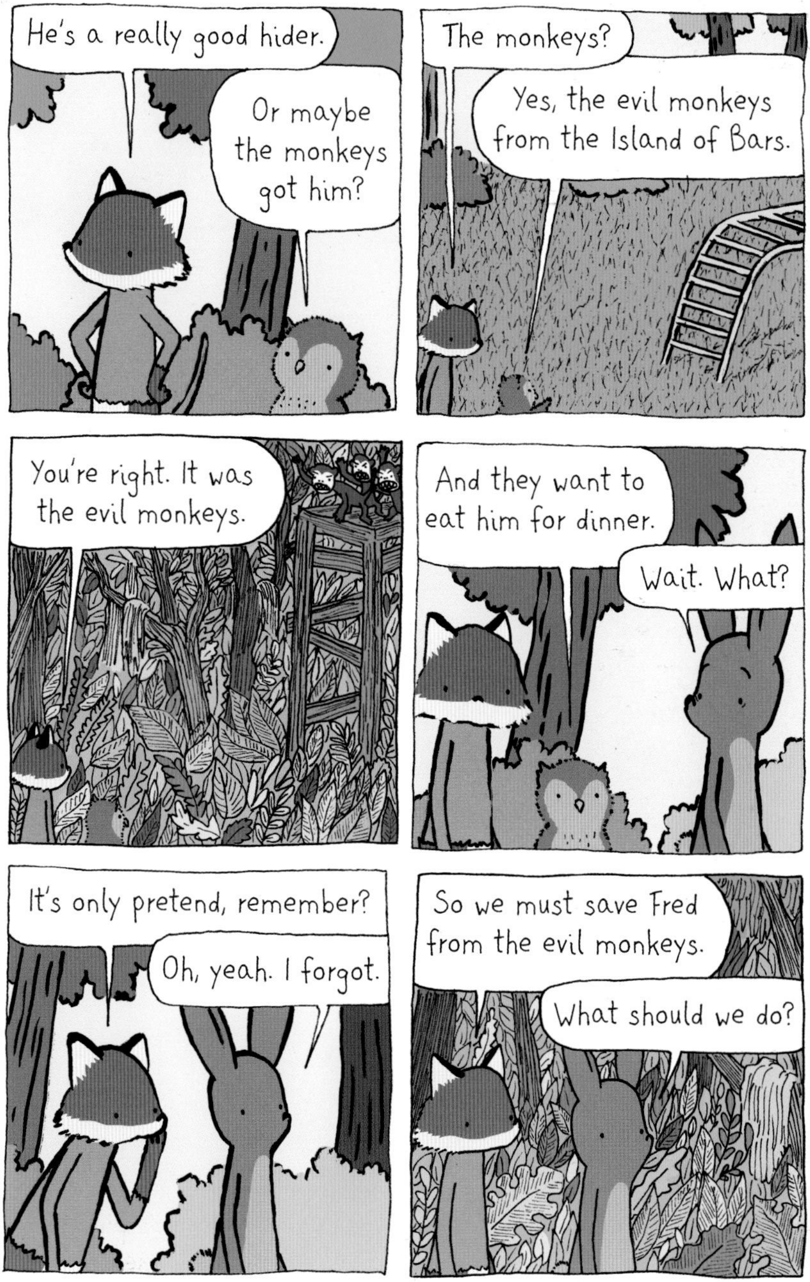
He's a really good hider.
Or maybe the monkeys got him?
The monkeys?
Yes, the evil monkeys from the Island of Bars.
You're right. It was the evil monkeys.
And they want to eat him for dinner.
Wait. What?
It's only pretend, remember?
Oh, yeah. I forgot.
So we must save Fred from the evil monkeys.
What should we do?

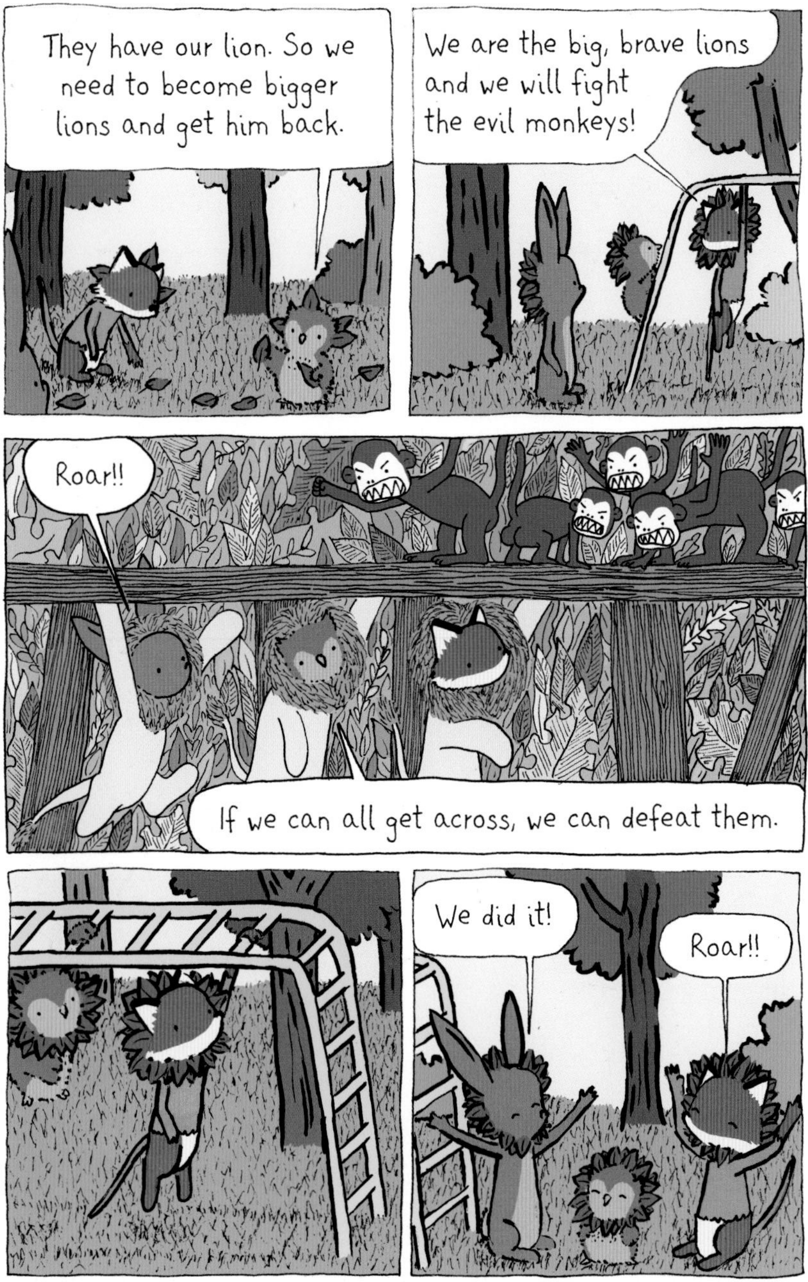
They have our lion. So we need to become bigger lions and get him back.
We are the big, brave lions and we will fight the evil monkeys!
Roar!!
If we can all get across, we can defeat them.
We did it!
Roar!!

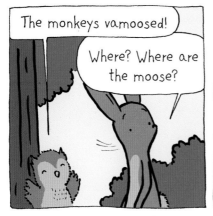

The monkeys vamoosed!

Where? Where are the moose?

No, no. "Vamoose" means to run away.

Phew! I don't know if I could handle a moose.

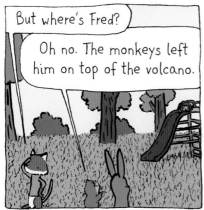

But where's Fred?

Oh no. The monkeys left him on top of the volcano.

And all the red leaves are bits of burning lava!

Hop over the red leaves of lava!!

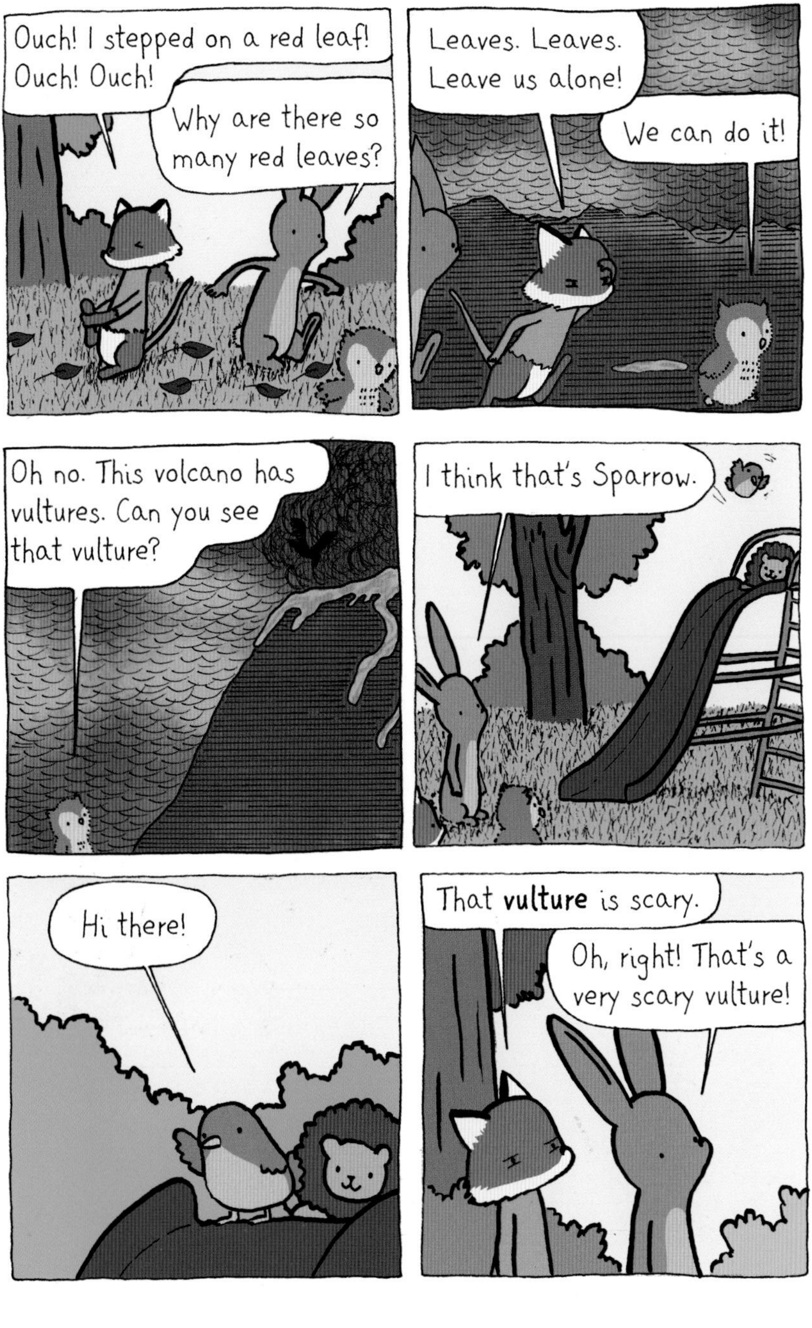
Ouch! I stepped on a red leaf! Ouch! Ouch!
Why are there so many red leaves?
Leaves. Leaves. Leave us alone!
We can do it!
Oh no. This volcano has vultures. Can you see that vulture?
I think that's Sparrow.
Hi there!
That **vulture** is scary.
Oh, right! That's a very scary vulture!

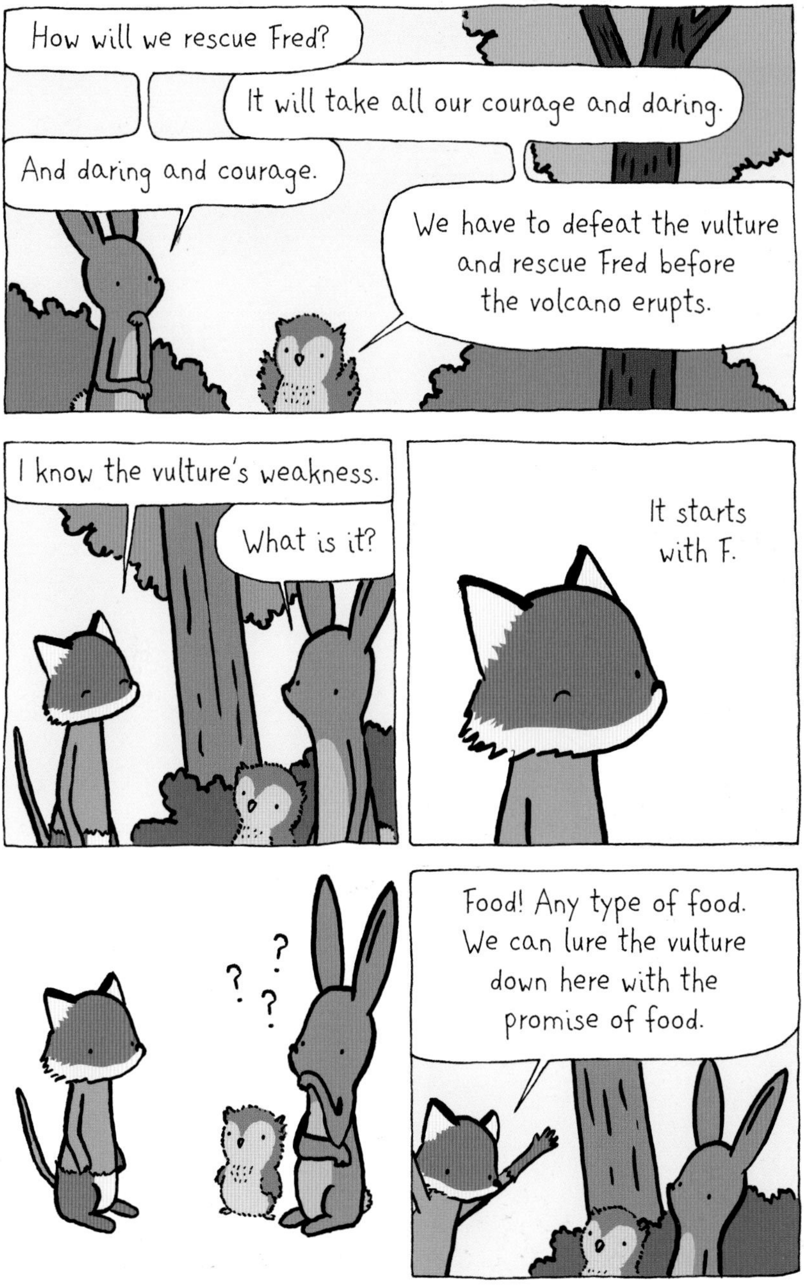
How will we rescue Fred?
It will take all our courage and daring.
And daring and courage.
We have to defeat the vulture and rescue Fred before the volcano erupts.
I know the vulture's weakness.
What is it?
It starts with F.
? ? ?
Food! Any type of food. We can lure the vulture down here with the promise of food.

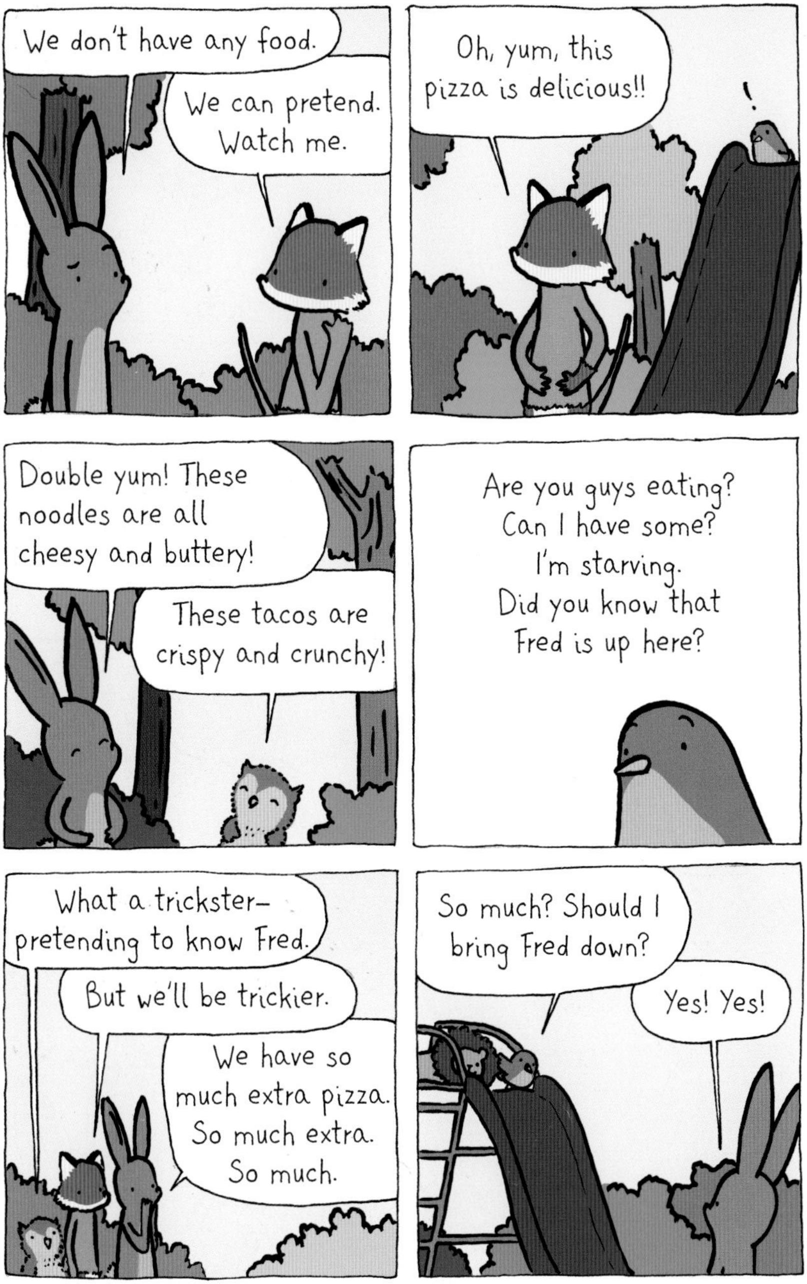
We don't have any food.
We can pretend. Watch me.
Oh, yum, this pizza is delicious!!
!
Double yum! These noodles are all cheesy and buttery!
These tacos are crispy and crunchy!
Are you guys eating? Can I have some? I'm starving. Did you know that Fred is up here?
What a trickster– pretending to know Fred.
But we'll be trickier.
We have so much extra pizza. So much extra. So much.
So much? Should I bring Fred down?
Yes! Yes!

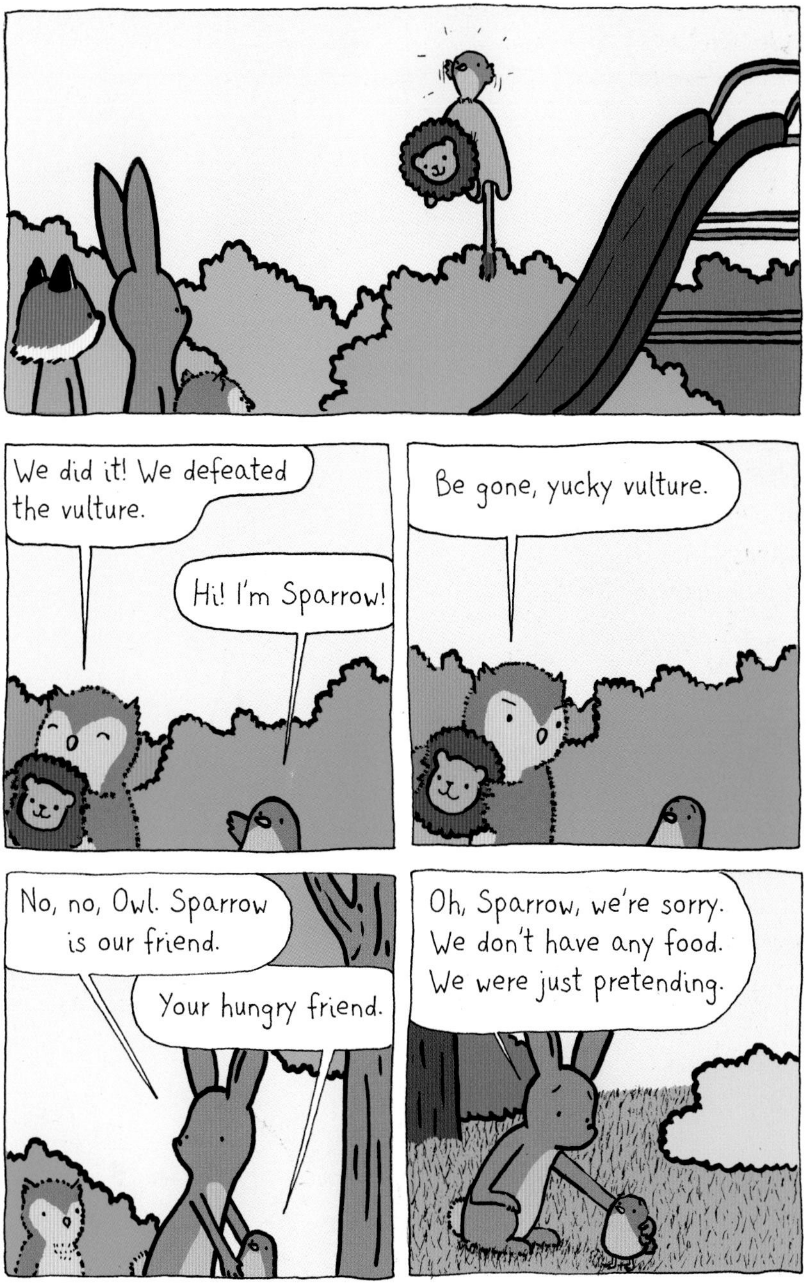
We did it! We defeated the vulture.
Hi! I'm Sparrow!
Be gone, yucky vulture.
No, no, Owl. Sparrow is our friend.
Your hungry friend.
Oh, Sparrow, we're sorry. We don't have any food. We were just pretending.

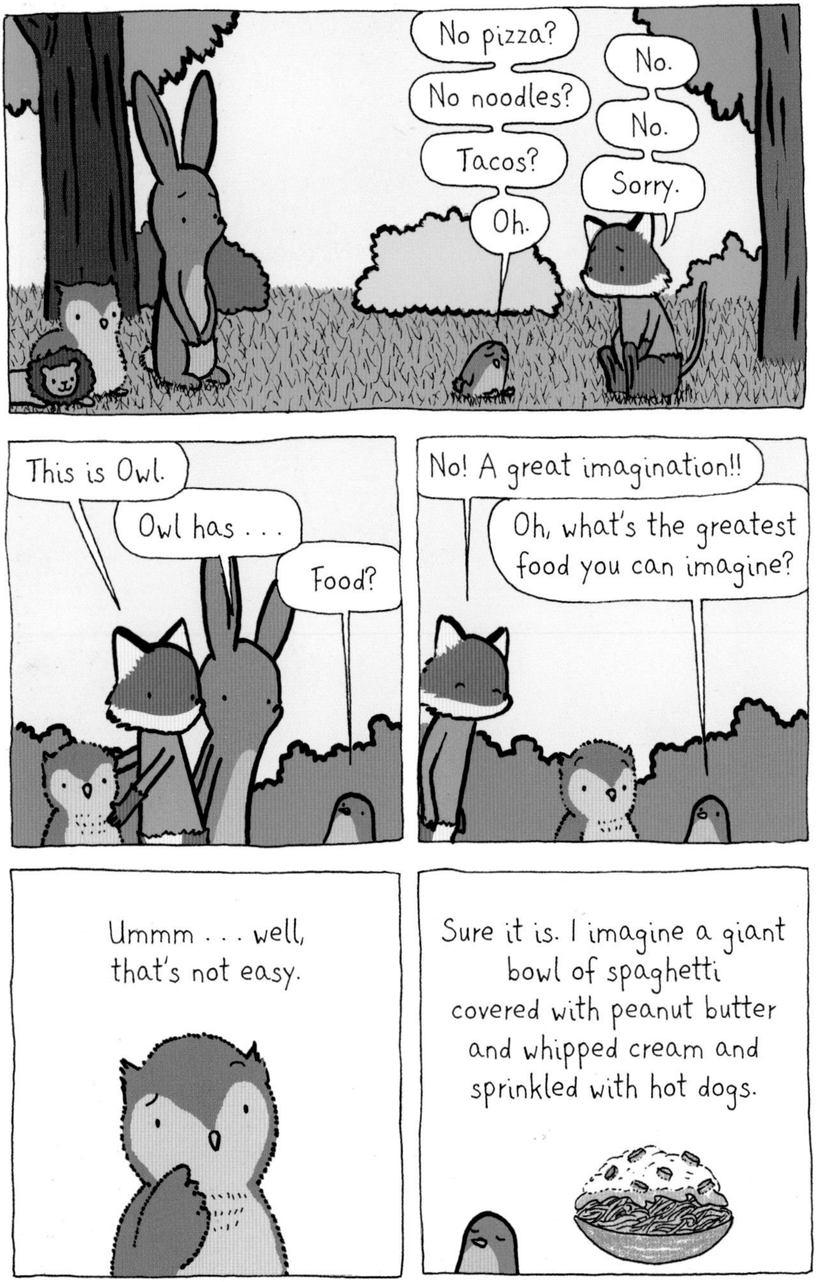
No pizza?
No.
No noodles?
No.
Tacos?
Sorry.
Oh.
This is Owl.
Owl has . . .
Food?
No! A great imagination!!
Oh, what's the greatest food you can imagine?
Ummm . . . well, that's not easy.
Sure it is. I imagine a giant bowl of spaghetti covered with peanut butter and whipped cream and sprinkled with hot dogs.

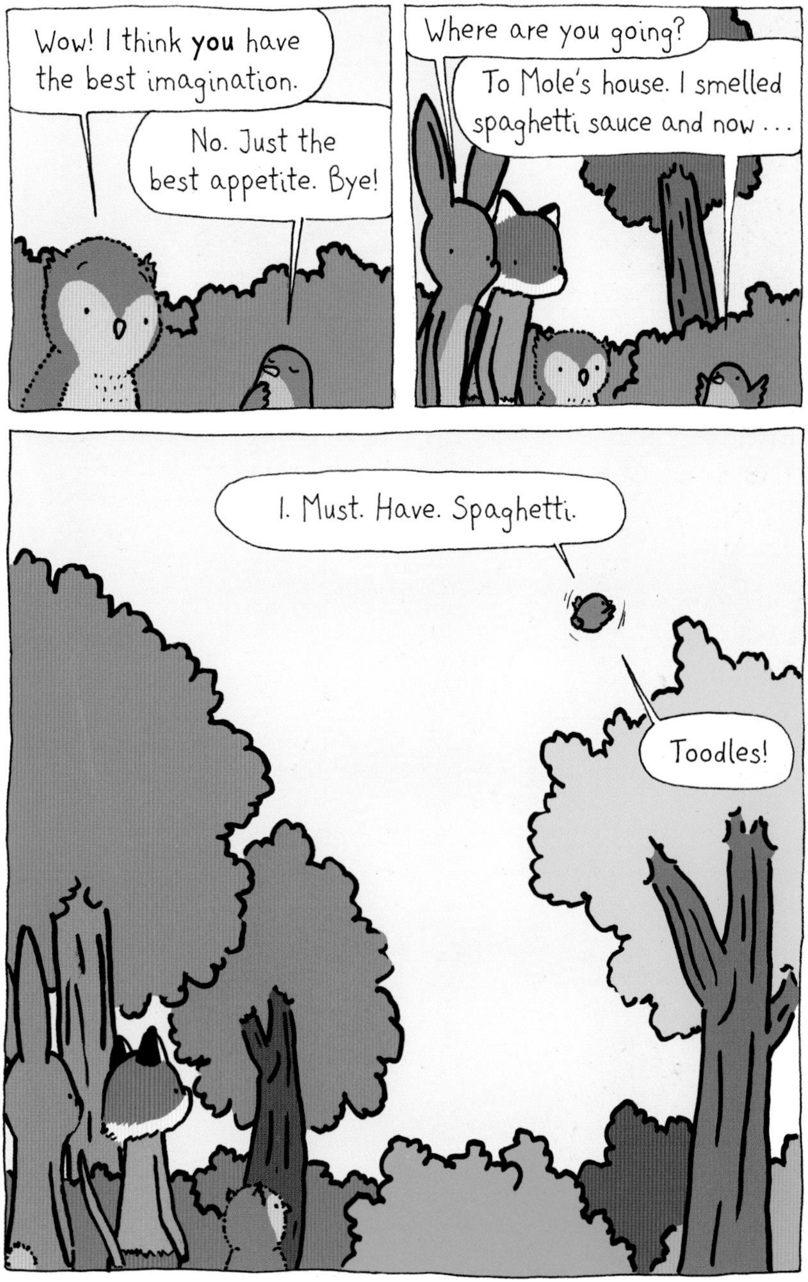
Wow! I think **you** have the best imagination.
No. Just the best appetite. Bye!
Where are you going?
To Mole's house. I smelled spaghetti sauce and now . . .
I. Must. Have. Spaghetti.
Toodles!

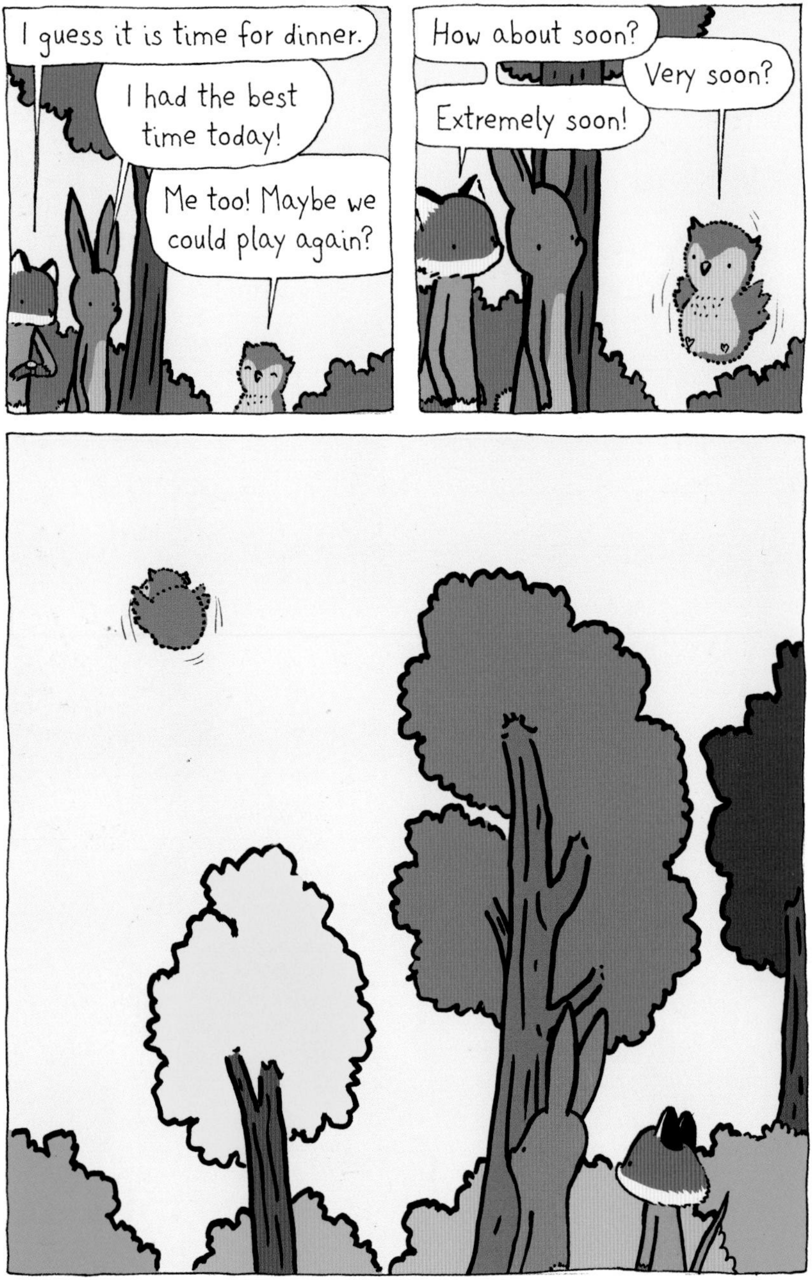
I guess it is time for dinner.
I had the best time today!
Me too! Maybe we could play again?
How about soon?
Very soon?
Extremely soon!

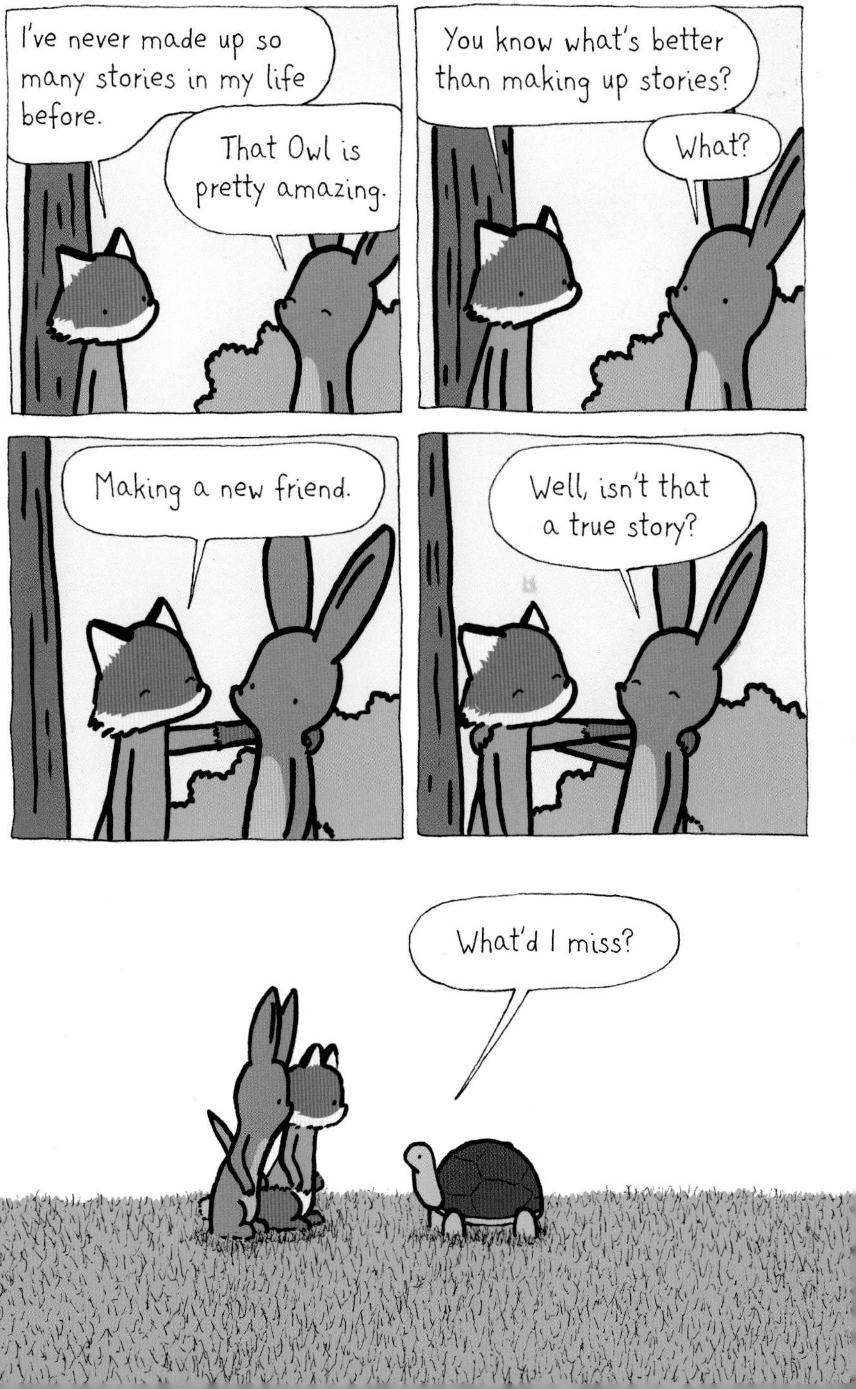
I've never made up so many stories in my life before.
That Owl is pretty amazing.
You know what's better than making up stories?
What?
Making a new friend.
Well, isn't that a true story?
What'd I miss?

STORY FOUR

FALL, FARM & FINICKY

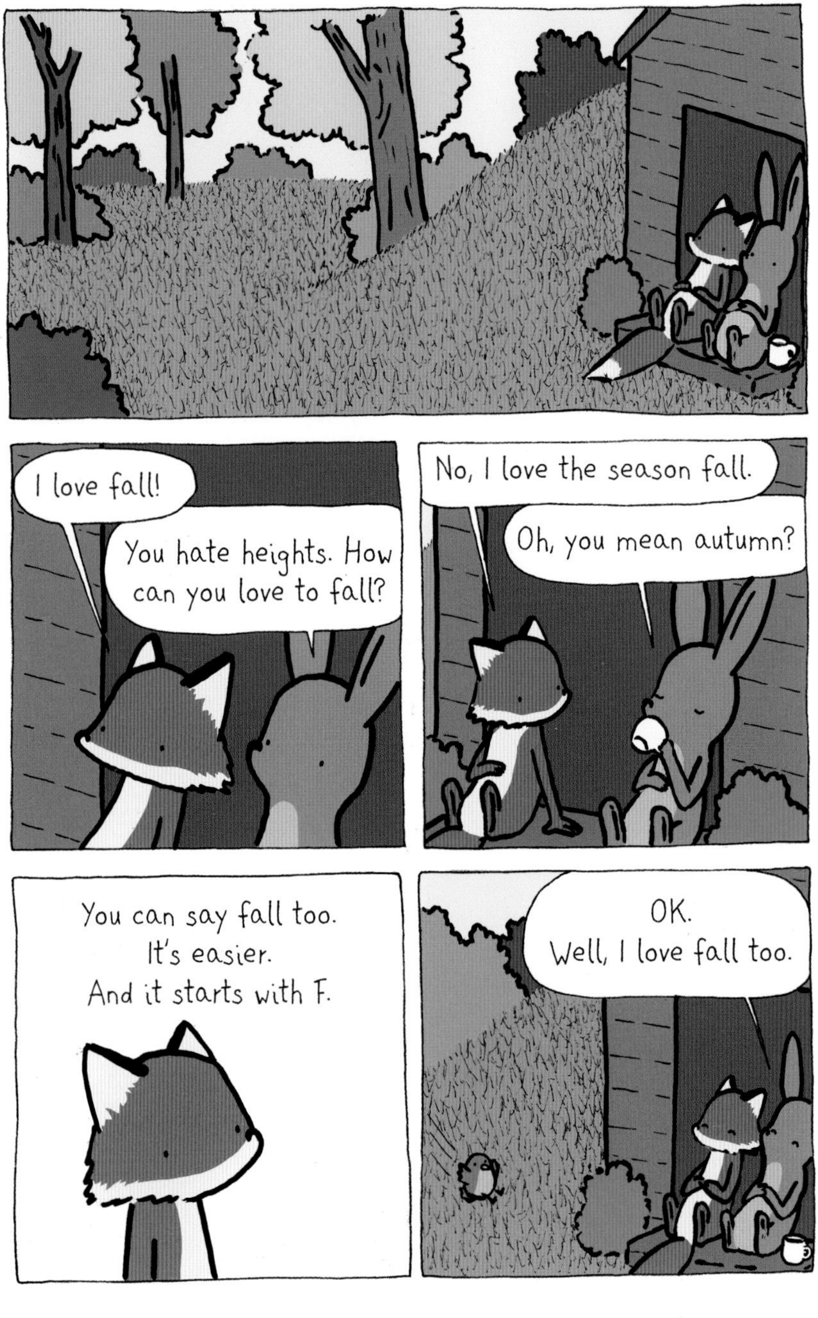
I love fall!
You hate heights. How can you love to fall?
No, I love the season fall.
Oh, you mean autumn?
You can say fall too. It's easier. And it starts with F.
OK. Well, I love fall too.

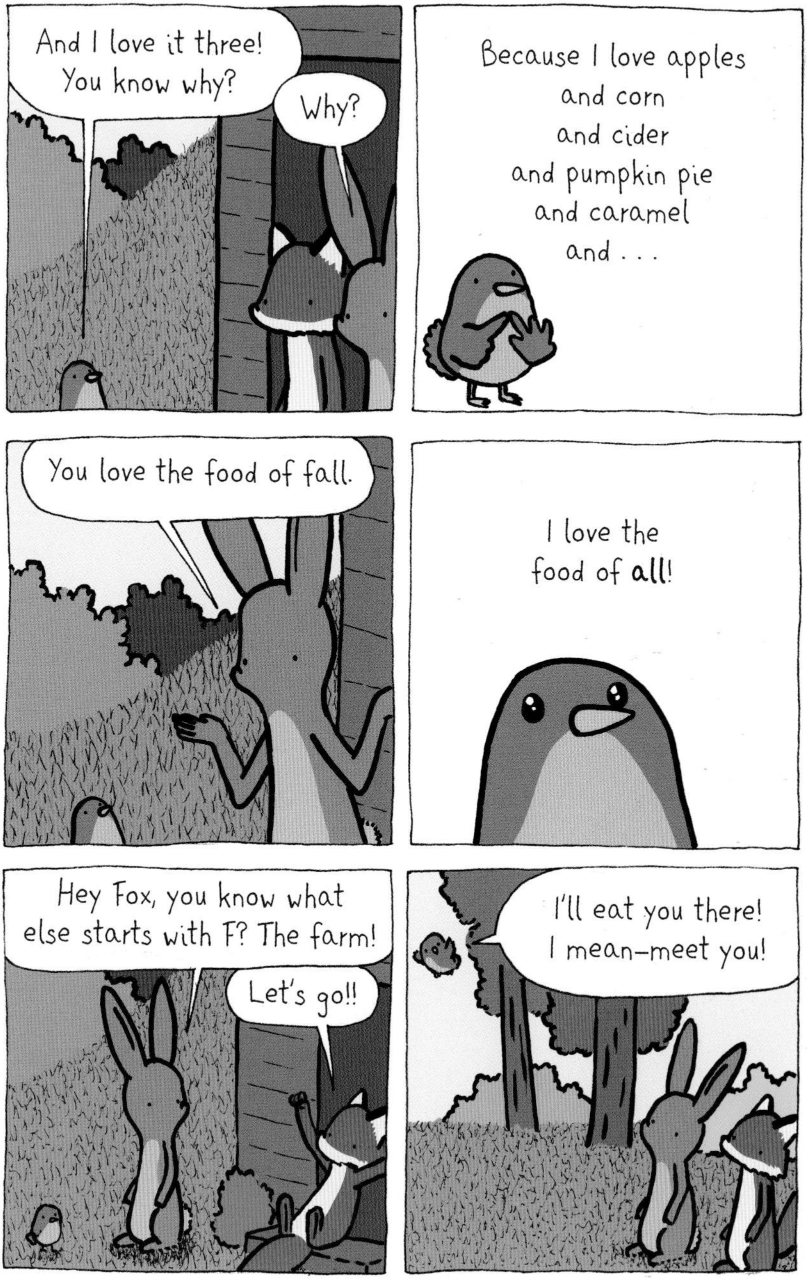
And I love it three! You know why?
Why?
Because I love apples and corn and cider and pumpkin pie and caramel and . . .
You love the food of fall.
I love the food of **all**!
Hey Fox, you know what else starts with F? The farm!
Let's go!!
I'll eat you there! I mean–meet you!

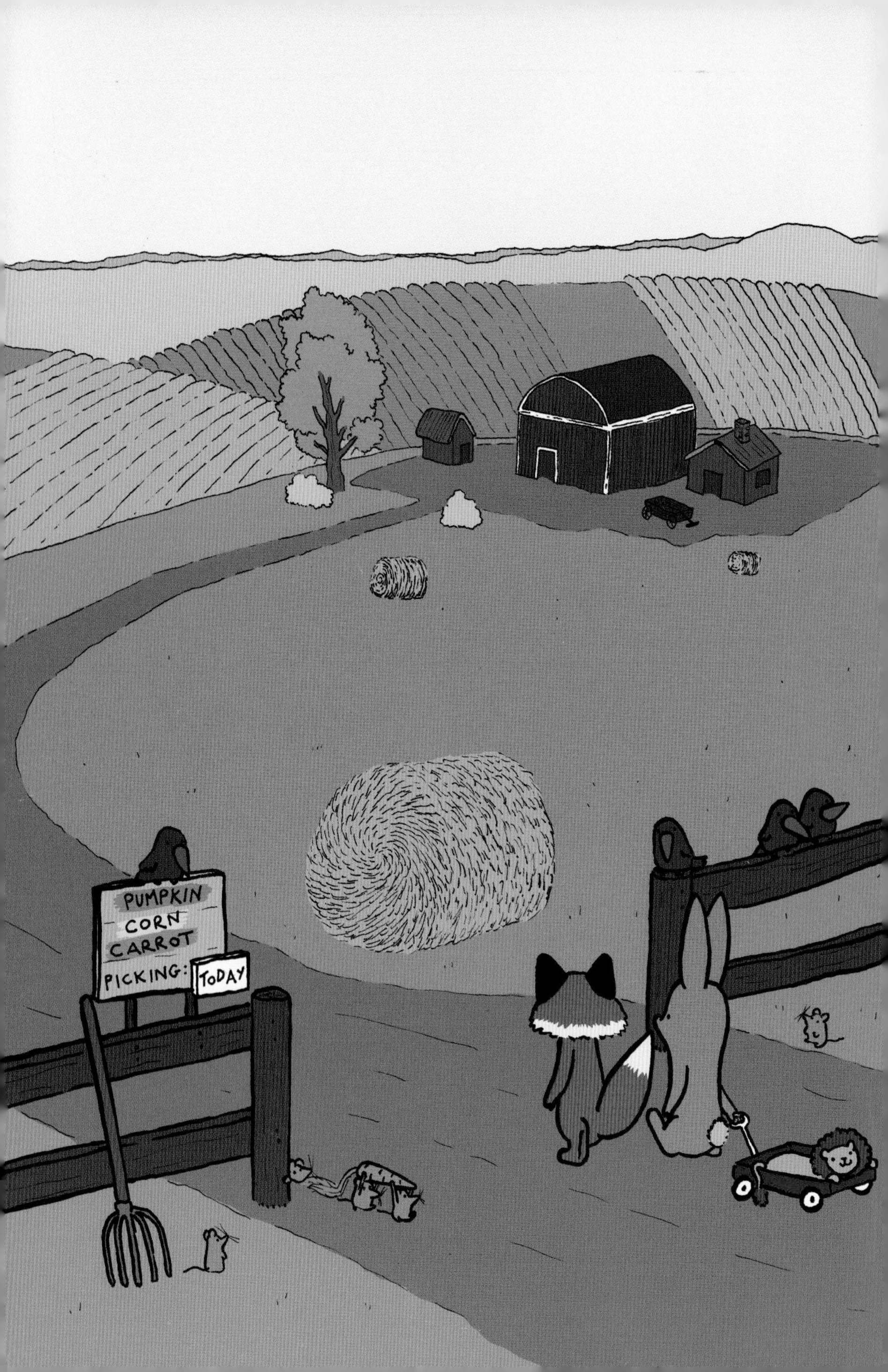
PUMPKIN
CORN
CARROT
PICKING:
TODAY

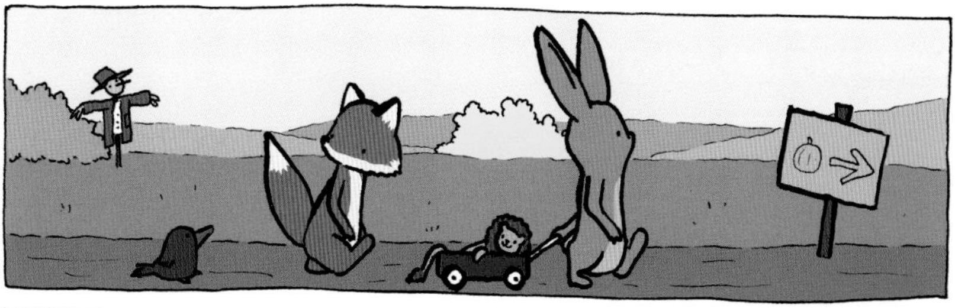

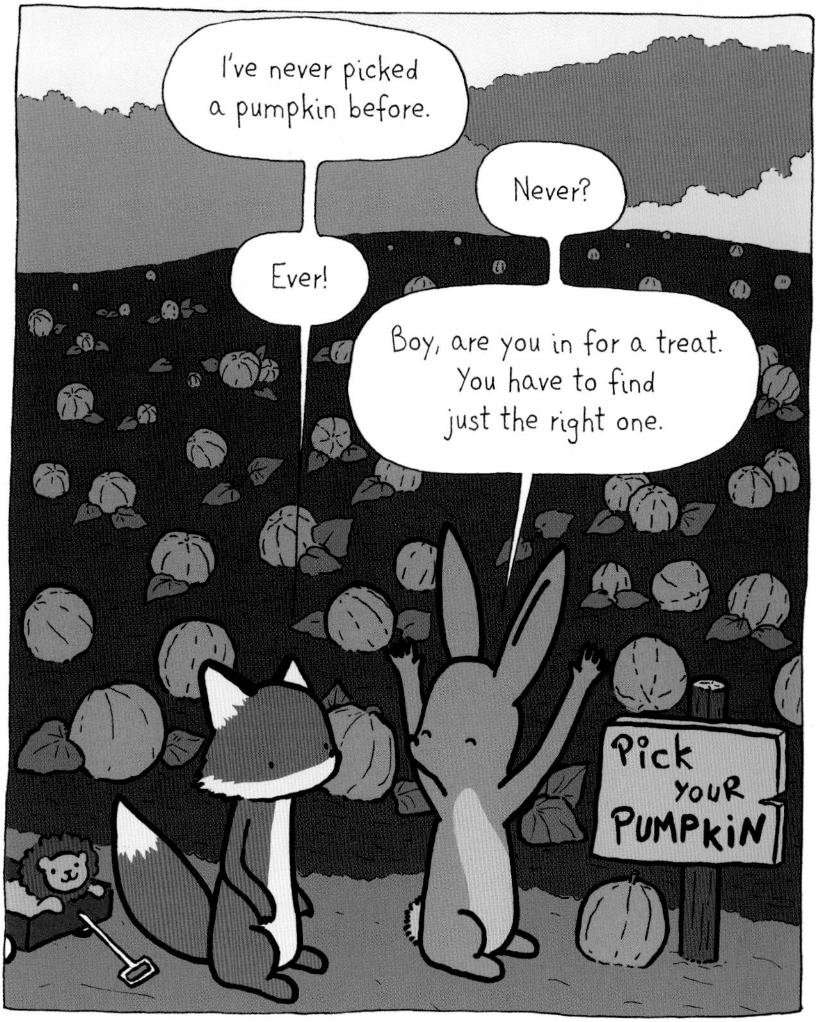
I've never picked
a pumpkin before.
Never?
Ever!
Boy, are you in for a treat. You have to find just the right one.
Pick YOUR PUMPKIN

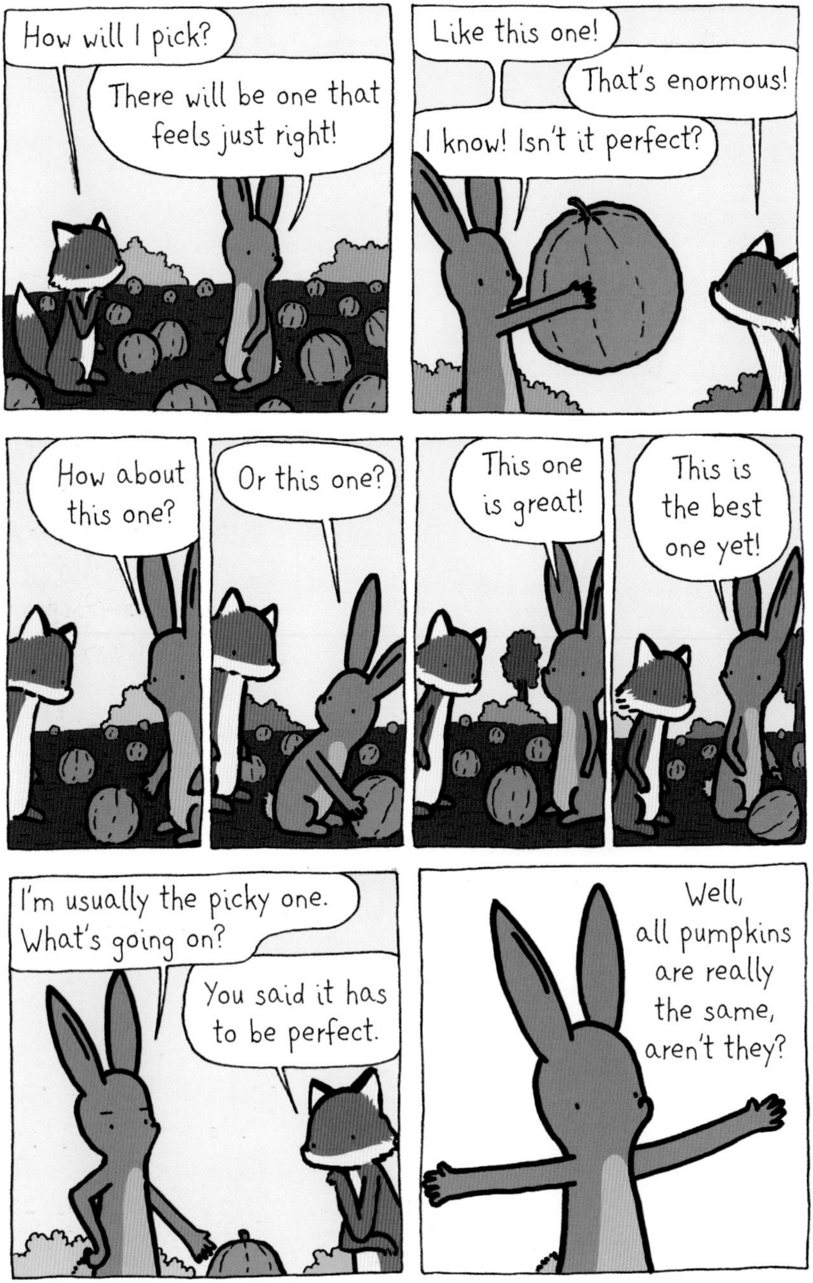
How will I pick?
There will be one that feels just right!
Like this one!
That's enormous!
I know! Isn't it perfect?
How about this one?
Or this one?
This one is great!
This is the best one yet!
I'm usually the picky one. What's going on?
You said it has to be perfect.
Well, all pumpkins are really the same, aren't they?

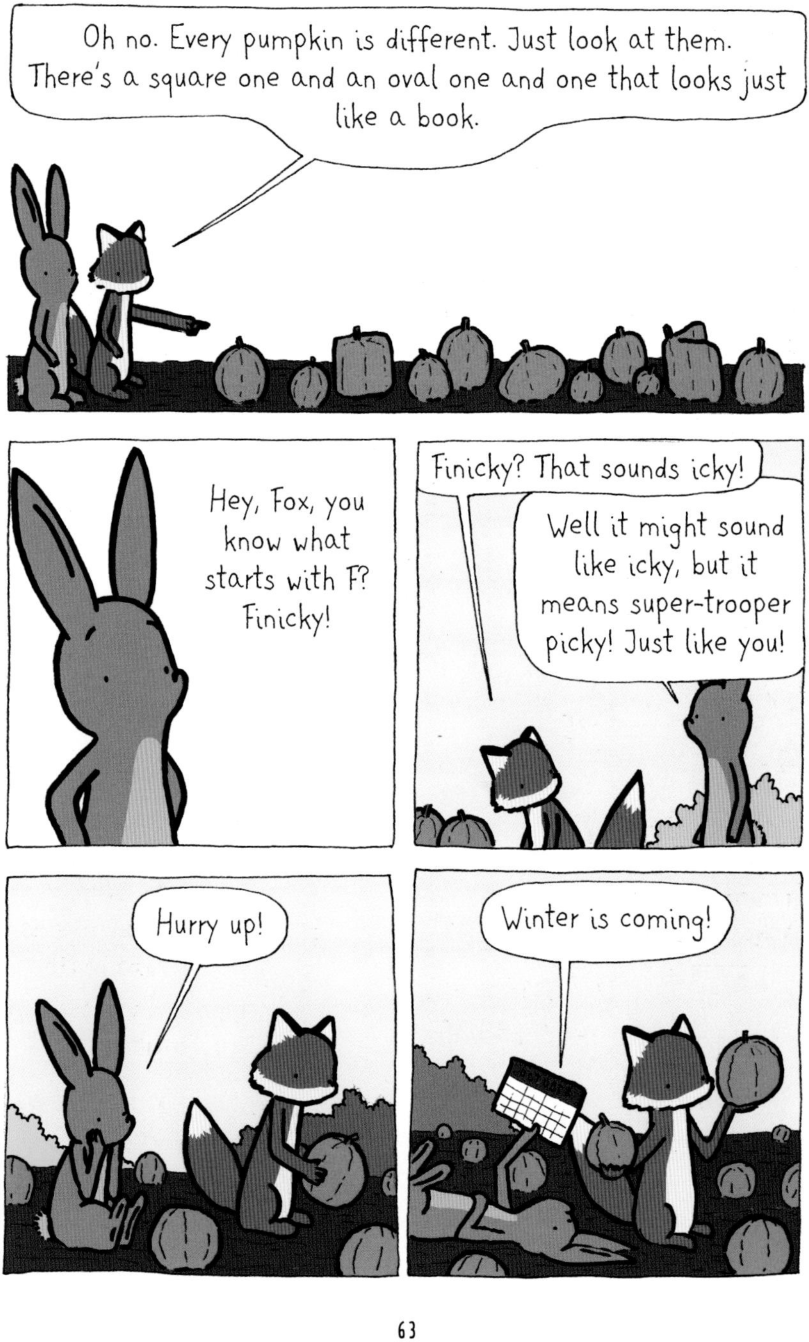
Oh no. Every pumpkin is different. Just look at them. There's a square one and an oval one and one that looks just like a book.
Hey, Fox, you know what starts with F? Finicky!
Finicky? That sounds icky!
Well it might sound like icky, but it means super-trooper picky! Just like you!
Hurry up!
Winter is coming!

Maybe you. Possibly you. Or you! Or you! Or you!

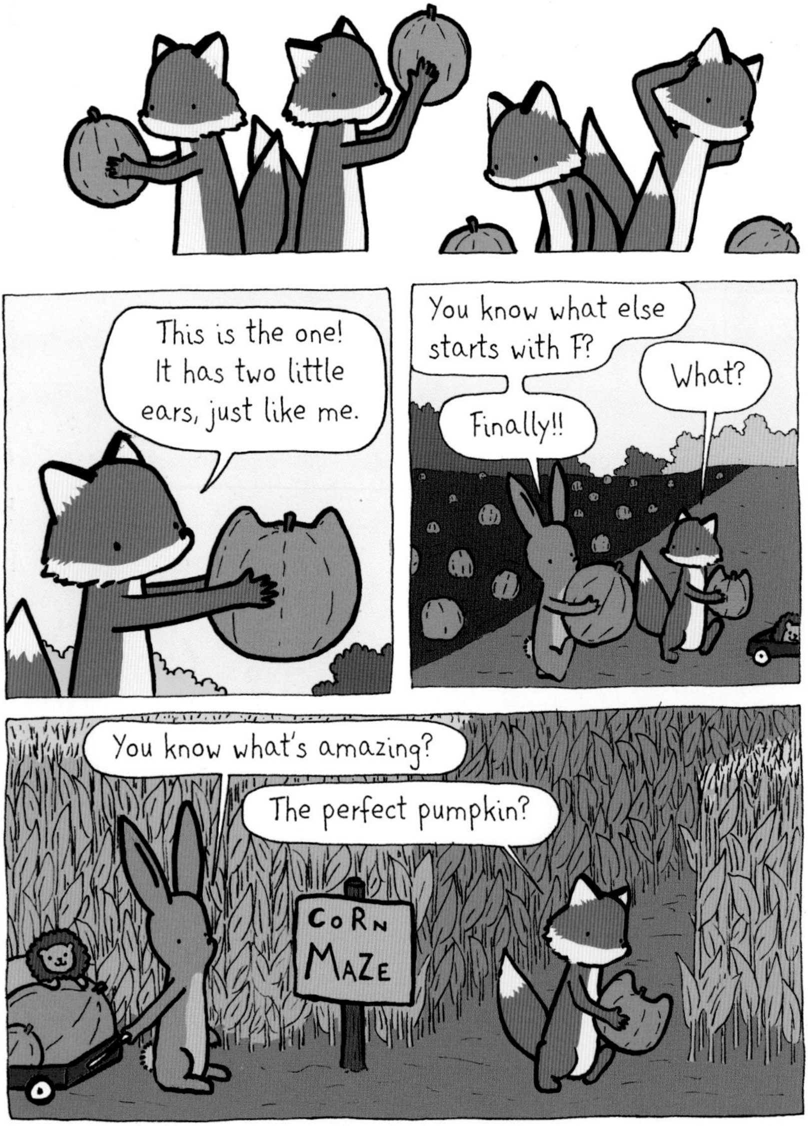
This is the one! It has two little ears, just like me.
You know what else starts with F?
Finally!!
What?
You know what's amazing?
The perfect pumpkin?
CoRN MaZE

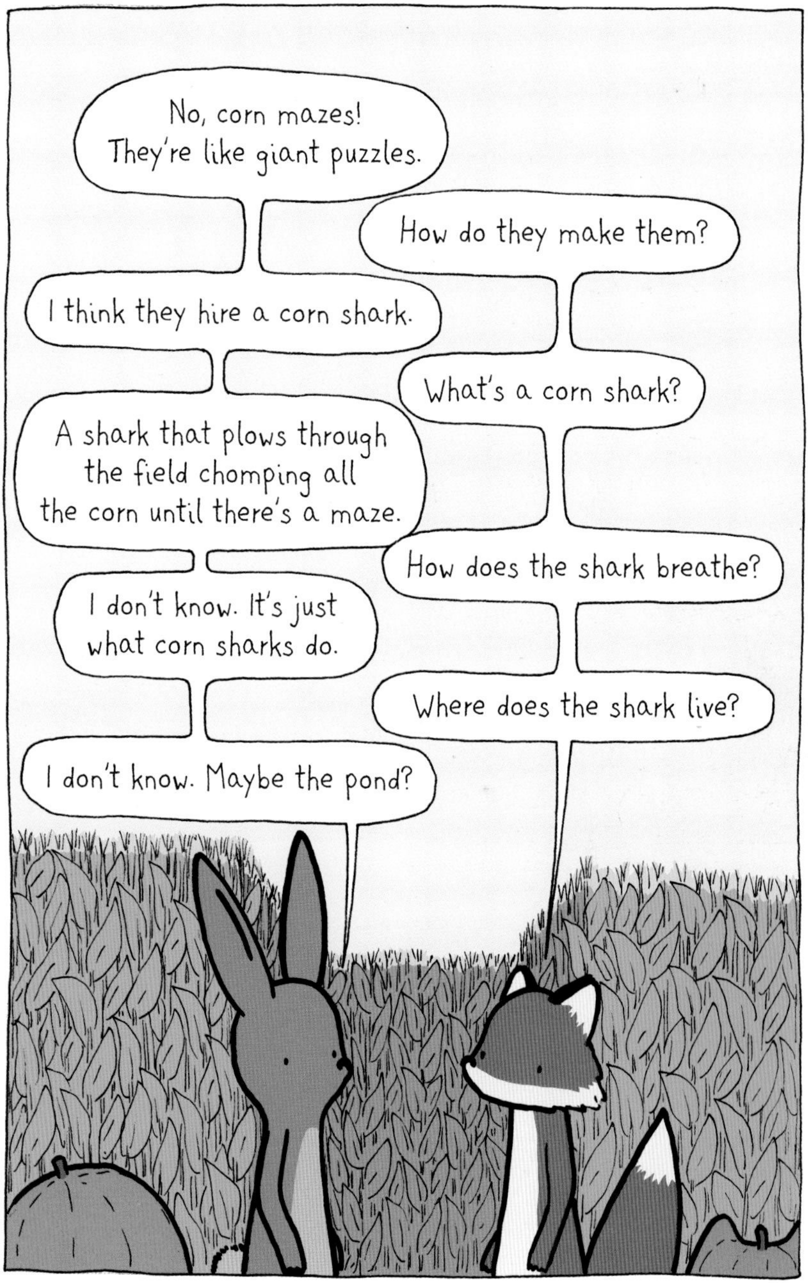
No, corn mazes! They're like giant puzzles.
How do they make them?
I think they hire a corn shark.
What's a corn shark?
A shark that plows through the field chomping all the corn until there's a maze.
How does the shark breathe?
I don't know. It's just what corn sharks do.
Where does the shark live?
I don't know. Maybe the pond?

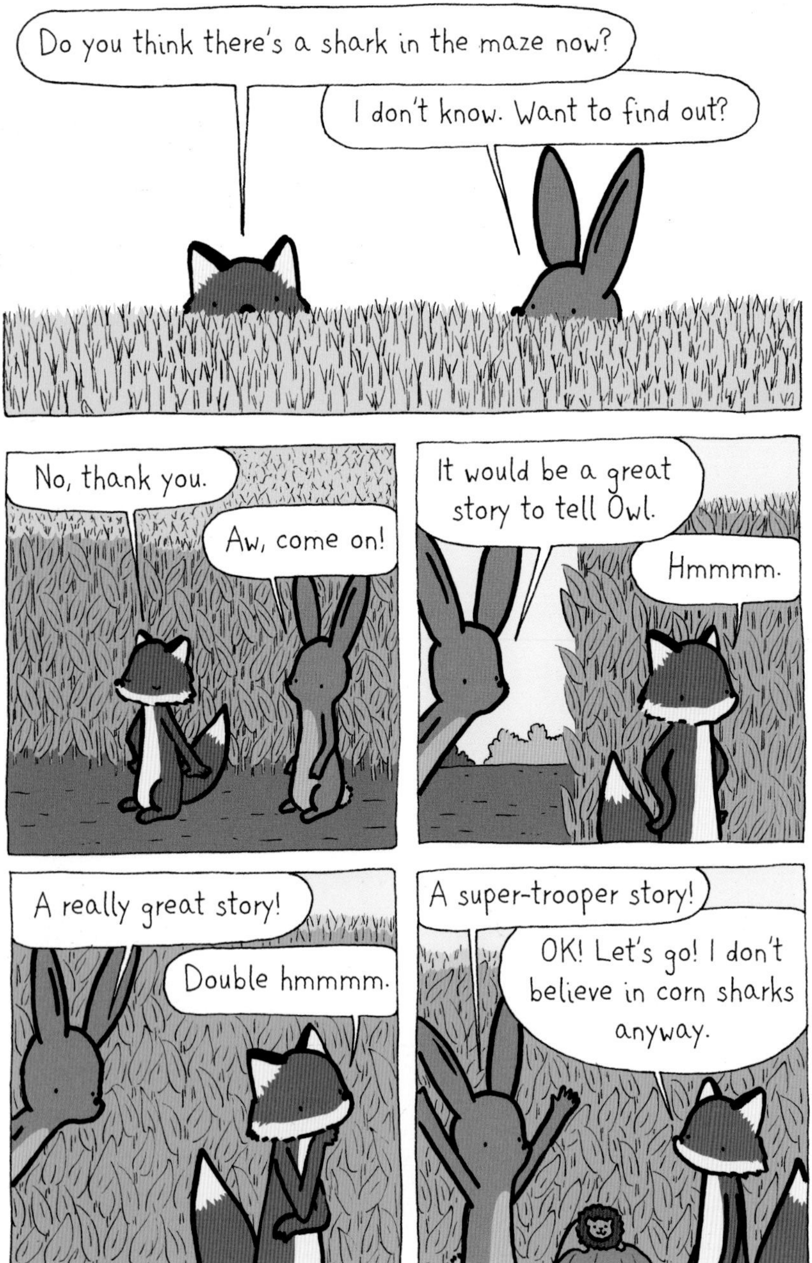
Do you think there's a shark in the maze now?
I don't know. Want to find out?
No, thank you.
Aw, come on!
It would be a great story to tell Owl.
Hmmmm.
A really great story!
Double hmmmm.
A super-trooper story!
OK! Let's go! I don't believe in corn sharks anyway.

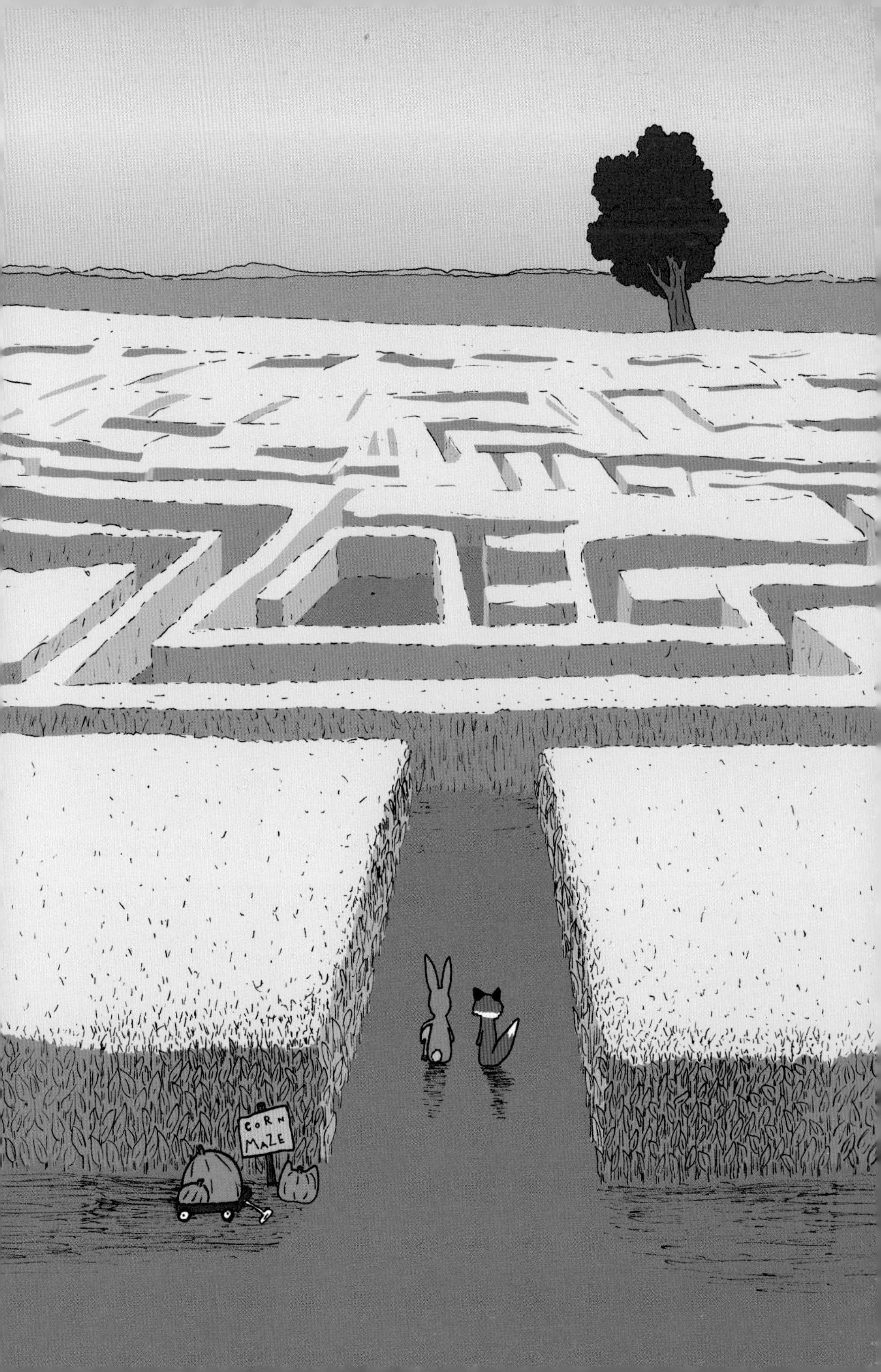
CORN MAZE

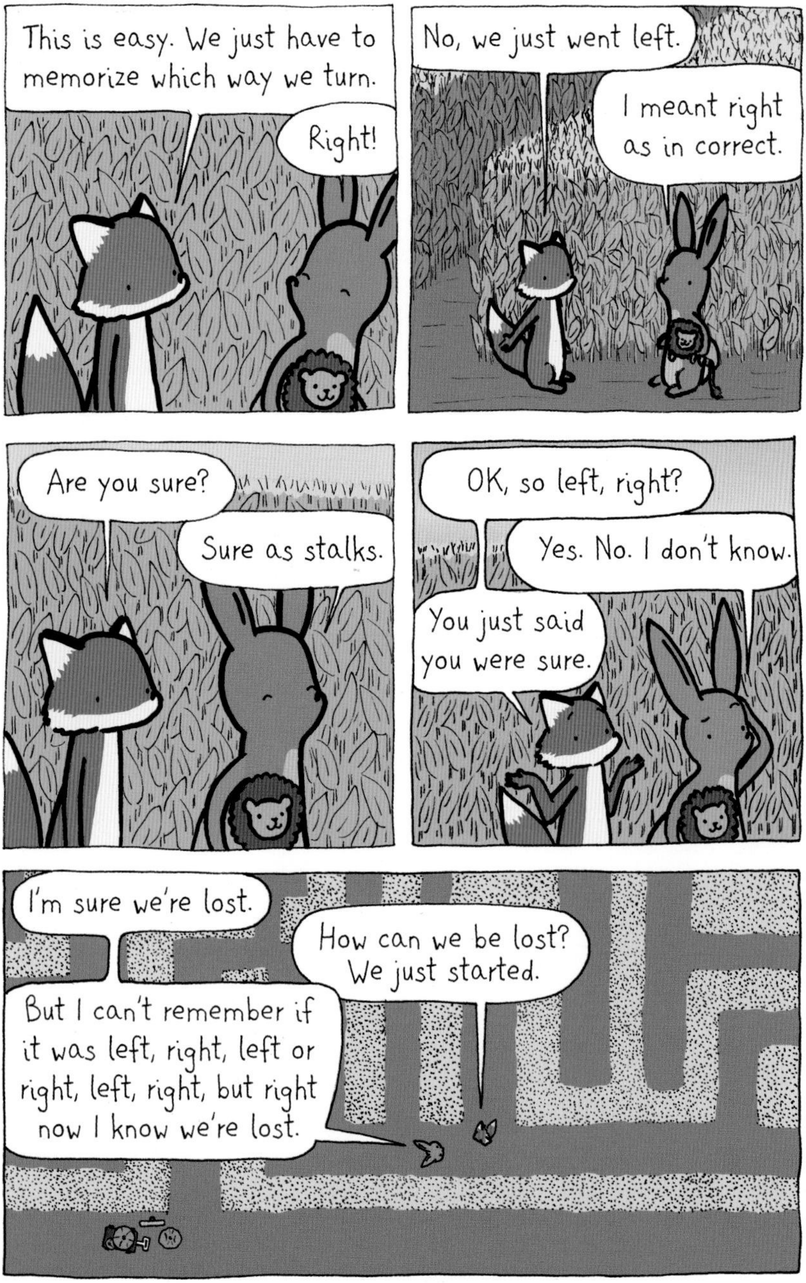
This is easy. We just have to memorize which way we turn.
Right!
No, we just went left.
I meant right as in correct.
Are you sure?
Sure as stalks.
OK, so left, right?
Yes. No. I don't know.
You just said you were sure.
I'm sure we're lost.
But I can't remember if it was left, right, left or right, left, right, but right now I know we're lost.
How can we be lost? We just started.

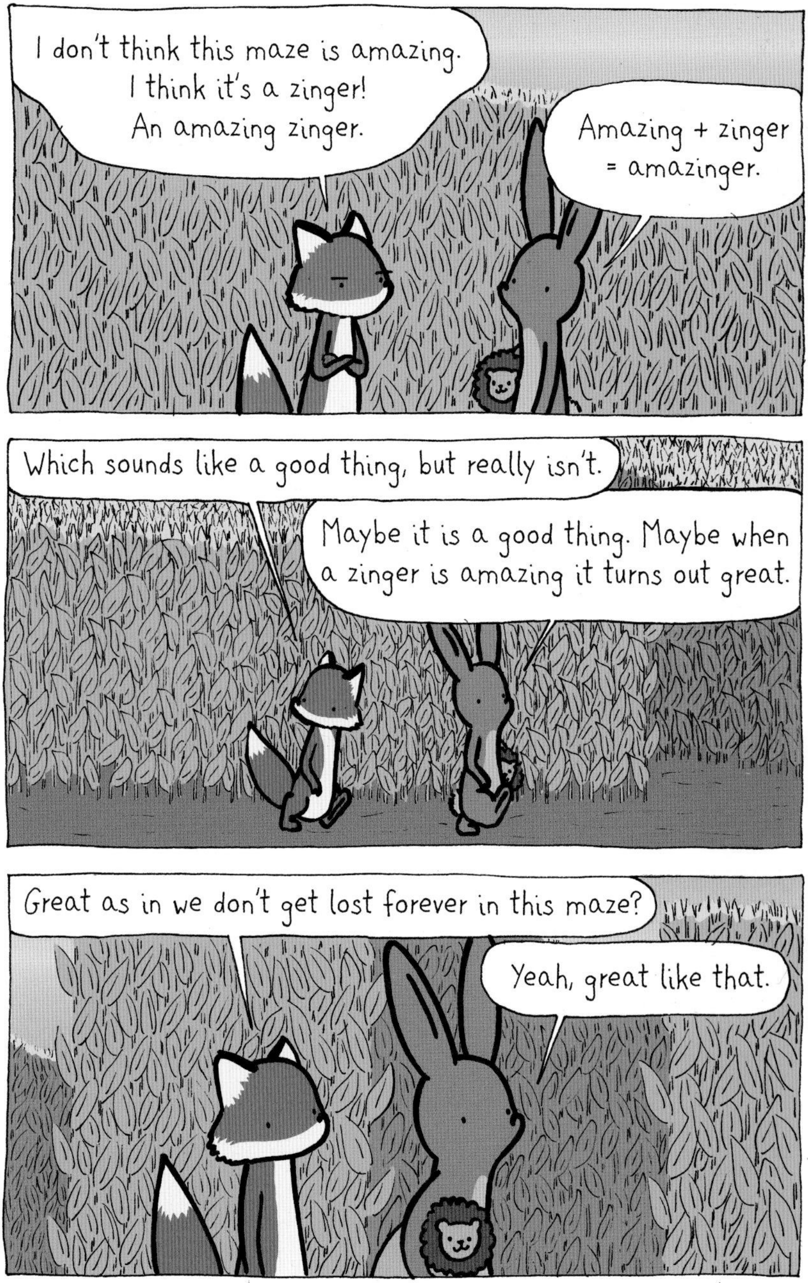
I don't think this maze is amazing. I think it's a zinger! An amazing zinger.
Amazing + zinger = amazinger.
Which sounds like a good thing, but really isn't.
Maybe it is a good thing. Maybe when a zinger is amazing it turns out great.
Great as in we don't get lost forever in this maze?
Yeah, great like that.

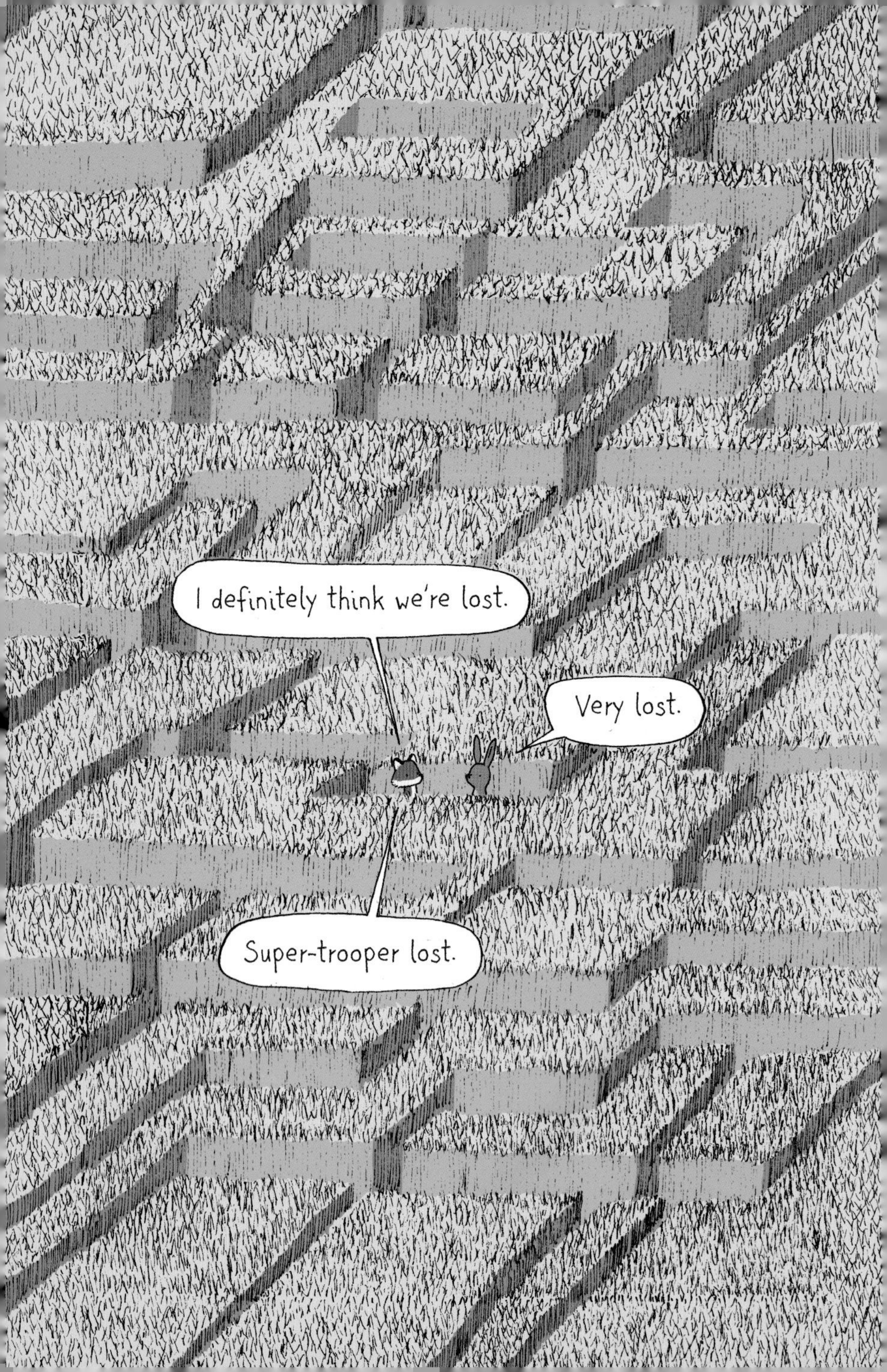
I definitely think we're lost.
Very lost.
Super-trooper lost.

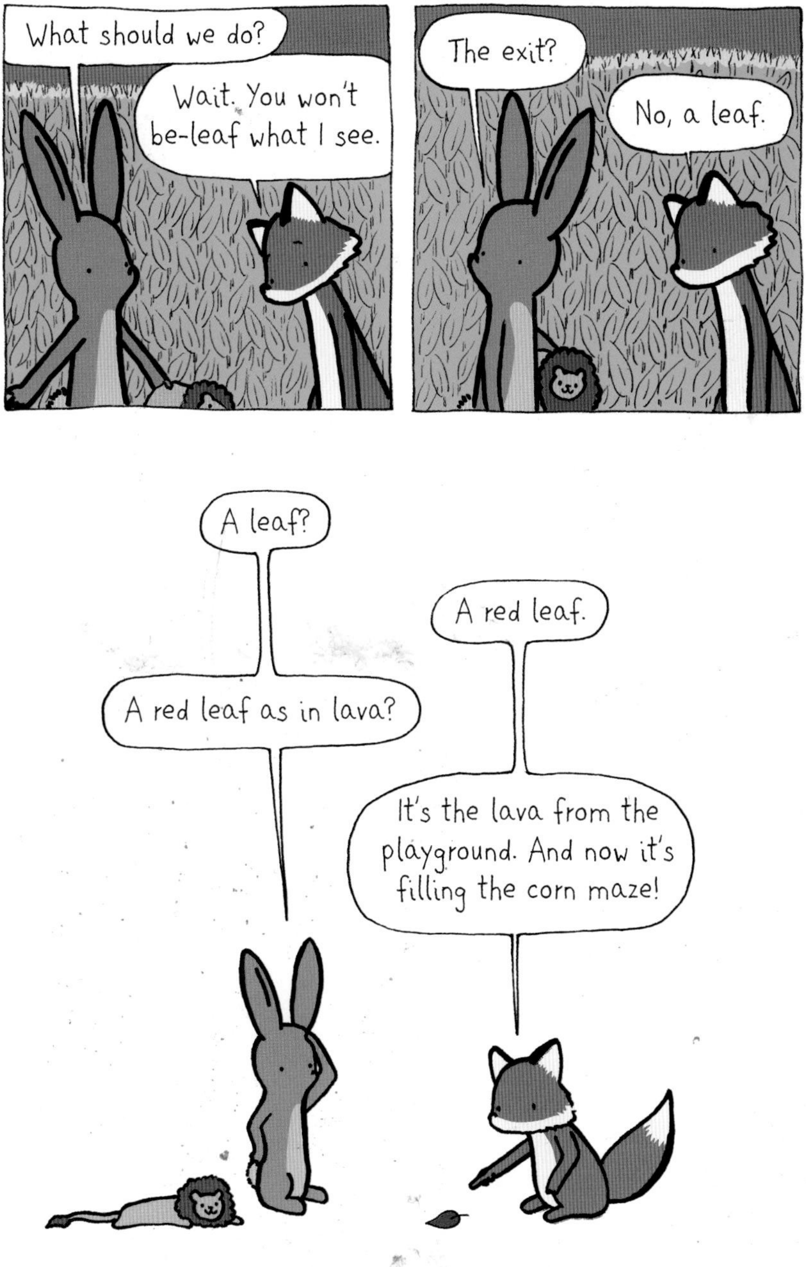
What should we do?
Wait. You won't be-leaf what I see.
The exit?
No, a leaf.
A leaf?
A red leaf.
A red leaf as in lava?
It's the lava from the playground. And now it's filling the corn maze!

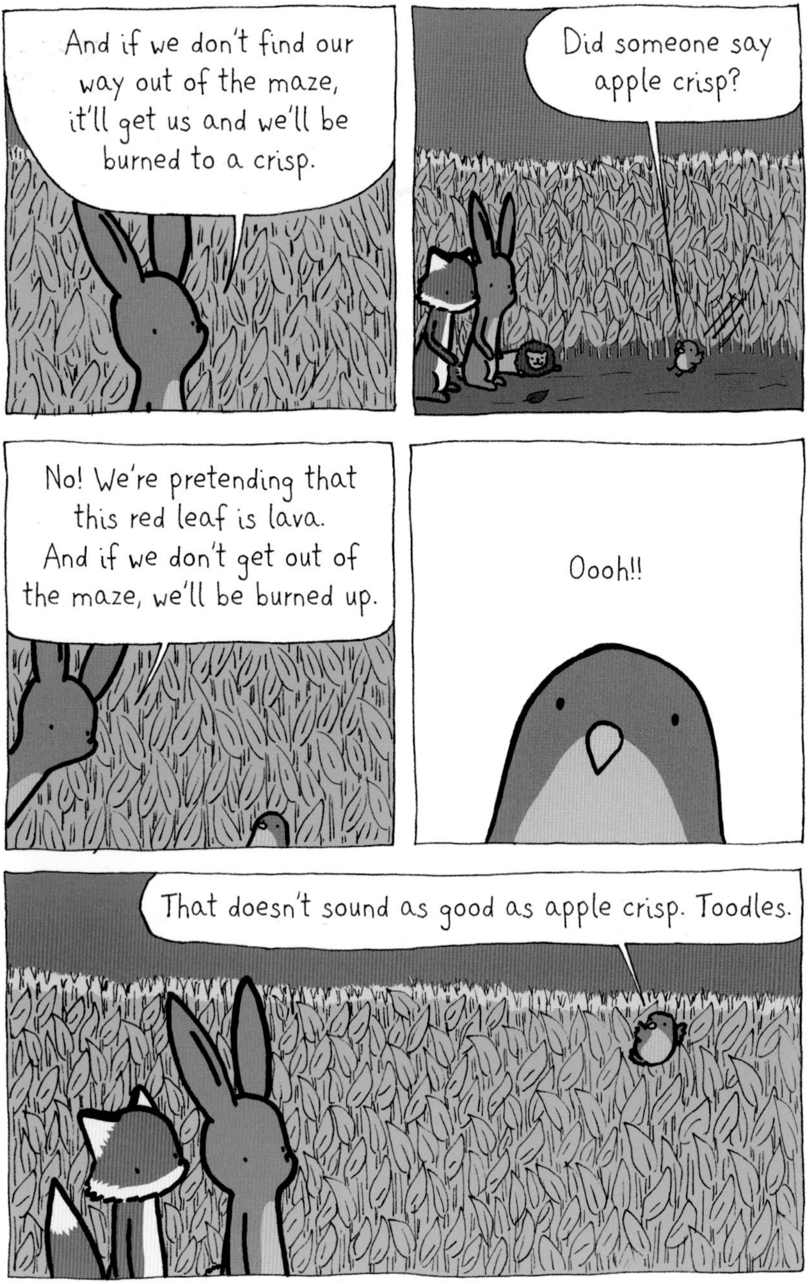
And if we don't find our way out of the maze, it'll get us and we'll be burned to a crisp.
Did someone say apple crisp?
No! We're pretending that this red leaf is lava. And if we don't get out of the maze, we'll be burned up.
Oooh!!
That doesn't sound as good as apple crisp. Toodles.

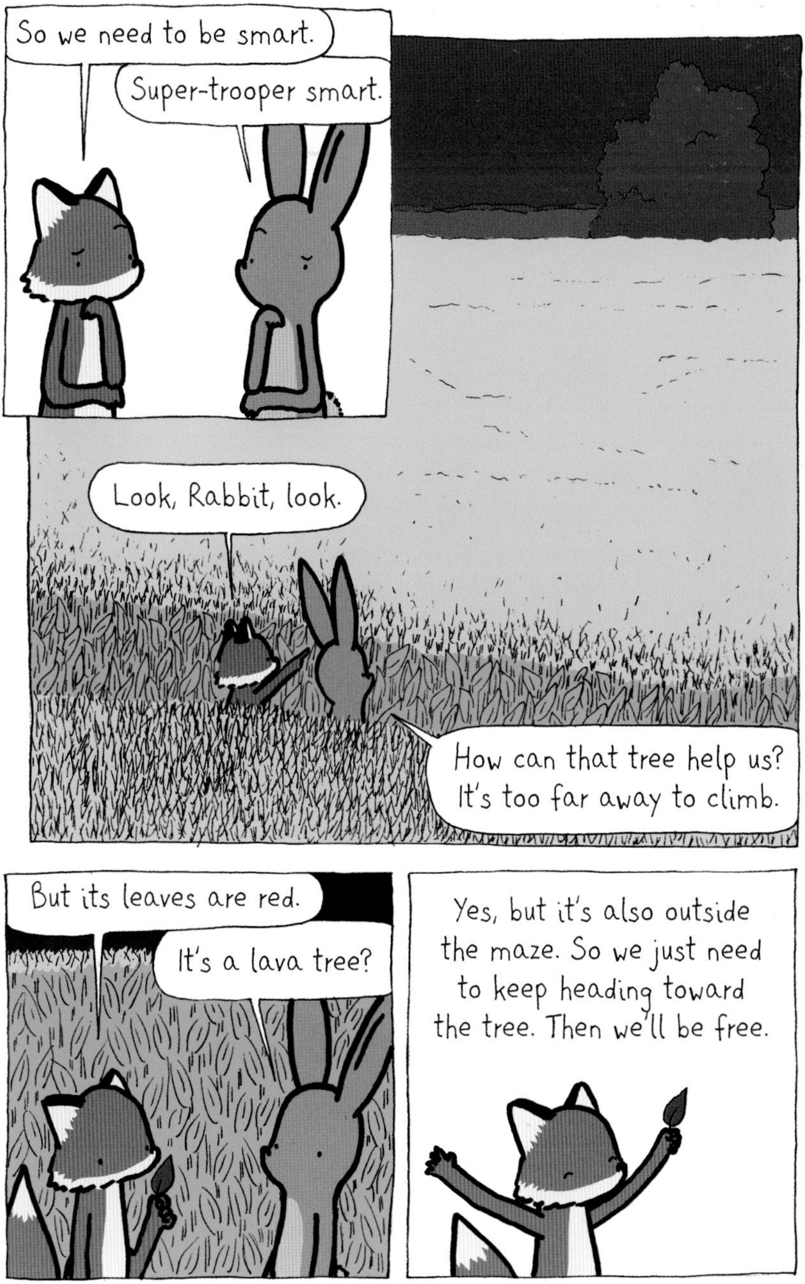
So we need to be smart.
Super-trooper smart.
Look, Rabbit, look.
How can that tree help us? It's too far away to climb.
But its leaves are red.
It's a lava tree?
Yes, but it's also outside the maze. So we just need to keep heading toward the tree. Then we'll be free.

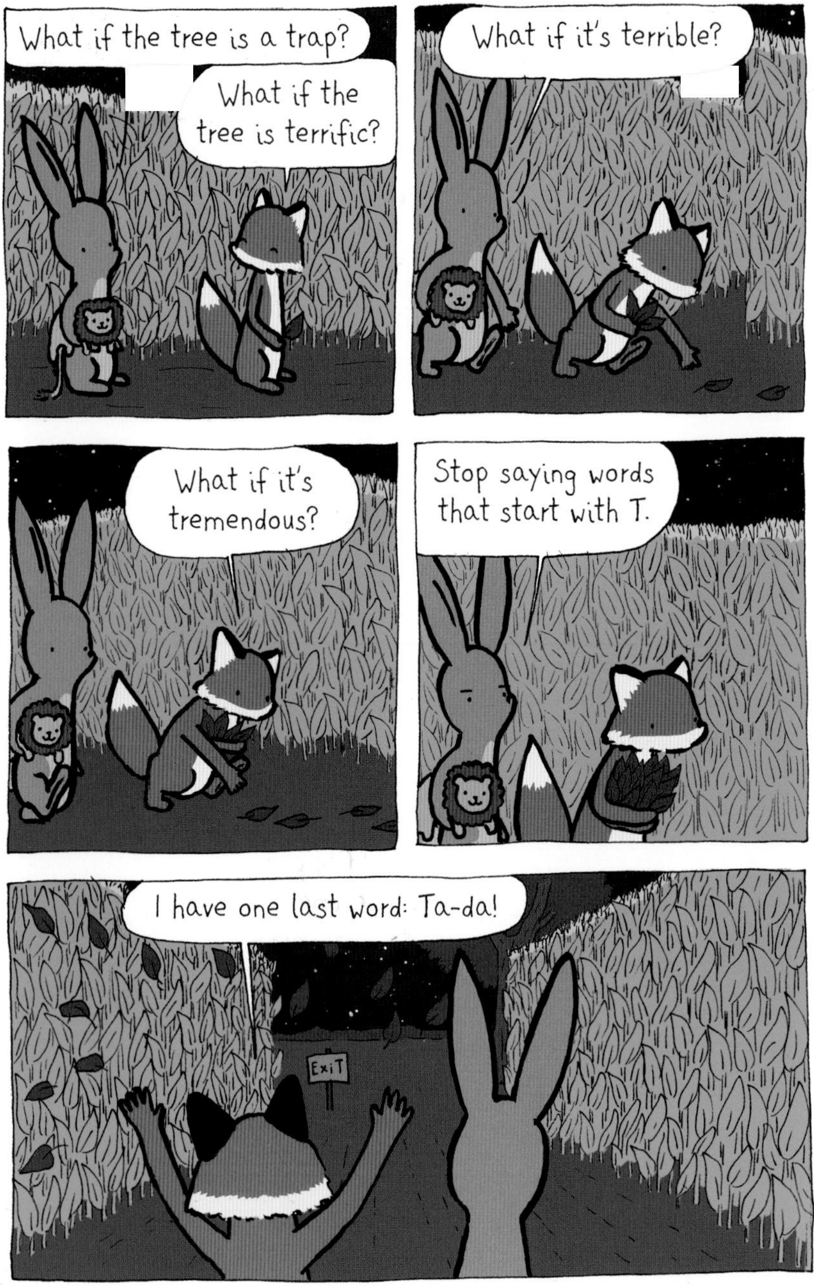
What if the tree is a trap?
What if the tree is terrific?
What if it's terrible?
What if it's tremendous?
Stop saying words that start with T.
I have one last word: Ta-da!
ExiT

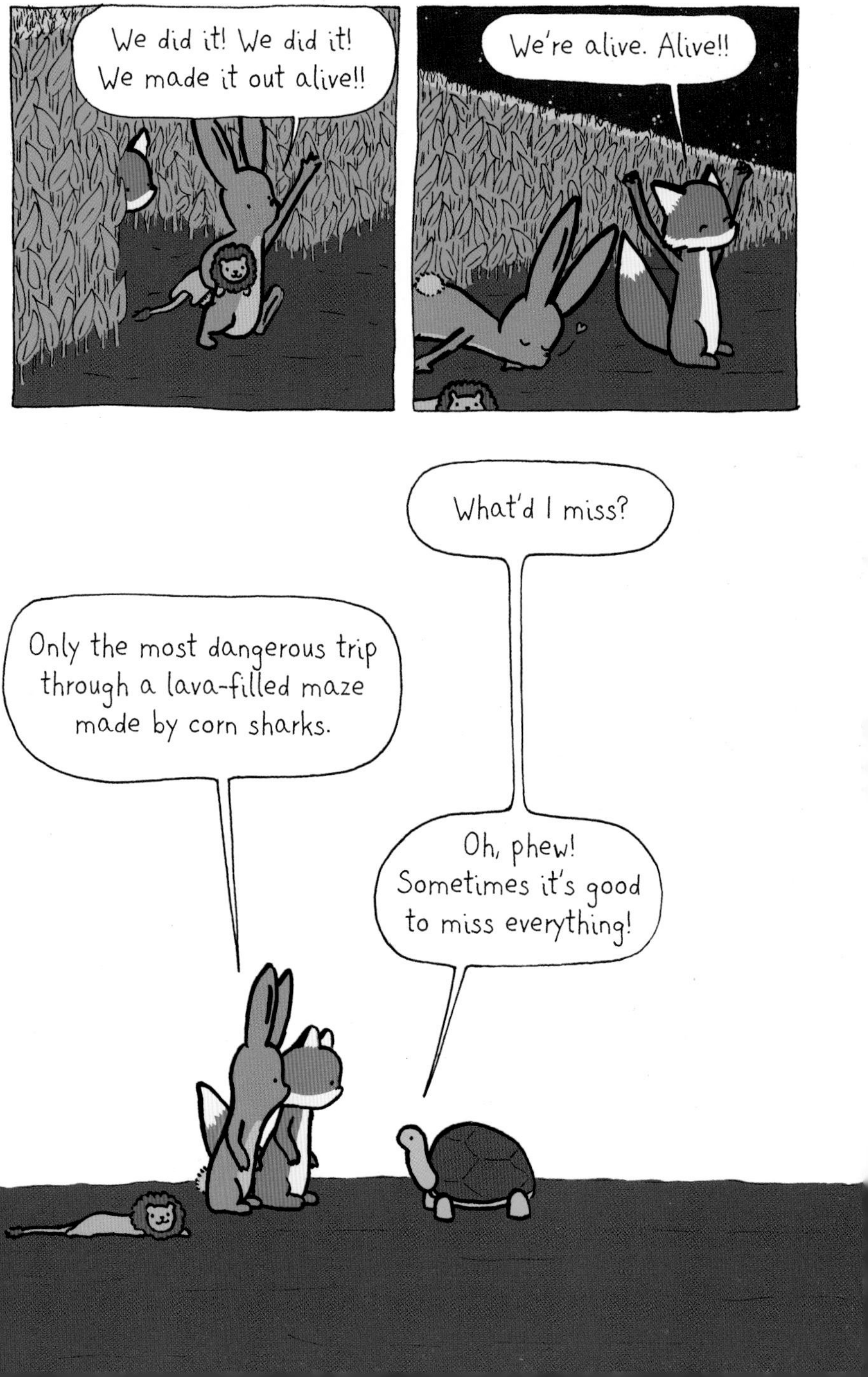
We did it! We did it! We made it out alive!!
We're alive. Alive!!
What'd I miss?
Only the most dangerous trip through a lava-filled maze made by corn sharks.
Oh, phew! Sometimes it's good to miss everything!

STORY FIVE

FRIENDS & FIREFLIES

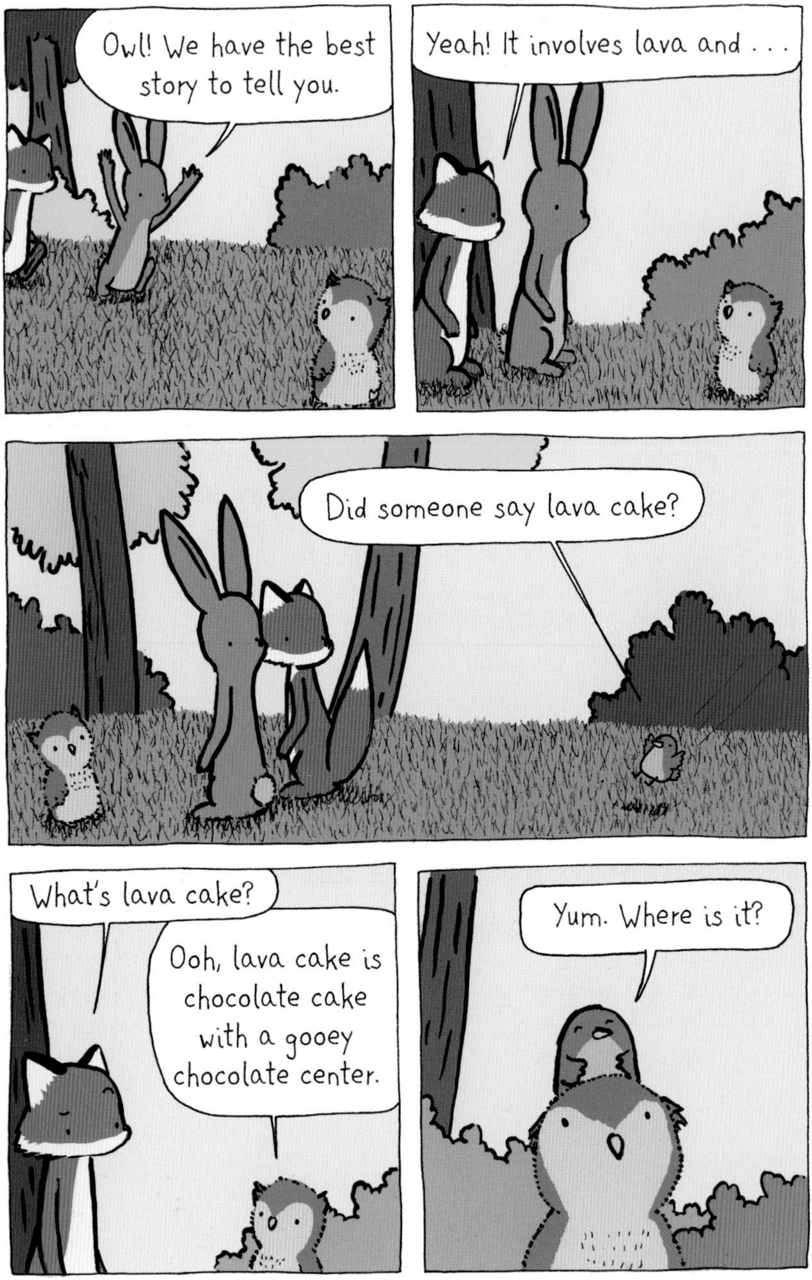
Owl! We have the best story to tell you.
Yeah! It involves lava and . . .
Did someone say lava cake?
What's lava cake?
Ooh, lava cake is chocolate cake with a gooey chocolate center.
Yum. Where is it?

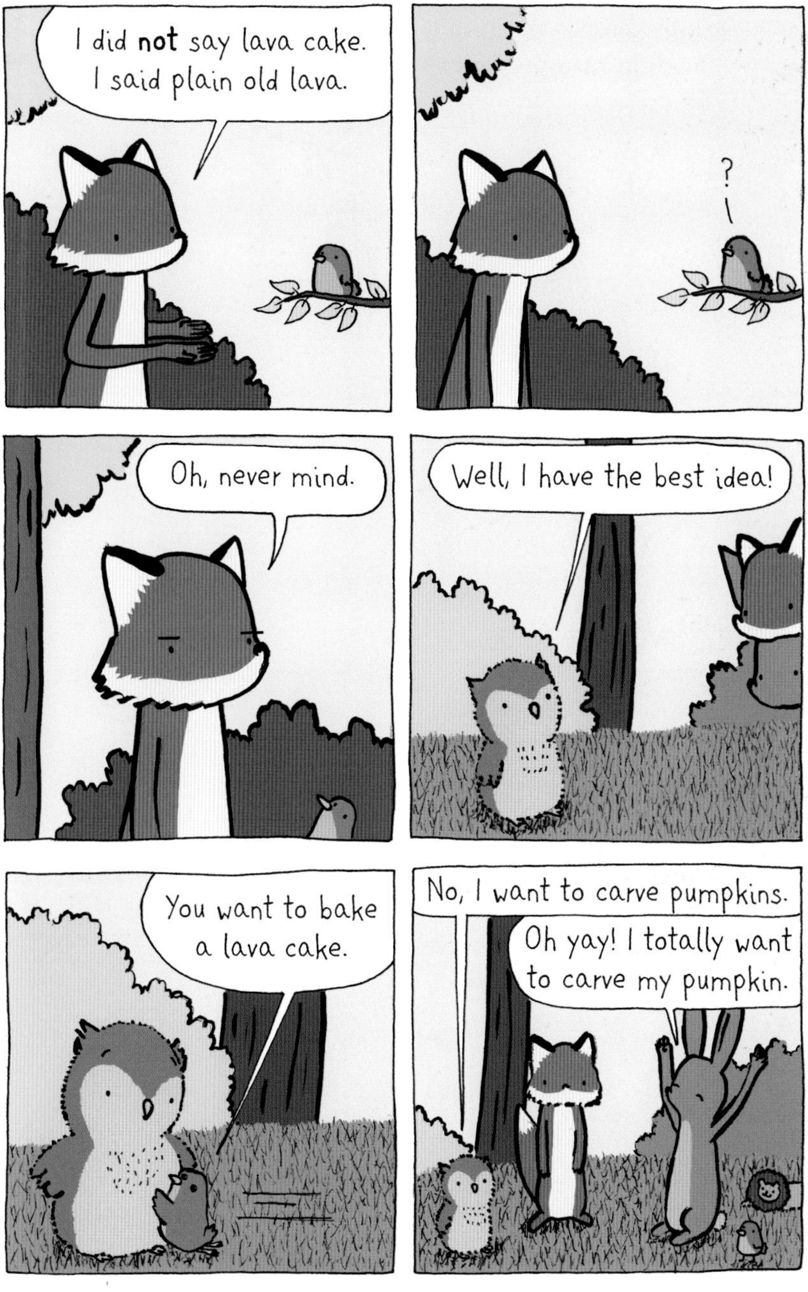
I did **not** say lava cake. I said plain old lava.
?
Oh, never mind.
Well, I have the best idea!
You want to bake a lava cake.
No, I want to carve pumpkins.
Oh yay! I totally want to carve my pumpkin.

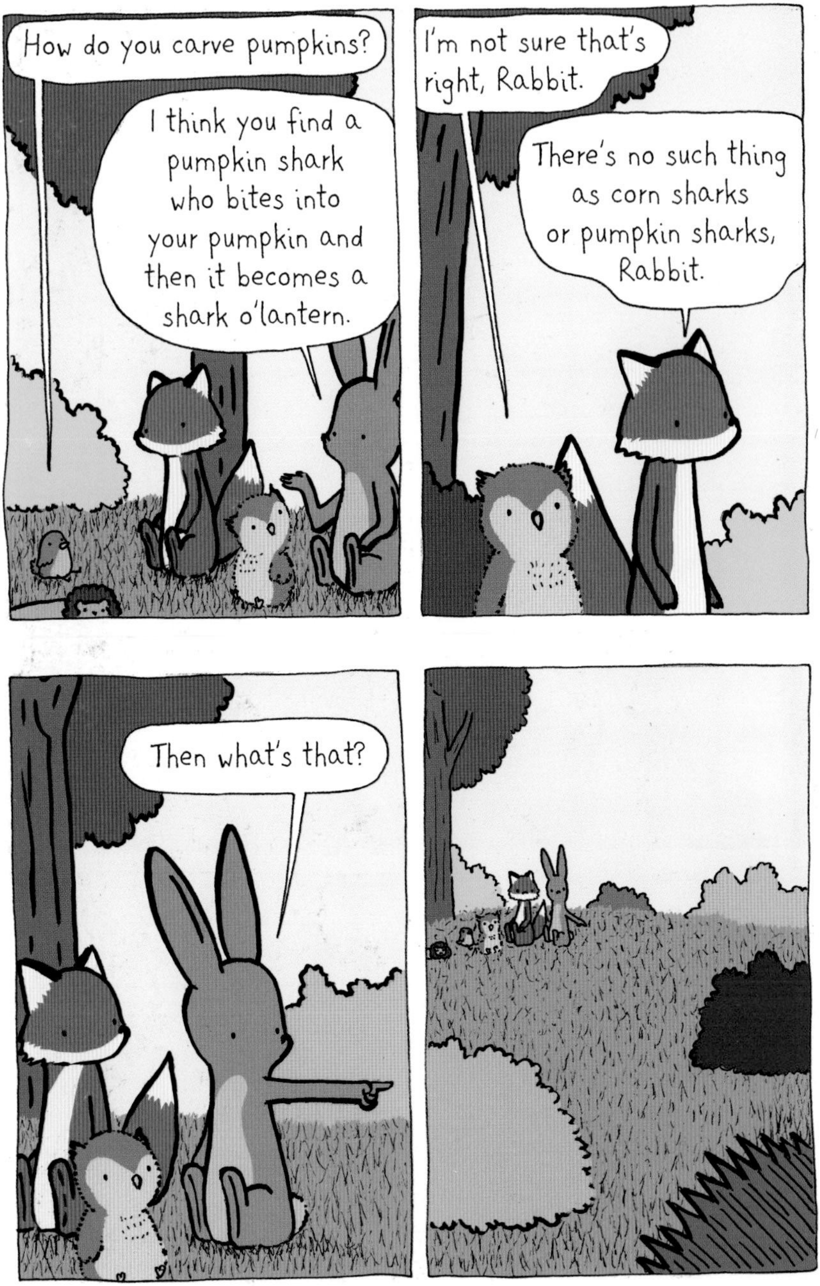
How do you carve pumpkins?
I think you find a pumpkin shark who bites into your pumpkin and then it becomes a shark o'lantern.
I'm not sure that's right, Rabbit.
There's no such thing as corn sharks or pumpkin sharks, Rabbit.
Then what's that?

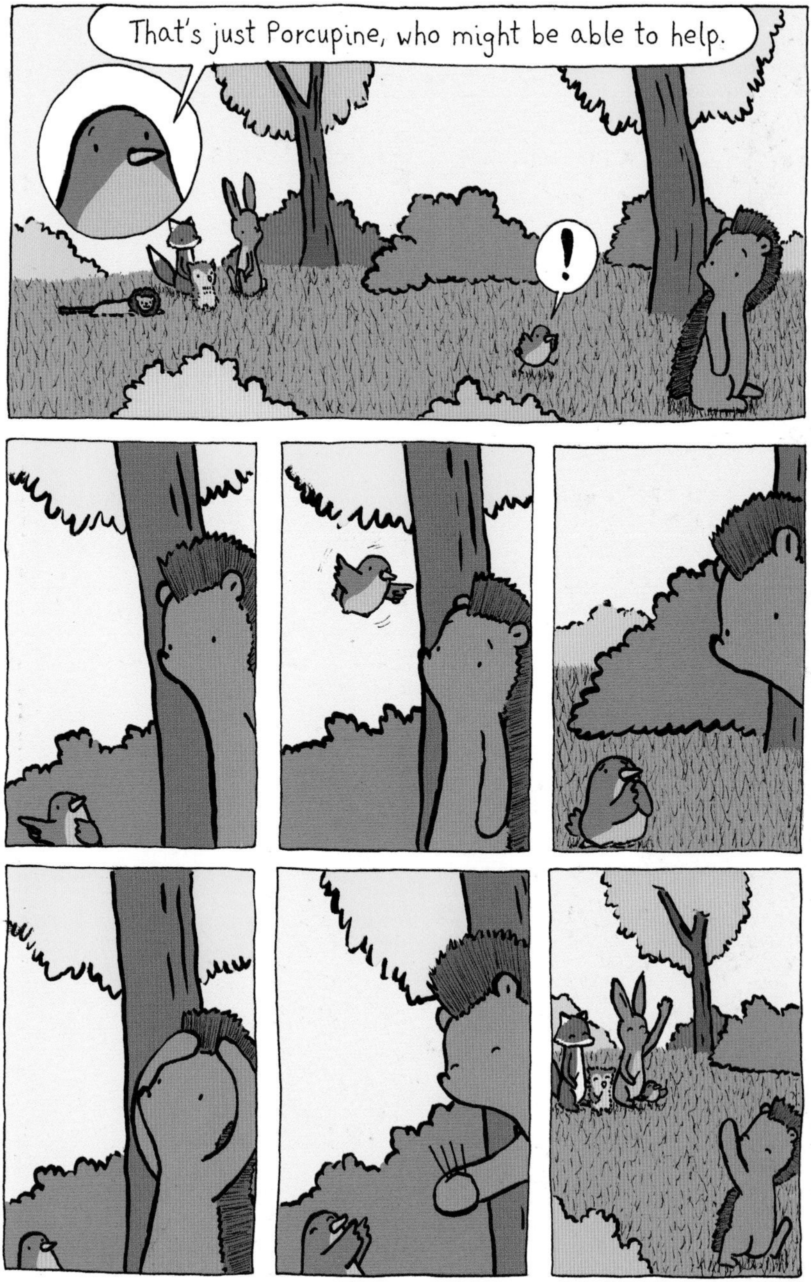
That's just Porcupine, who might be able to help.
!

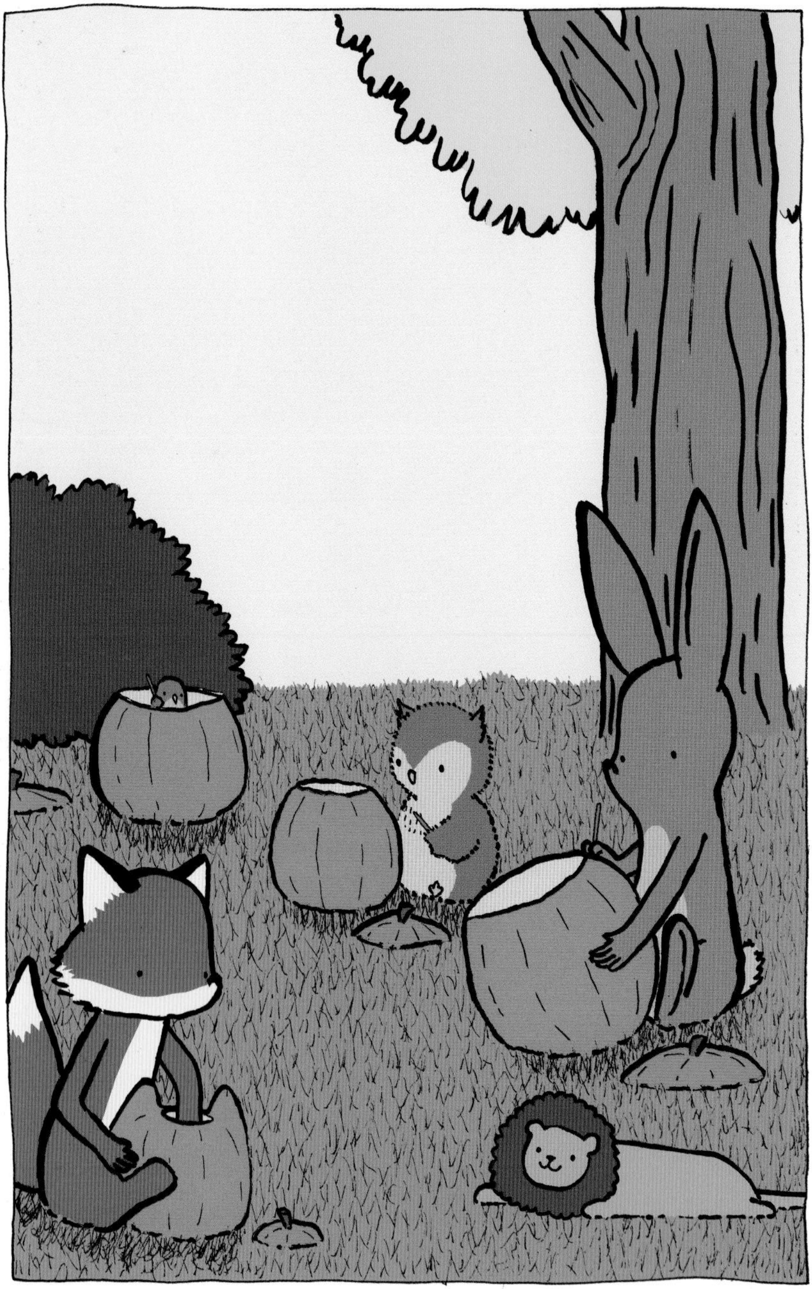

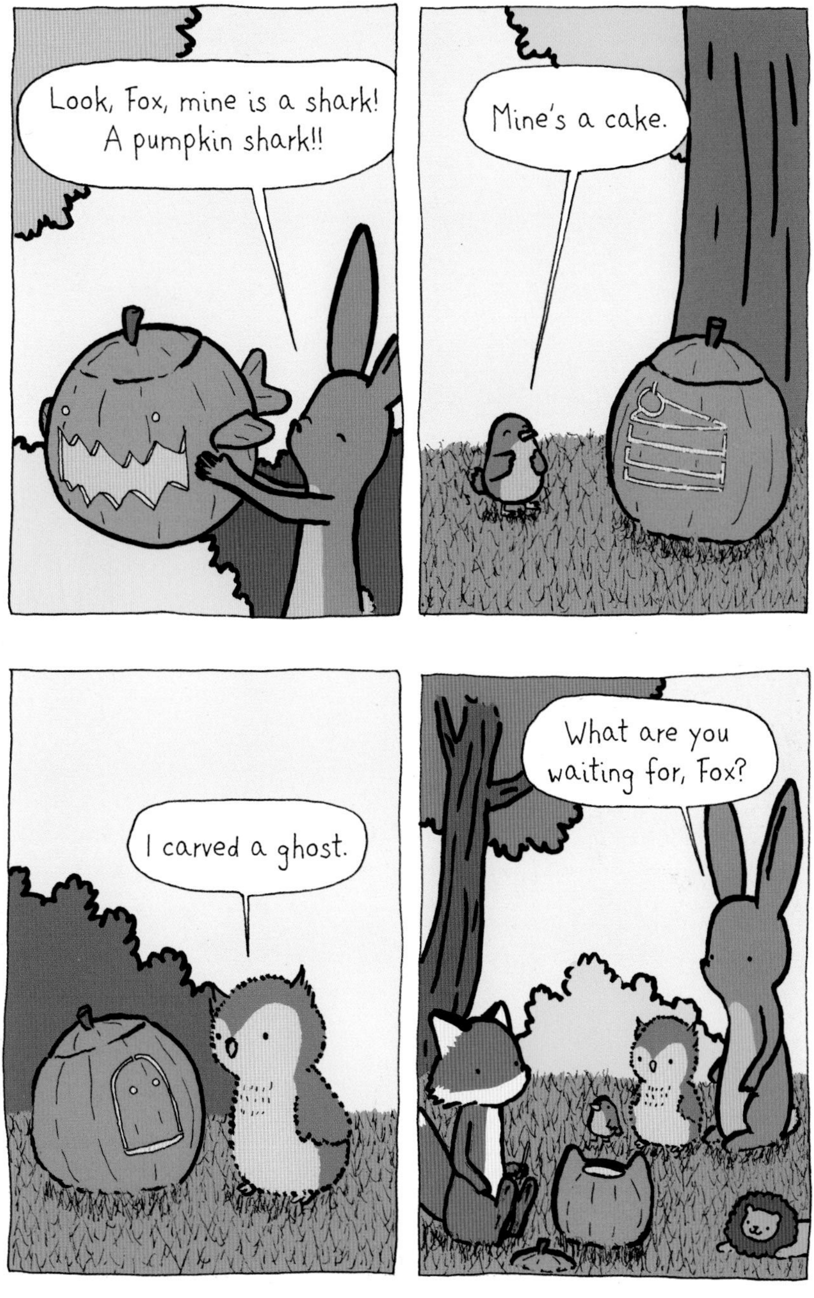
Look, Fox, mine is a shark! A pumpkin shark!!
Mine's a cake.
I carved a ghost.
What are you waiting for, Fox?

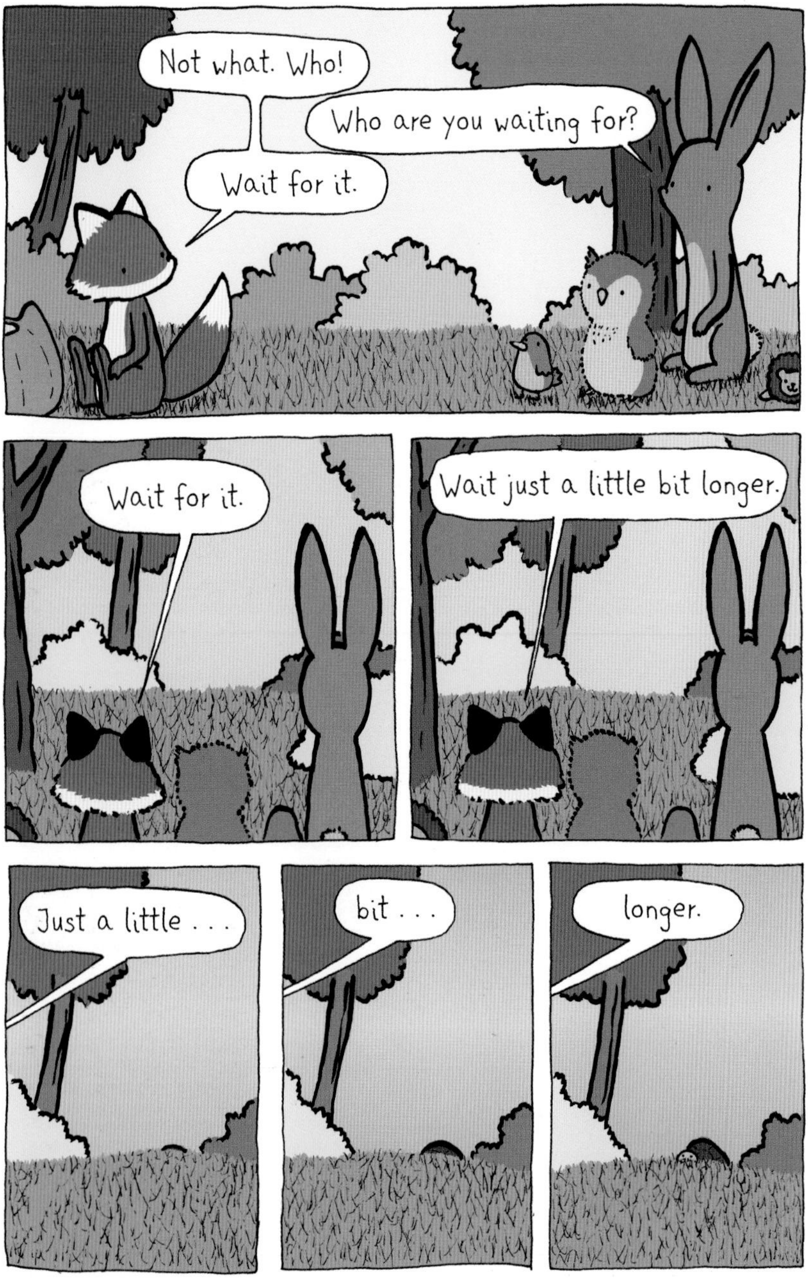
Not what. Who!
Who are you waiting for?
Wait for it.
Wait for it.
Wait just a little bit longer.
Just a little . . .
bit . . .
longer.

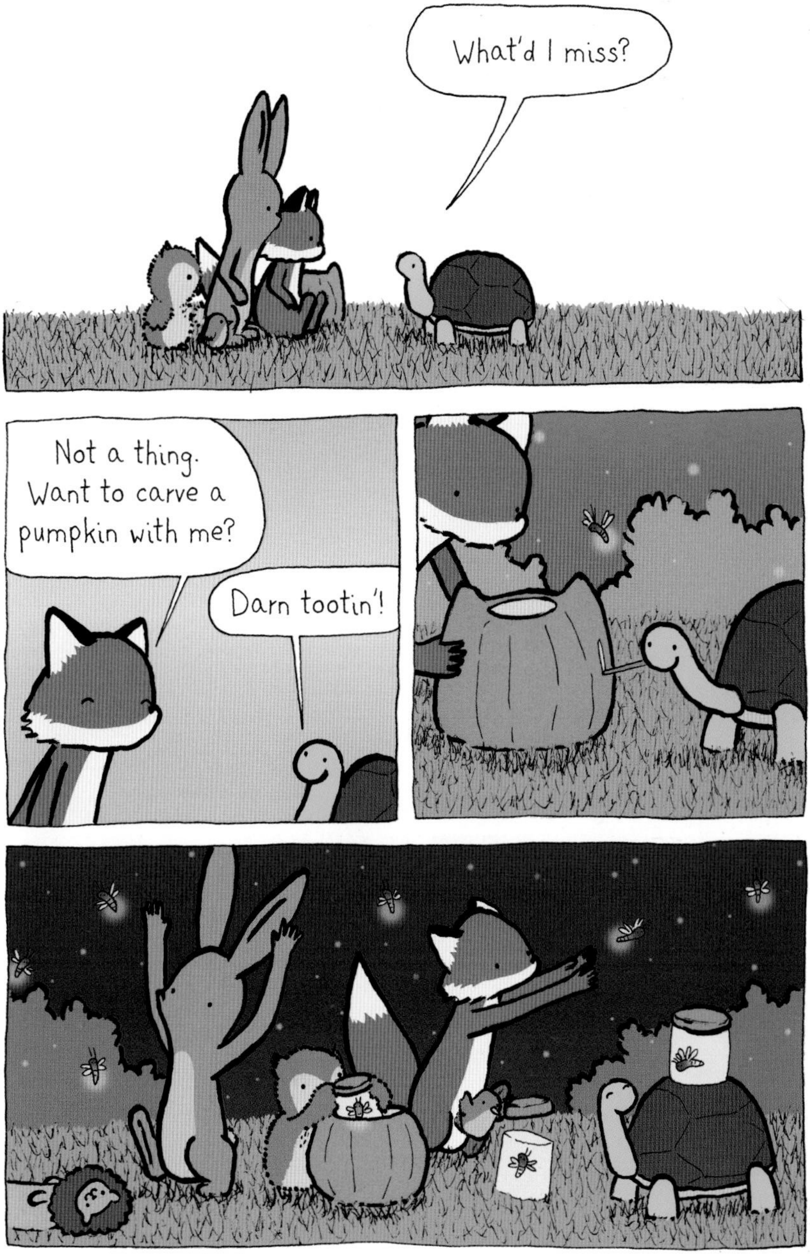
What'd I miss?
Not a thing. Want to carve a pumpkin with me?
Darn tootin'!

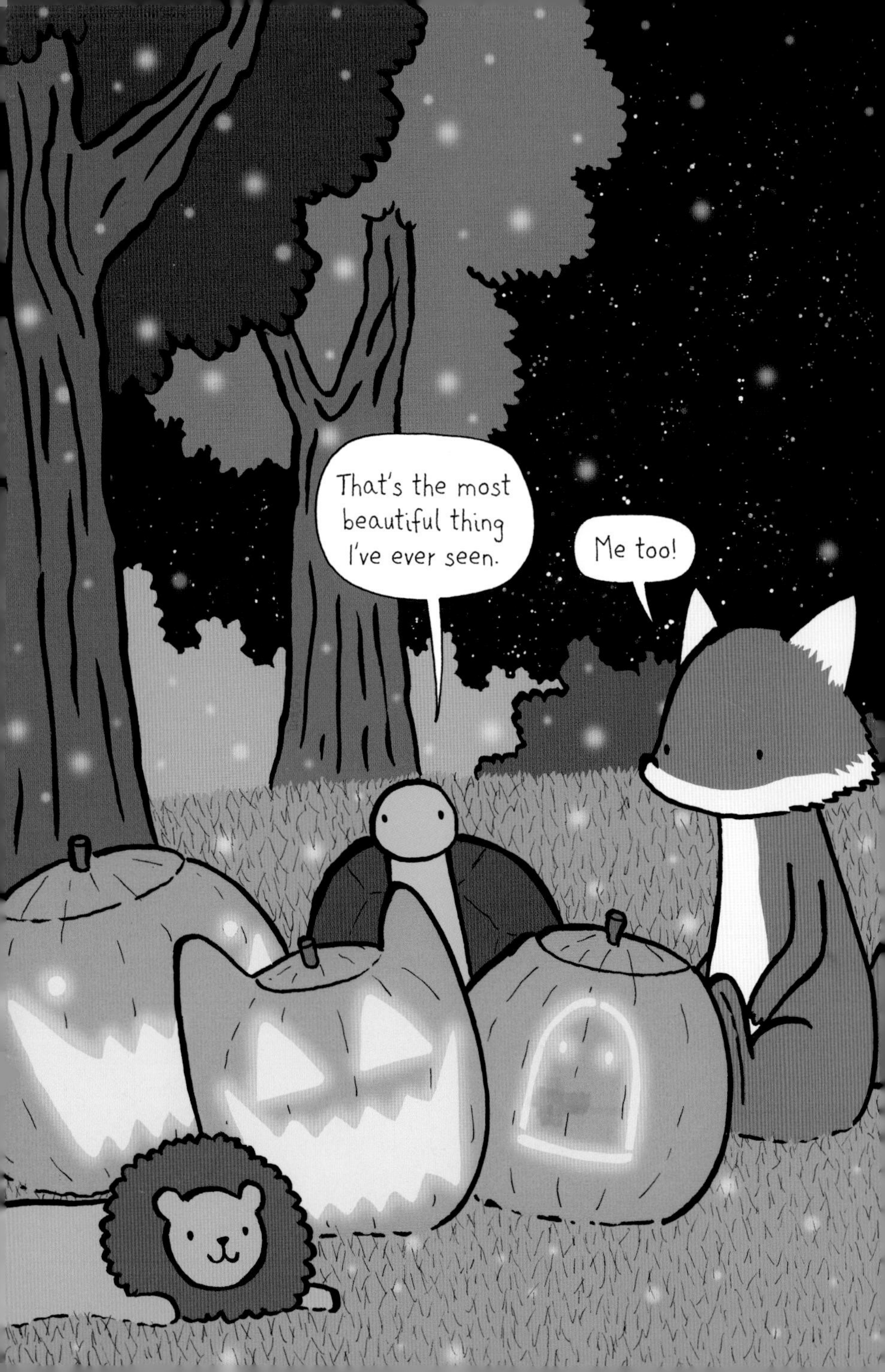
That's the most beautiful thing I've ever seen.
Me too!

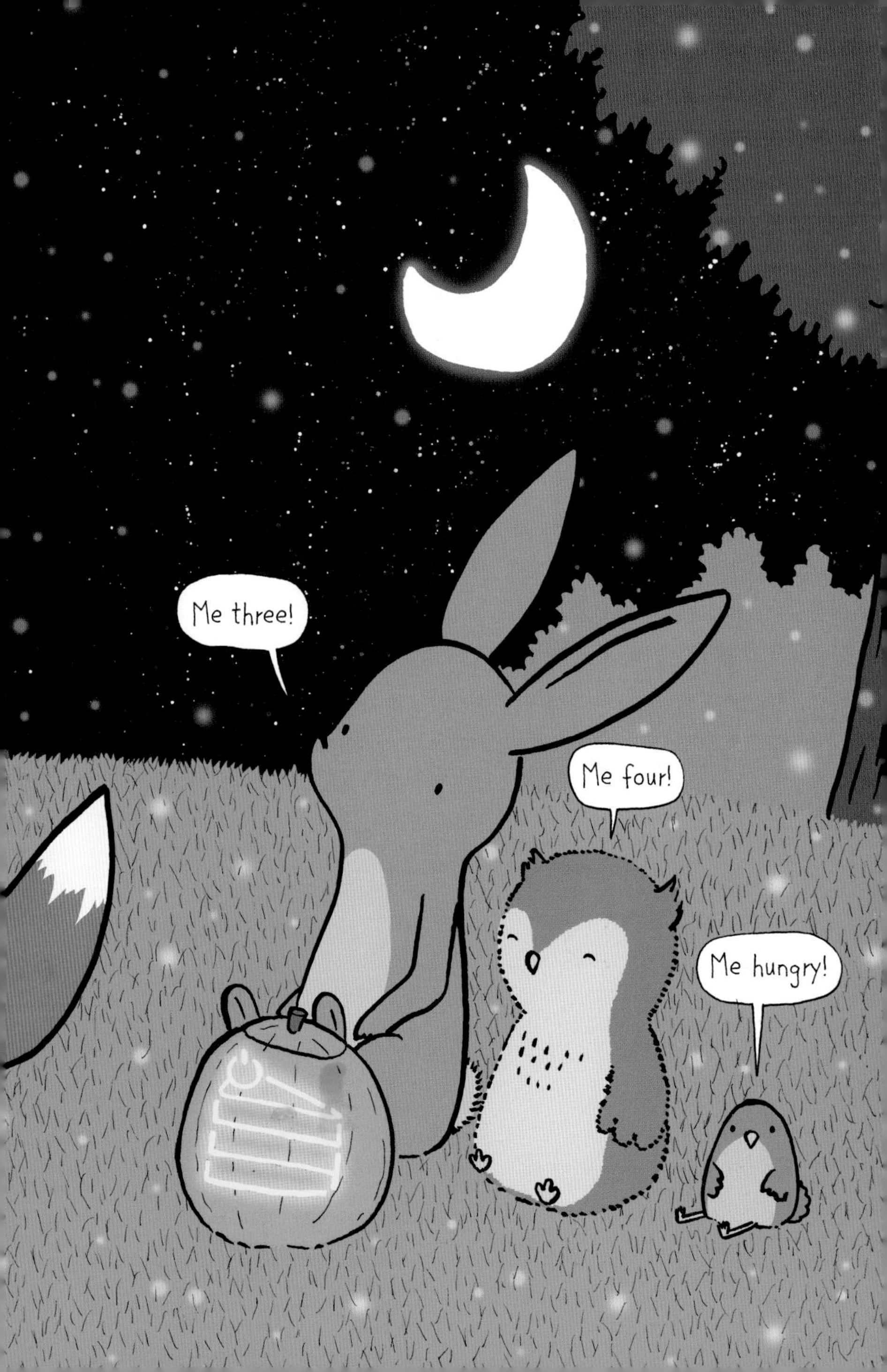
Me three!
Me four!
Me hungry!

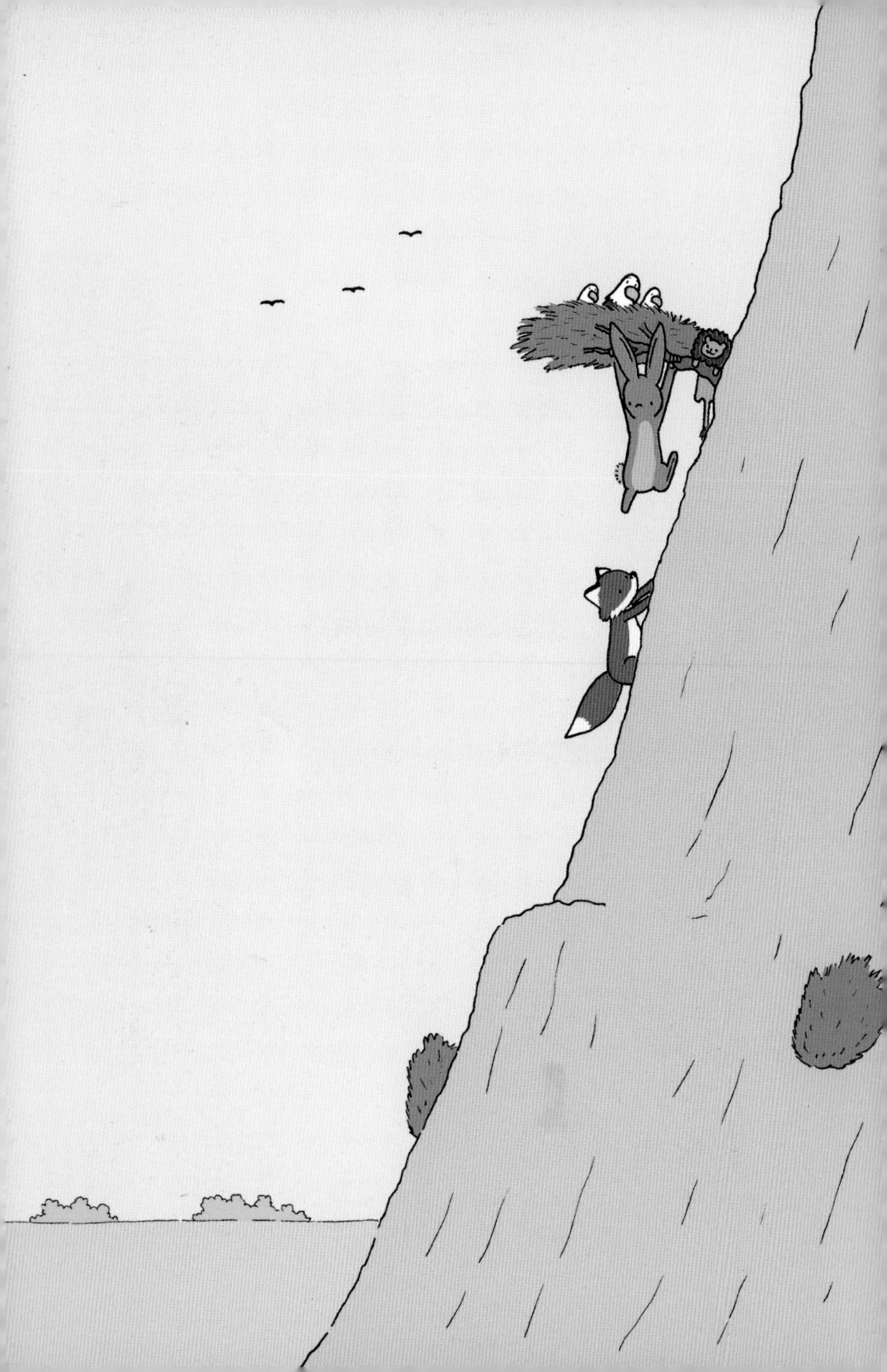

READ ON FOR A SNEAK PEEK OF
FOX AND RABBIT'S NEXT ADVENTURE IN

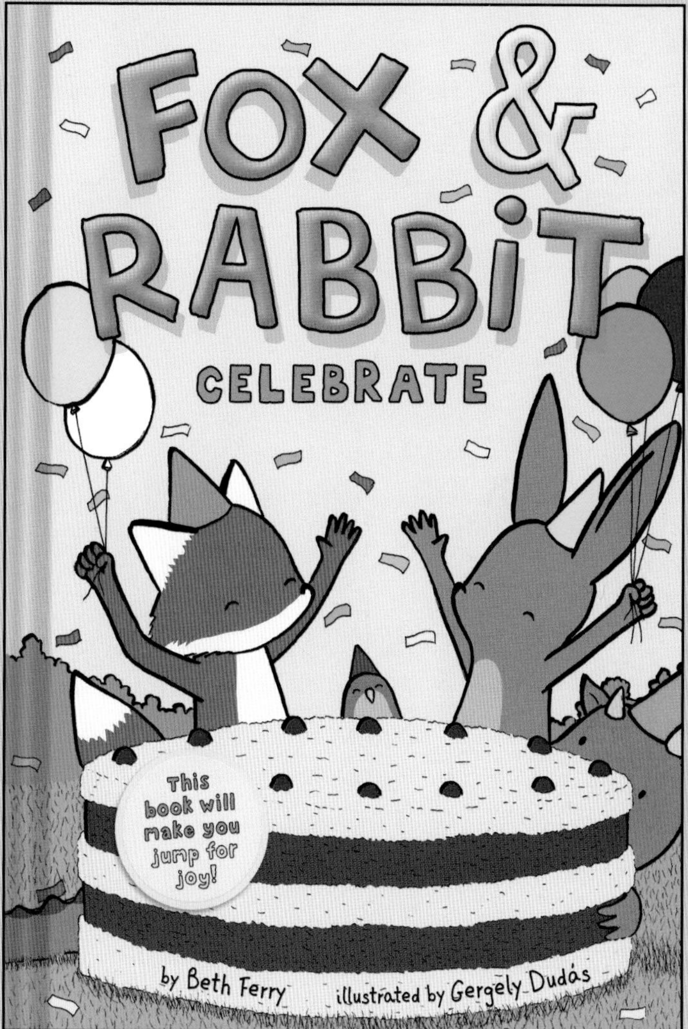
FOX & RABBIT
CELEBRATE
This book will make you jump for joy!
by Beth Ferry
illustrated by Gergely Dudás

PARTY, PIZZA
& PLANS

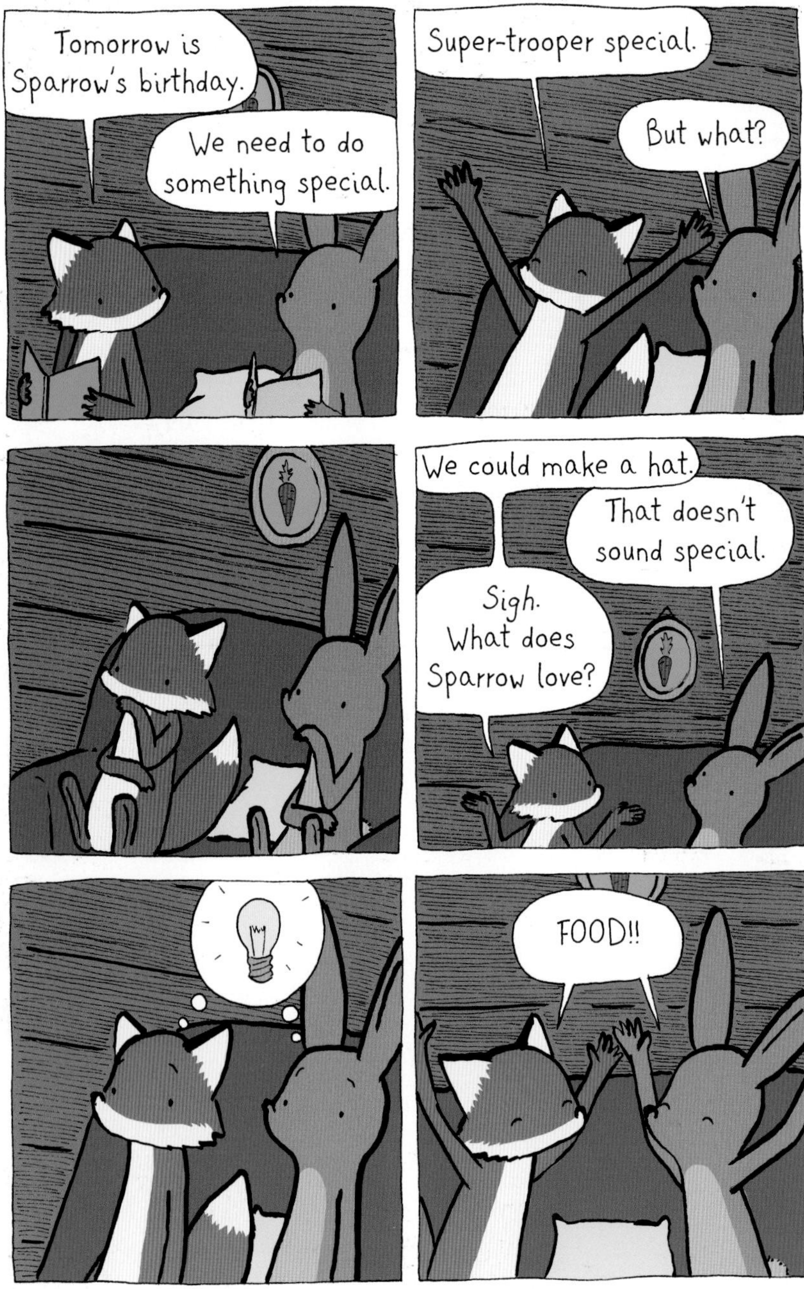
Tomorrow is Sparrow's birthday.
We need to do something special.
Super-trooper special.
But what?
We could make a hat.
That doesn't sound special.
Sigh. What does Sparrow love?
FOOD!!

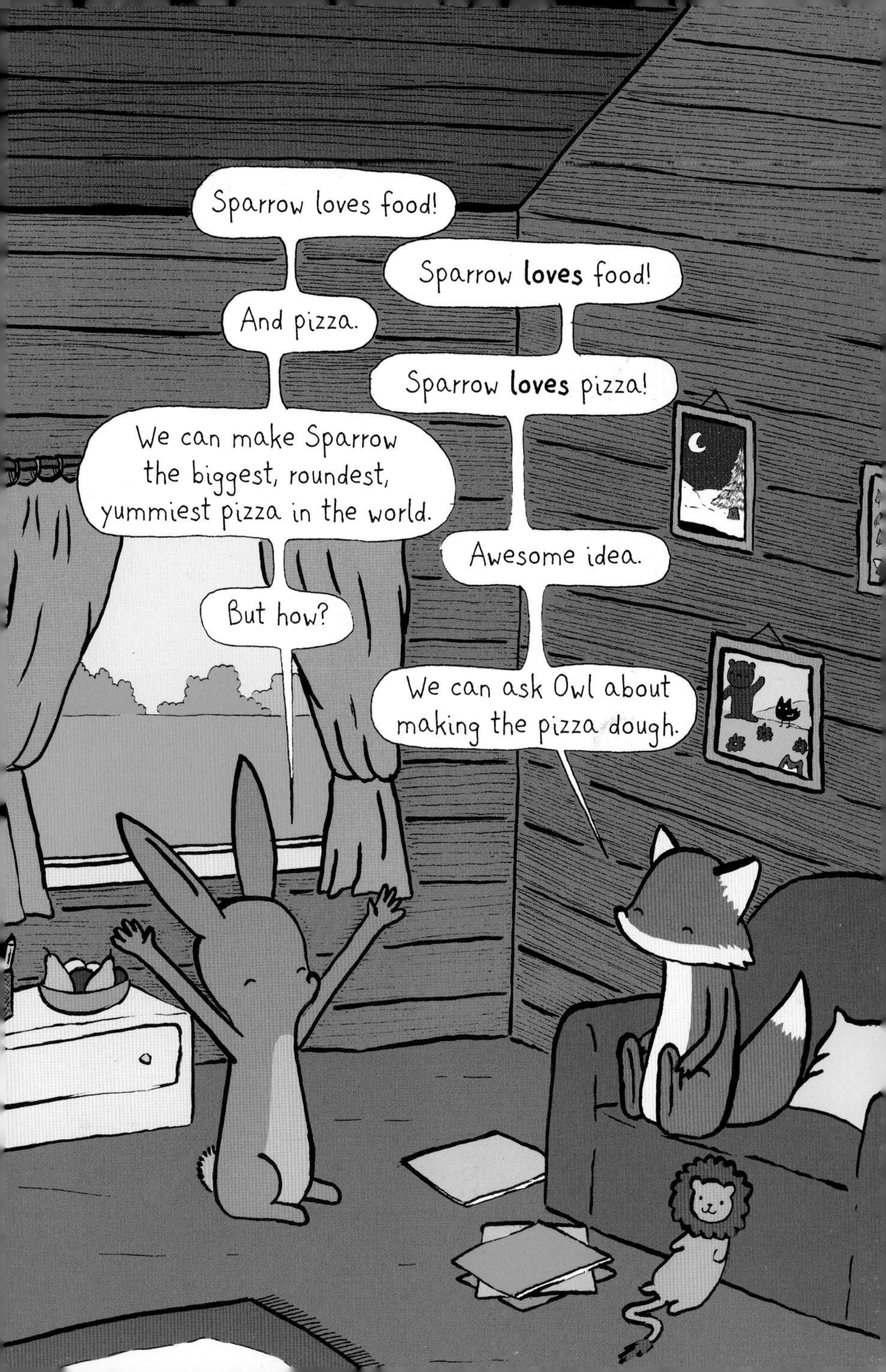

Sparrow loves food!
Sparrow **loves** food!
And pizza.
Sparrow **loves** pizza!
We can make Sparrow the biggest, roundest, yummiest pizza in the world.
Awesome idea.
But how?
We can ask Owl about making the pizza dough.

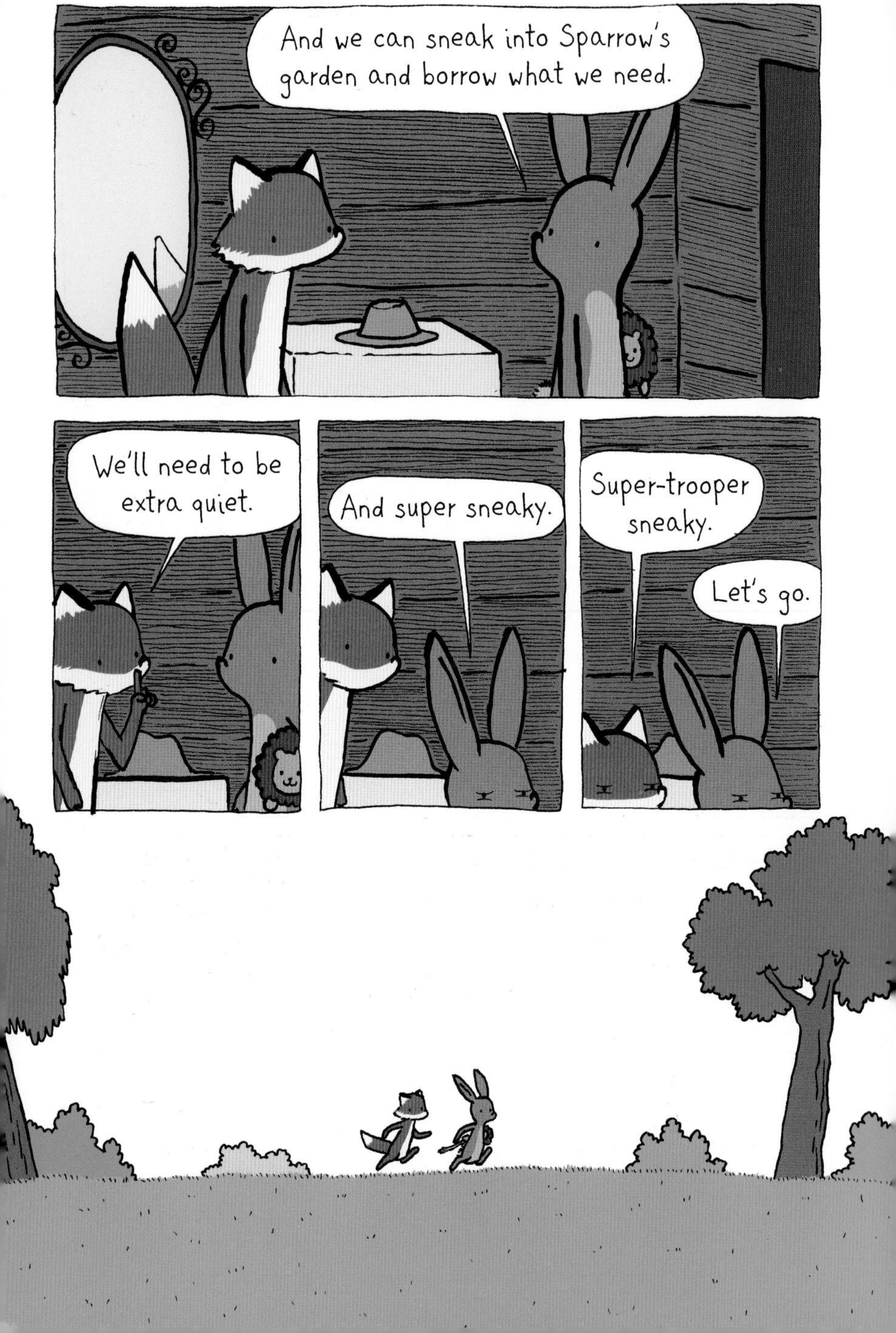
And we can sneak into Sparrow's garden and borrow what we need.
We'll need to be extra quiet.
And super sneaky.
Super-trooper sneaky.
Let's go.

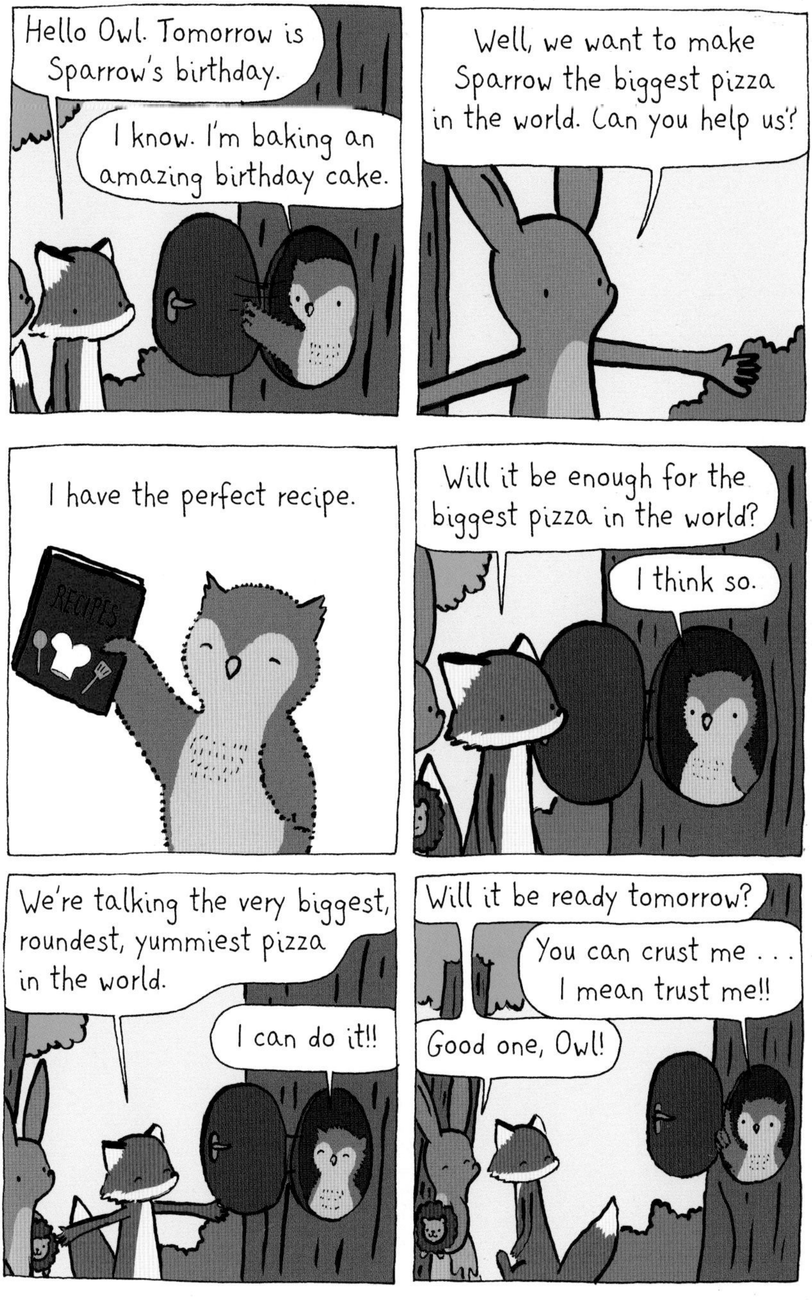
Hello Owl. Tomorrow is Sparrow's birthday.
I know. I'm baking an amazing birthday cake.
Well, we want to make Sparrow the biggest pizza in the world. Can you help us?
I have the perfect recipe.
RECIPES
Will it be enough for the biggest pizza in the world?
I think so.
We're talking the very biggest, roundest, yummiest pizza in the world.
I can do it!!
Will it be ready tomorrow?
You can crust me . . . I mean trust me!!
Good one, Owl!

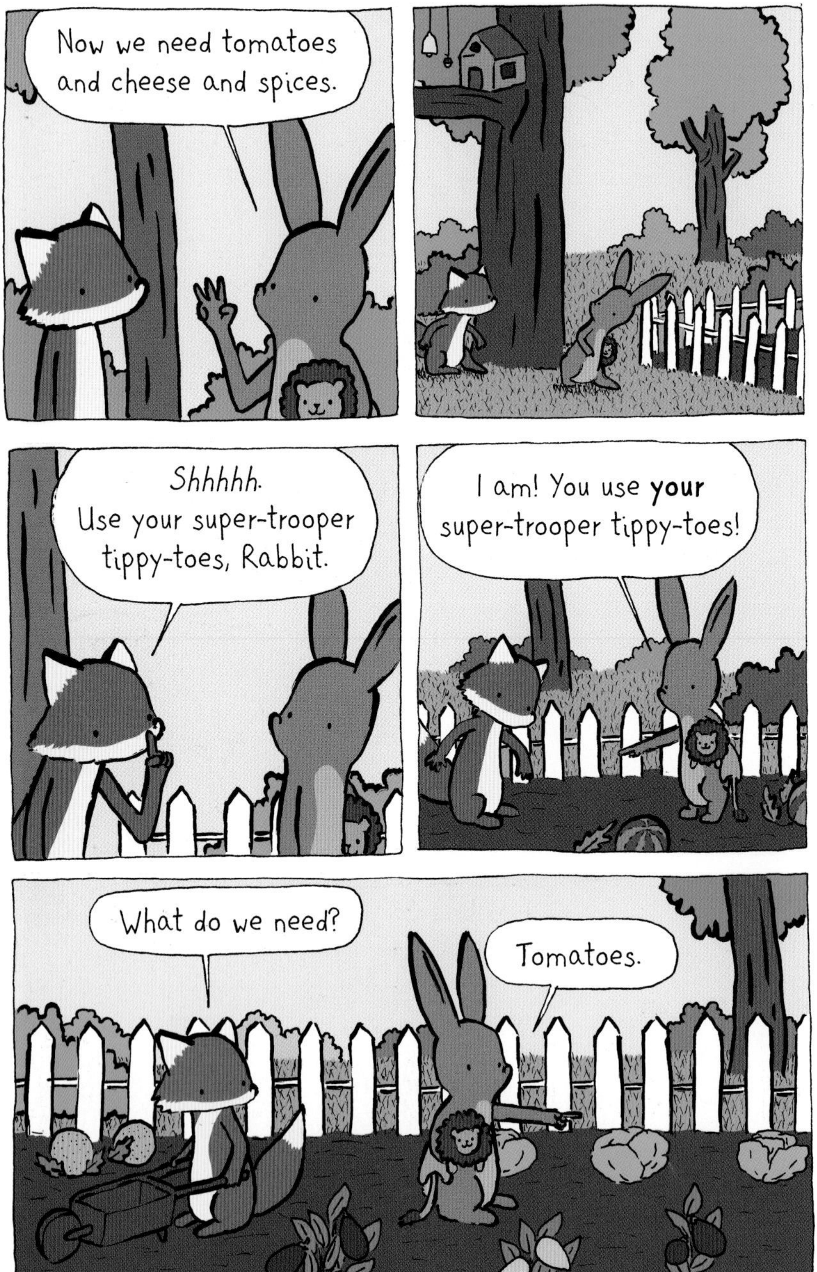
Now we need tomatoes and cheese and spices.
Shhhhh.
Use your super-trooper tippy-toes, Rabbit.
I am! You use **your** super-trooper tippy-toes!
What do we need?
Tomatoes.

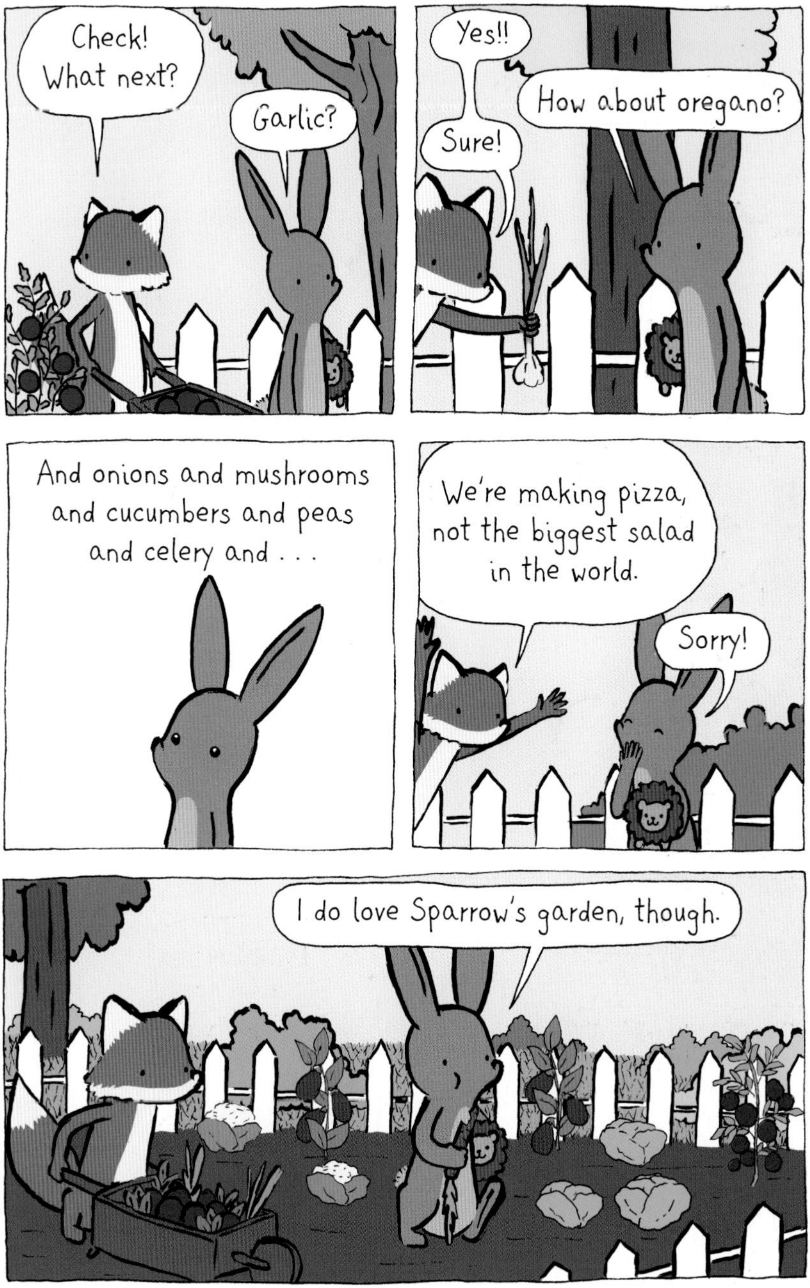
Check! What next?
Garlic?
Yes!!
Sure!
How about oregano?
And onions and mushrooms and cucumbers and peas and celery and . . .
We're making pizza, not the biggest salad in the world.
Sorry!
I do love Sparrow's garden, though.

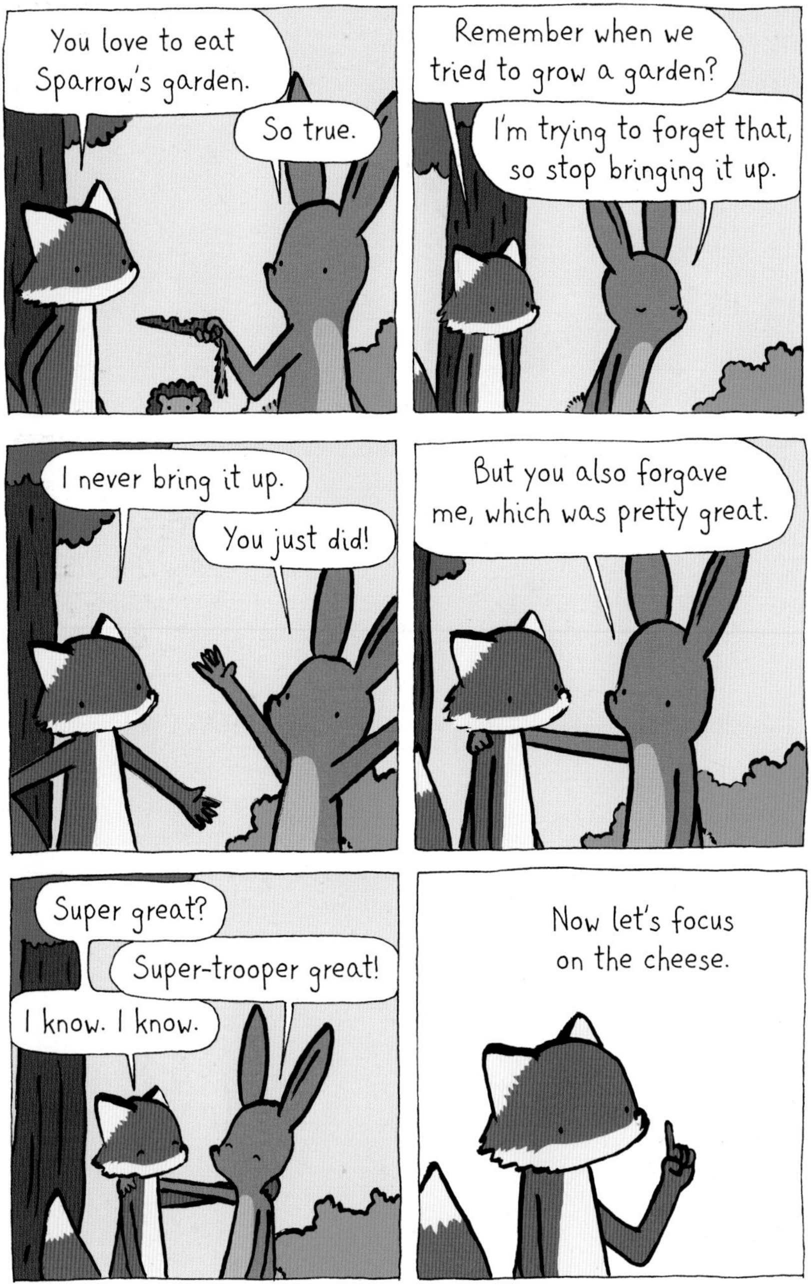
You love to eat Sparrow's garden.
So true.
Remember when we tried to grow a garden?
I'm trying to forget that, so stop bringing it up.
I never bring it up.
You just did!
But you also forgave me, which was pretty great.
Super great?
Super-trooper great!
I know. I know.
Now let's focus on the cheese.

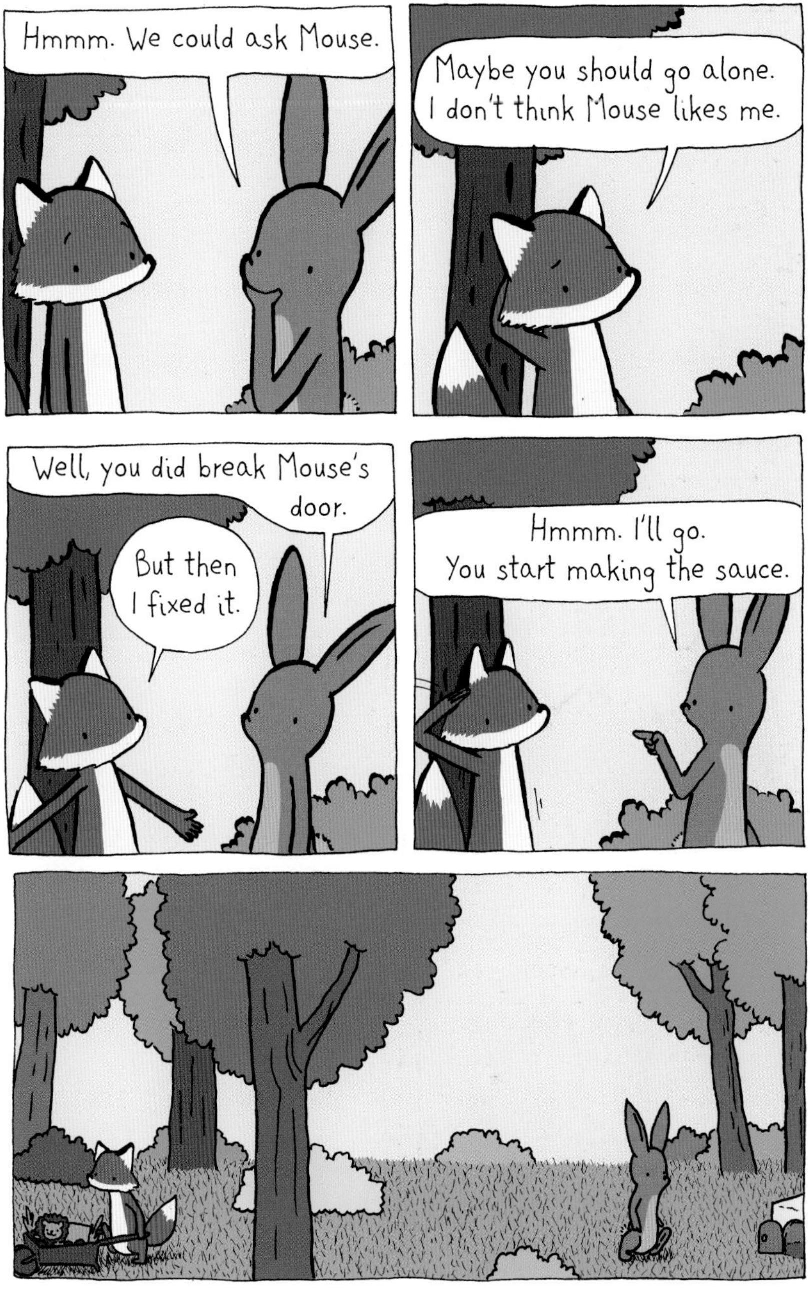
Hmmm. We could ask Mouse.
Maybe you should go alone. I don't think Mouse likes me.
Well, you did break Mouse's door.
But then I fixed it.
Hmmm. I'll go. You start making the sauce.

Hello, Mouse. I'm wondering if I could ask you a favor.

Hello!! I never got the chance to thank Fox. Ever since Fox "fixed" my door, I began leaving it open. I've made so many new friends.

Wow! That's . . . surprising.

Isn't it wonderful? Now, how can I help you?

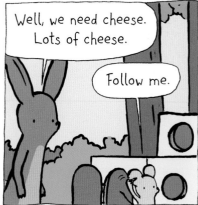

Well, we need cheese. Lots of cheese.

Follow me.

Chamber of Cheese

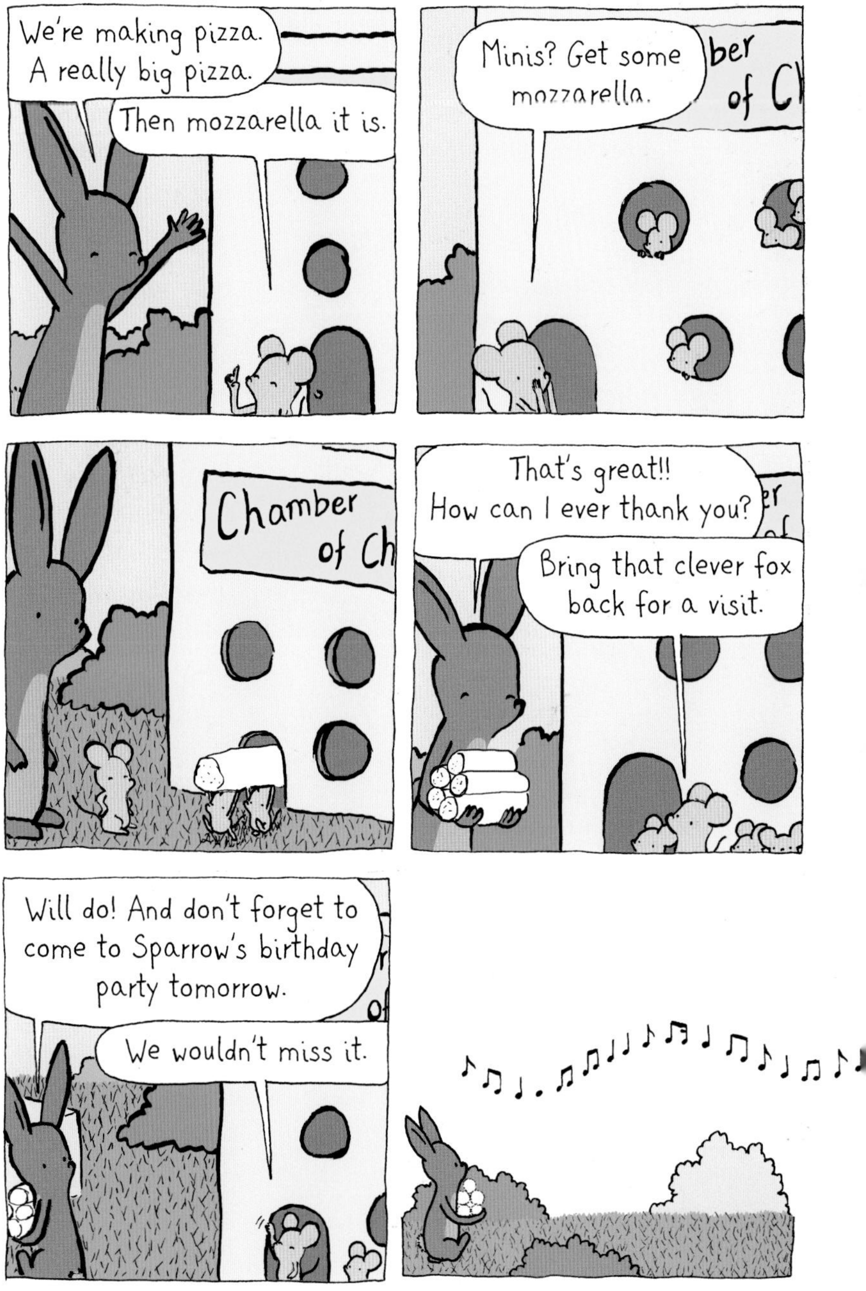

We're making pizza. A really big pizza.
Then mozzarella it is.
Minis? Get some mozzarella.
ber of Ch
Chamber of Ch
That's great!! How can I ever thank you?
Bring that clever fox back for a visit.
Will do! And don't forget to come to Sparrow's birthday party tomorrow.
We wouldn't miss it.

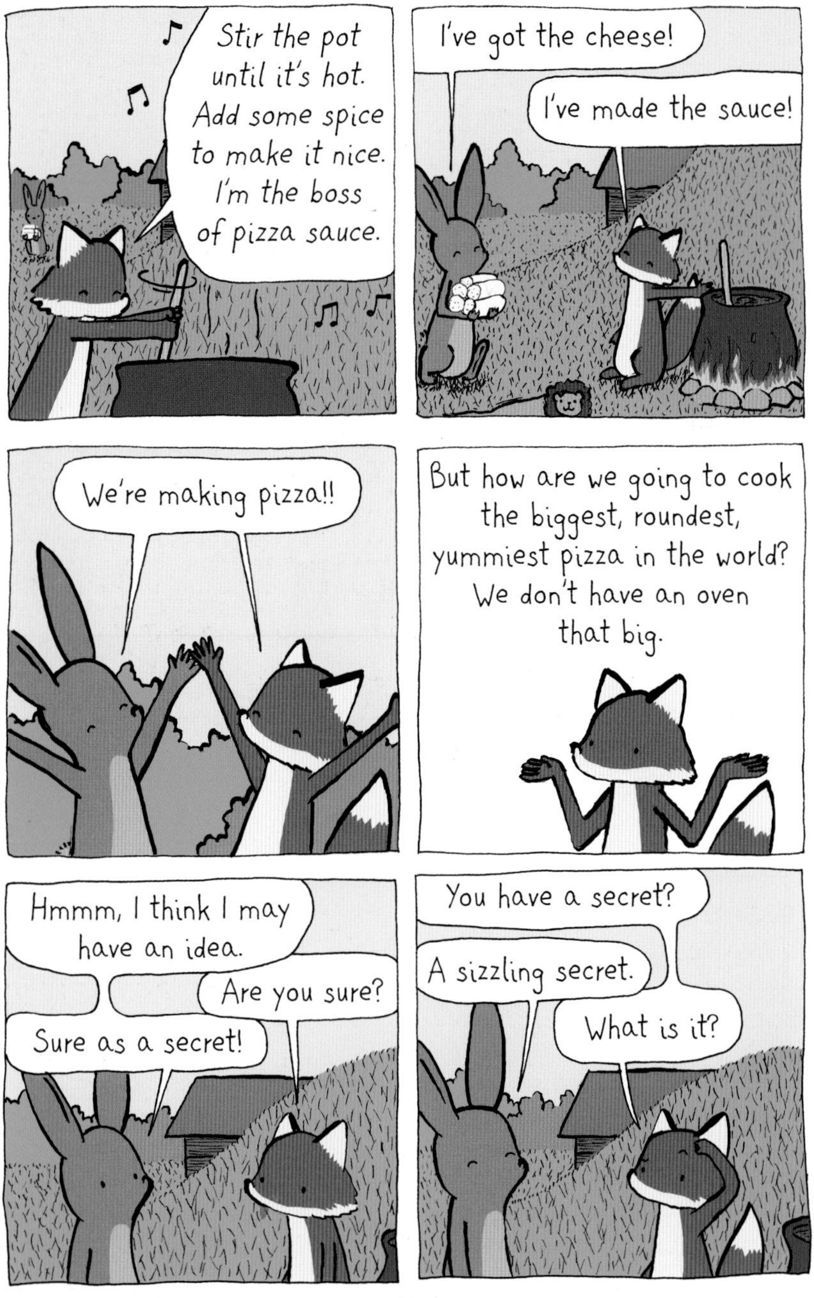
Stir the pot until it's hot. Add some spice to make it nice. I'm the boss of pizza sauce.
I've got the cheese!
I've made the sauce!
We're making pizza!!
But how are we going to cook the biggest, roundest, yummiest pizza in the world? We don't have an oven that big.
Hmmm, I think I may have an idea.
Are you sure?
Sure as a secret!
You have a secret?
A sizzling secret.
What is it?

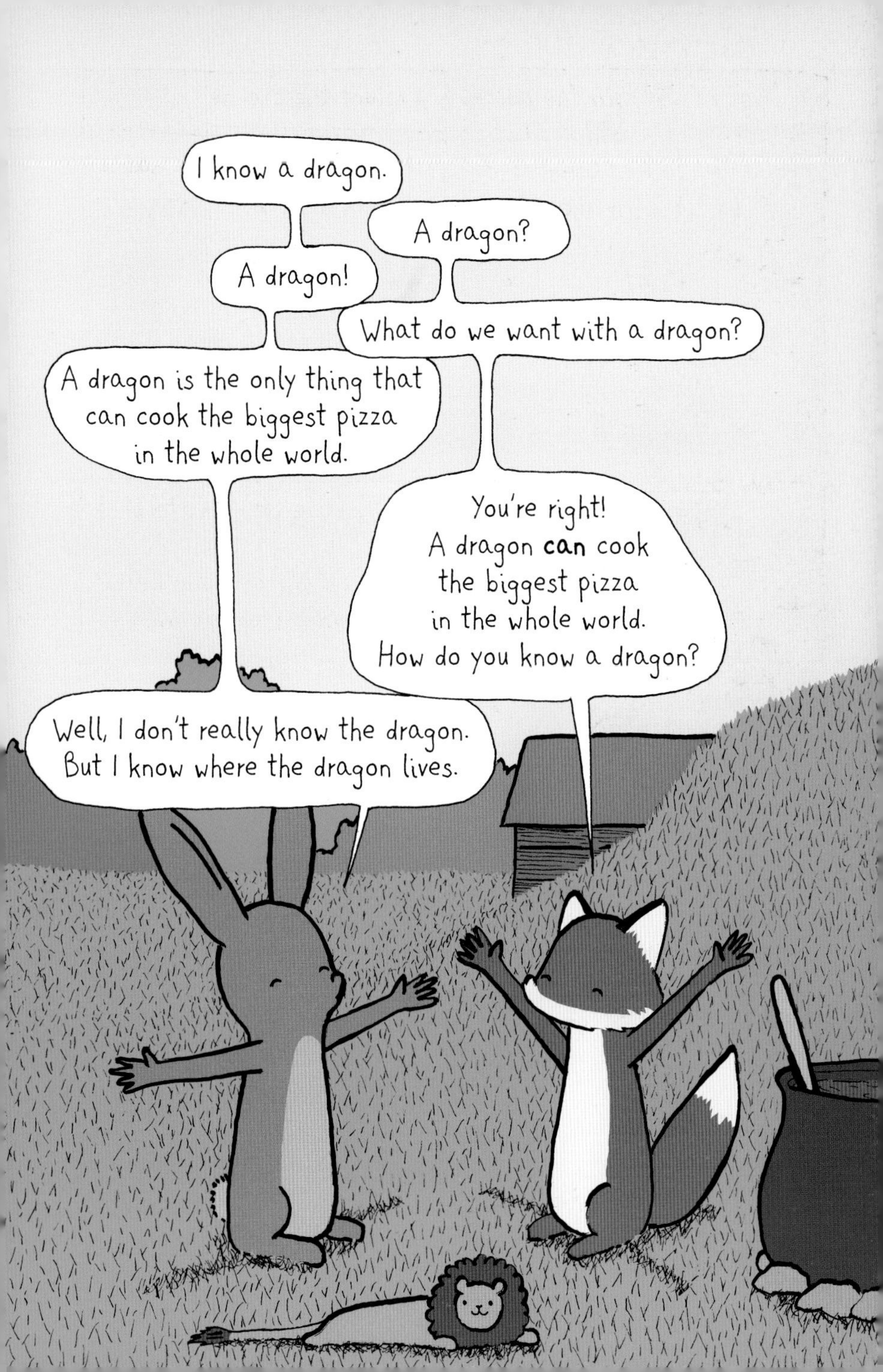
I know a dragon.
A dragon?
A dragon!
What do we want with a dragon?
A dragon is the only thing that can cook the biggest pizza in the whole world.
You're right! A dragon **can** cook the biggest pizza in the whole world. How do you know a dragon?
Well, I don't really know the dragon. But I know where the dragon lives.

ABOUT THE AUTHOR

Beth Ferry only grows pumpkins in her garden, which makes fall her second-favorite season. If she is lucky, her dog will not have eaten all the pumpkins before she's had a chance to carve them—often into characters from her books, which include *The Scarecrow*, *Swashby and the Sea*, and *Stick and Stone*. All these books begin with the letter S, which is Beth's favorite letter because it begins many of her favorite words, including *sunshine*, *sand*, and *sea*. S also begins the words *sweet* and *silly*, which are the main flavors of the world of Fox and Rabbit. Sparrow would argue that sweet and salty are the best flavors, and Beth just might agree. You can learn more at bethferry.com

ABOUT THE ILLUSTRATOR

Gergely Dudás is a self-taught illustrator. He was born in July 1991. His artwork in the early 1990s was a lot more abstract than it is today. He is the creator of the Bear's Book of Hidden Things seek-and-find series.

Like Fox, Rabbit, and Owl, Gergely spent almost every afternoon of his childhood at the playground, playing pretend with his friend Dani. And, like Fox, he loves fall because of the many warm colors that appear on the trees and bushes.

He lives with his girlfriend and a dwarf rabbit called Fahéj.

Gergely's work is inspired by the magic of the natural world. You can see more from him at dudolf.com.

FOR ZACH, WHOSE IMAGINATION
IS AN INSPIRATION
—B.F.

FOR MY DEAR FRIEND JANÓ, WHO LIKES
ADVENTURES AS MUCH AS I DO
—G.D.

The art in this book was created with graphite and ink and colored digitally.

PUBLISHER'S NOTE: This is a work of fiction. Names, characters, places, and incidents are either the product of the author's imagination or used fictitiously, and any resemblance to actual persons, living or dead, business establishments, events, or locales is entirely coincidental.

Library of Congress Control Number for the hardcover edition: 2020937895

Paperback ISBN 978-1-4197-4972-8

Text copyright © 2020 Beth Ferry
Illustrations copyright © 2020 Gergely Dudás
Book design by Steph Stilwell

Printed and bound in China
10 9 8 7 6 5 4 3 2 1

Amulet Books are available at special discounts when purchased in quantity for premiums and promotions as well as fundraising or educational use. Special editions can also be created to specification. For details, contact specialsales@abramsbooks.com or the address below.

Amulet Books® is a registered trademark of Harry N. Abrams, Inc.

ABRAMS The Art of Books
195 Broadway, New York, NY 10007
abramsbooks.com